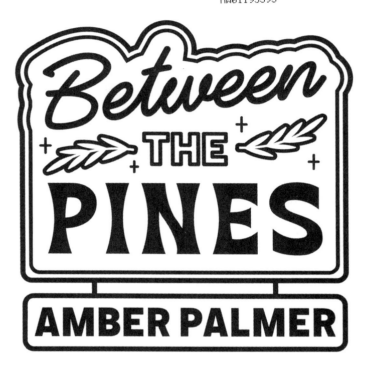

Between THE PINES

AMBER PALMER

Amber &
Palmer

Complete Editing Services performed by Heather Nix

Alpha/Beta: Liz Mayer, Rose Santoriello, Lauren Cox, Megan Laffey

Cover Design: Kaja McDonald (aka Bookish Averil)

Probably Smut Special Edition 2025

For Holly and Lauren -
This book exists because of you. Your support and friendship have been my
anchor, and I'm endlessly grateful.

To those who find themselves trapped in a mind that lies to you -
I hope you know you can always find your way out. I hope you know it's
okay to run, to doubt, to be scared before pulling yourself out of the
trenches and dusting yourself off.

Find your people and let them love you hard. I <u>promise</u> it's worth
it in the end.

playlist

For the full playlist, scan the QR code!

Neon Moon - Brooks and Dunn
Oh, Tonight - Josh Abbott Band, Kacey Musgraves
Risk - Gracie Abrams
The Bones - Maren Morris, Hozier
My Home - Myles Smith
Break Up With Him - Old Dominion
Worst Way - Riley Green
Spin You Around - Morgan Wallen

content warning

josie

· · ·

IF HEARTBREAK INSURANCE WAS A THING, my premium would be sky-high.

My relationship roadmap was littered with head-on collisions and fender benders galore, and it would appear from the severe case of whiplash I was currently sporting, I hadn't learned my lesson.

Stumbling upon my boyfriend balls-deep in a blonde buckle bunny after one of the largest rodeos of his career was one hell of a lesson to learn.

The asshole hadn't even had the sense of self-preservation to stop and ask himself if fucking her against *my* trailer—a trailer I'd stupidly let him borrow—was a good idea or not.

Clearly, it was not.

I'd taken one look at his bare ass seated between her thighs before my self preservation kicked in. I turned on my heels, called my sister, and got the hell out of dodge.

My mom always said that when the going gets tough, I would get going. She insisted it was a joke, but some days, like today, it didn't feel like one. In fact, it felt like a goddamn truth I didn't want to face.

Maybe that was why I climbed into my sister's car and hit the ground running.

Or driving, I suppose.

I tapped my fingers against the steering wheel as George Strait sang about all his exes living in Texas. I couldn't help but laugh as I drove as far away from Texas and my exes as I could.

The last thing I remembered seeing were his wide eyes in my rearview mirror as he chased after me, one hand desperately clinging to his jeans while the other was waving for me to stop.

I didn't know what I had seen in the guy, what made me think this one would be different from the string of others. His red flags were a mile long, flying high for all to see from the very beginning.

But red was my favorite color, and I had a stubborn streak a mile long.

Wyatt Walker was too smooth, too polished, for a cowboy. He came in from the city, sweeping into our small town like he was god's gift to the rodeo scene—even though his rides left something to be desired.

But what he lacked in skill, he made up for in looks and swagger. He sauntered up to me at my favorite local bar, turning on his megawatt smile and Southern charm. After a few heated glances and just as many beers, I found myself staring up at his ceiling the next morning with my hair mussed and his arm slung around my waist.

A one-night stand turned into a full-fledged relationship, and eight months later, I was going with him to every rodeo and event he'd attended. He'd met my parents, and I'd met his.

Hell, we'd even talked about moving in together.

And now, I was running away as fast as I could to a cabin in the mountains of Tennessee to pull myself together.

Did I think Wyatt was going to be my one true love? Eh, the odds had never been in our favor.

But I was woman enough to admit that I'd been charmed by

deep blue eyes and a pair of dimples. His betrayal stung more than I wanted to admit, but I knew some fresh mountain air would do me good.

It always had.

Looking up ahead, I saw a sign for a gas station and pulled in when the driveway came into view. I'd barely stopped on the way, wanting to get as far away from Texas and the boy who had broken my heart as quickly as possible.

My phone buzzed on the passenger seat as I turned off the ignition. I groaned, falling back against the headrest before reaching over and grabbing the damn thing. There weren't many people I wanted to talk to right now and even fewer who knew where I was headed, but I checked it, nevertheless.

The words 'Do Not Answer' flashed across my screen, complete with red alarm emojis that I had thought drove my point home in the heat of the moment. It may have been a bit immature to change Wyatt's contact as soon as I found myself alone, but I just didn't trust myself not to answer in a vulnerable state.

I'd lost count of how often he'd called since leaving him in the dust last night. He'd filled my voicemail full of tearful apologies and half-hearted excuses, most of which I'd never listen to. I should have let this one roll, too, but call me curious… I wanted to know what he thought he could say to make up for what he'd done.

I swiped my thumb across the screen, bringing it to my ear and cringing as Wyatt's slurring, drunken voice came across the line.

"Josieeeeee, baby, you finally answered!"

"What do you want, Wyatt?" I asked, rubbing my temples to disband the tension headache that threatened to surface.

"Baby, you gotta listen to me"—hiccup—"she means nothing to me. I dunno what I was thinkin'. I wasn't thinkin'—"

"Yes, you were," I said, stepping out of the car into the chilly evening air and taking in my surroundings. The sun was setting behind the pines, washing the Tennessee sky in pink and orange hues. "You were just thinking with the head between your legs versus the one on your shoulders."

"Never again," he slurred. "Never, ever again, Josie. Starting right now, I'm your man and your man only."

I stepped inside the store, ignoring the bell as it jingled overhead. The clerk looked up from their phone, mumbling a hello before turning their attention back to their doom scroll. My shoes stuck to the floor as I hunted the aisles for junk food and energy drinks. I hadn't slept in well over twenty-four hours, and I was still at least two hours from the cabin.

"Honestly, Wyatt... You should have 'been my man' since the beginning. I shouldn't have to catch you with your dick in someone else for you to have an epiphany about our relationship."

"No, I swear it. You're the one for me. You're it. I wanna get married."

I couldn't stop the laugh from bubbling up as I reached into the fridge and grabbed two energy drinks. "Yeah, I don't think that's going to happen. Let's just call it, okay? We gave it a shot and—"

"But your dad was going to sponsor me in the upcoming season..."

The words were a shot to my chest, sending my heart crashing into the pit of my stomach. Of course, it all boiled down to a stupid sponsorship. Wyatt didn't regret cheating on me. He didn't regret getting caught. It was all about losing what I assumed was a large chunk of money.

As a retired world champion team roper, my dad made a name for himself through horse training. People had traveled from all over the country to attend his clinics, and his stables were always full of yearlings in need of a guiding hand.

And since his name still held significant weight on the rodeo circuit, having his endorsement could've catapulted Wyatt's already budding career into something he could only dream of.

Too bad the cheating bastard would never see a dime of my dad's money now.

I added four bags of chips and a bag of mini SweeTarts to my haul and took it to the counter. The cashier looked just as bored as they had when I walked in, putting their phone down with a sigh before scanning each item.

"Well, maybe you should have thought about that before you fucked Trisha Lawson out in the open for God and all his children to see."

He tried pleading with me, but I didn't listen.

"Have a nice life, Wyatt."

I hung up, quickly cursing myself for my stupidity. The clerk stared with wide eyes and a slack jaw, their hand outstretched, my bag hanging between us.

"Cowboys," I mumbled before swiping the food and heading back to the safety of my car.

lincoln

. . .

"HOW ABOUT ANOTHER ROUND, STUD?" The blonde standing in front of me placed her hands flat on the bar top, trying and failing to push her tits together as she gave me a saccharine sweet smile.

Was that supposed to be alluring? I guess for some men, it was, but I'd done this job for a long time. This woman was on the prowl, looking for someone to show her a good time.

Unfortunately for her, that wasn't going to be me.

"Sure thing. What'll you have?" I asked, pulling out a line of glasses and filling them with ice.

She tapped her long, manicured finger against her lips in thought. I didn't know who she was trying to fool, but it wasn't me. She'd been sipping on vodka and cranberry juice all night, one of the most basic drink requests I could think of.

My dad always said you could tell a lot about a woman based on her drink of choice. I used to laugh him off because there were a lot of reasons for people to drink weird shit. Hell, every now and then, even I enjoyed a fruity little cocktail over a beer.

But working at this run-down bar in the middle of nowhere

opened my eyes to the truth. I realized I'd spent too much time chasing after the vodka cranberry women over ones who knew how to shoot their whiskey.

As if on cue, the woman turned over her shoulder to the rowdy group of girls in the corner. "Who wants another vodka cran?" She was met with a chorus of cheers, and I smiled as I grabbed the bottle of clear liquor and began to pour.

They all wore bright pink sashes with different sayings in gold glittering letters. I couldn't tell if it was a birthday celebration or maybe just a bunch of girls from the city running away to the mountains to "find themselves" at some kind of bullshit yoga retreat the hippies up there like to put on.

The woman, little miss *Sexy & Single* according to the words across her chest, turned back and slid her card across the sticky bar top when I told her the total. "Can I start a tab?"

"Absolutely, ma'am. Just be sure to stop by and close it out before you go. Wouldn't want you to forget it," I called over my shoulder, walking to the computer to input her payment. I slipped the card between the tabs of the Rolodex, noting the man's name engraved into the card she'd given me.

Sexy and single, my ass.

I'd always liked working behind the bar. It was methodical. Practiced. Most of the time, the place was filled with local patrons who'd known me since I was a boy. They'd order a beer, and we'd chat the shit about this, that, or the other until closing time. But tourist season was in full swing since the weather was changing. Summer was coming, and as much as I hated to admit it, our little slice of heaven in the mountains was beautiful.

Pinecrest was a close-knit community, filled to the brim with that small-town charm most city folk sought when taking their family on vacation. The town held festivals once a month during the tourist season, and there was a local farmers market every weekend. Everyone participated in some capacity, usually wrangled into helping by Joan Wilkins, the chairwoman of special events who looked like the fucking crypt keeper.

"Oh-Em-Geeeeee!" a brunette squealed, running up to the bar and slinging an arm around her friend. According to her sash, this one was supposed to be the *Dancing Queen*. "I just love vodka crans. They're the best. Don't you just *love* them?" Each word is over the top and exaggerated, but she didn't seem to notice or care about the looks the locals shot their way. She grabbed the drink and brought it to her lips before calling, "Girls, come get your drinks!"

The sound of screeching chairs and cheers for alcohol drowns out the sound of Hank Williams on the ancient jukebox. Each woman grabbed a cocktail, profusely thanking me for doing my job, before returning to their table.

"Goddamn tourists," Frank mumbled, downing the rest of his beer with a grimace. "Why do they have to come here? To this bar?"

"I don't know, old man. Maybe you should raise your prices to drive them away," I said, smirking as I collected the empty glasses and placed them into the dishwasher.

Frank hadn't worked behind the bar in years. These days, he was more of a silent partner, sitting on a stool and drinking his own stock while I ran the day-to-day operations.

If you'd asked me five years ago if I would've seen myself handing out beers to the same men I once looked up to, I would've told you my ambitions ran deeper. But all it took was one day, *one mistake*, for me to give up on all my dreams.

"Kid, this bar is more yours than mine. I tell you that nearly every damn day. I don't know what else I could do."

I held out my hand for his empty glass, filling it with a local craft brew before sliding it back his way. "Am I still considered a kid at 35? What's the cutoff? When do I become an adult?"

"Fuckin' smartass."

I opened my mouth to live up to my reputation but was quickly stopped by a dark-headed bombshell walking through the front door. She stood in the entryway, clutching her purse strap with a white-knuckle grip. Her eyes flitted around the bar, taking in her surroundings.

I didn't recognize her, and she sure as shit didn't look like she belonged in a small town like Pinecrest. This girl was the kind to turn every head in a room without trying, even if there was something wild in her eyes I couldn't quite place.

I considered myself a good judge of character. Working this job had some perks, and that was one of them. I saw people in all their glory. I celebrated their highs and mourned their lows right alongside them.

And this woman? She was running from something or someone, of that I was sure.

When her gaze landed on the bar, she pulled her shoulders back and strode forward with a confidence I'd only seen a handful of times. She dropped her bag at her feet, sliding onto the worn leather stool. Her shoulders drooped a fraction, a hint of vulnerability peeking through before she turned steely eyes on me.

"*Goddamn*," Frank muttered for the second time in less than five minutes. He really was a man of few words. "They don't make'em like that 'round here."

I wiped my hands on the towel, throwing it over my shoulder. "What were you saying not even five minutes ago about tourists getting the hell outta your bar?"

The men behind me laughed, and I was sure Frank flipped me the bird as I passed by, but I didn't care. Not when that beauty was staring up at me through long lashes, scanning my body in a way that made me want to fucking preen.

I'd never been that guy before. Sure, I wasn't a fool. I wasn't ignorant of the way women had stared at me my whole life. I took care of my body and my mind, but I wasn't one to walk around like I was god's gift to the female population.

"What can I getcha, darlin'?" I asked, placing my palms on the counter. "We've got the basics, and—"

"Whiskey on the rocks," she paused, closing her eyes before chuckling. "Actually, make it a double."

josie

. . .

STOPPING at a bar in the middle of nowhere hadn't been a part of my plan. I'd had a one-track mind since leaving Texas, telling myself everything would be fine once I made it to the cabin and had a moment to myself.

I hadn't thought about how silent it would be once I got there or how depressing it would feel to pull up in the middle of the night to an empty house, and I didn't want to find out.

Truth be told, I wasn't ready to be alone with my thoughts. Who knew what bullshit my mind would try and spin? I didn't have the best track record when it came to being level-headed. Overthinking was my middle name, and I'd damn well earned it.

That was when the flickering neon sign for *Frank's* had cut through the pitch-black sky like some kind of beacon.

As I pulled off the road, the small dirt parking lot was nearly full. Luckily, I found a spot near the treeline. I wasn't sure what to expect as I walked through the doors, but at this point, I didn't care. Anything was better than being alone.

And the hot-as-sin bartender staring at me as though I was his last meal wasn't half-bad either.

He wasn't handsome in the way most men were these days. There was something distinctly rugged about him, something I'd always been attracted to but had never found. Day-old stubble lined his jaw, and his dark hair was tucked beneath a backward baseball cap. He wore a black t-shirt that hugged a well-defined chest. The sleeves tightened around his biceps as he worked.

And his *hands*.

God, I'd never considered how hot something like that could be? I'd been around my fair share of cowboys, and while their hands were rough and worn like this man's were, I'd never had a visceral reaction to them before.

I wanted to know what they'd feel like against my skin. Would he caress my body gently? Or would his calloused palms dig into my flesh like a man possessed?

One thing was for sure... I needed to get a fucking grip before I jumped across this bar and answered my own dangerous questions.

"Rough night?" he asked, grabbing a bottle with a time-worn label off the shelves. It looked a bit dusty, but I didn't care. The burn was all I needed to get my mind off what awaited me once I left this dive.

I scoffed, running a hand through my hair as he pushed the glass forward. "You could say that." I brought the glass to my lips, savoring that sweet sting as it traveled down my throat, leaving only a warm tingle behind.

The bartender raised his brows in surprise. "Damn, killer. I've seen grown men struggle to take a shot of that."

I smiled, lifting my glass in a fake toast. "Well, my daddy taught me to handle my whiskey. Nothing can be worse than the rye bullshit he keeps on hand."

"Noted," he said, offering a little salute. "So, you're obviously not from around here."

I waited a beat, wondering if he would follow up his observation with a question, but he said nothing more. "That obvious, huh?"

The corners of his mouth lifted in a smirk. "I'd remember your face if I'd ever run into it before."

The heat from the liquor had nothing on the blush creeping across my cheeks. "Is that right?"

He leaned forward, dark eyes raking over my face before dipping lower. The scent of fresh forest and aged whiskey was a punch to the gut. It should be illegal to smell that good. I wanted to bottle it up and keep it forever.

"Sure is," he said. "Now, the question is... What brought you to Pinecrest?"

I sighed, running my finger along the rim of the glass. He was asking a loaded question, and I didn't know if I wanted to give him the answer. Usually, I was an open book. I wore my heart on my sleeve, and my face always betrayed my emotions. "I guess you wouldn't believe me if I told you I was on vacation?"

"Nope."

"Okay, what about one of those soul-searching retreats that are always advertised on social media? You know, the kind that swears they can change your life just by reading your cards."

His deep, throaty laughter would've made me weak in the knees if I hadn't been sitting down already. "Cards?"

I shrugged. "Tarot cards or whatever. I don't know; it sounded good in my head. My sister is into all that shit."

"Which brings us back to the question at hand." He pushed off the counter, pulling a glass down and pouring himself two fingers of the same liquor he'd offered me.

I brought my drink to my lips, savoring the subtle sweet flavor. "Should you really be drinking on the job? Isn't that kind of illegal?"

He pointed the bottle in my direction. "Anyone ever tell you you're mighty good at deflecting, darlin'?"

The name shouldn't have sounded so good falling from his lips, but I was a goner. I clenched my thighs together to stifle the blooming ache. "Maybe a time or two. Is it so wrong to want to keep you guessing?"

"Fair point," he said with a chuckle. "How about you tell me your name? After all, I may be willing to let you off with one free drink, but my boss is a stickler for the rules, and he's sitting right behind me."

I peered around his tall frame in time to see a group of men in their sixties suddenly diverting their attention to the beers in front of them. The one in the middle looked up momentarily, and I could see the blush creeping from under his thick beard. "Oh yeah, he seems like a real ball buster." I leaned down, digging through my purse until I grabbed my wallet and placed a twenty-dollar bill on the counter. "Will this buy me another round?"

"You haven't even finished—"

But his words died when I grabbed the half-empty glass and downed the contents. The liquor was making me bold, so I playfully opened my mouth to show I'd swallowed every drop. His eyes darkened, pinning me to the spot as I closed my mouth and smiled. "What about now? Have I earned another drink?"

He cursed under his breath, trading my empty glass for a full one. "Guess this means you aren't starting a tab?"

"Leave the girl alone, Lincoln! Give'r what she wants."

I smiled at the old man's ribbing, while the delicious man before me closed his eyes and mumbled something about old fools who get drunk in bars.

"I have enough cash to last at least another hour," I said, licking my lips and leaning forward. "*Lincoln.*" His gaze dropped, tracking the movement with hungry eyes as I said his name. "Maybe if you're good, I'll tell you my name."

"Oh yeah?" he asked, dropping his voice. "And what's your definition of good, darlin'?"

I shrugged, trying to keep control of my rapidly beating heart. "Keep me company and find out."

lincoln

. . .

"YOU DID NOT!" I couldn't tear my gaze away as the woman in front of me laughed, covering her face in embarrassment. "With the preacher's daughter?"

It was nearly two in the morning, but I wasn't tired. The bar closed half an hour ago, and she and I were still going strong. Each second I spent in her presence was fucking intoxicating. I didn't even know her name; she'd still refused to tell me, and somehow, it became inconsequential when she looked at me like I hung the moon.

Maybe, for her, I wanted to.

I leaned back in my seat, tucking my arms behind my head. "Oh yeah. Let's just say that Sunday morning sermons with my grandma became pretty awkward. I'm surprised he even let me back inside his church."

Her melodic laughter turned into a horrible cackle. For a moment, I was just drunk enough to be worried that whatever spell she'd weaved was wearing off. But no, it was the same beautiful devil sitting before me.

We'd traded the whiskey in for beers a few rounds ago, and I was glad because the girl could drink like a sailor. She was going toe-to-toe with me, and I wondered when she would hit a wall. Maybe she already had, and I was the one who was too drunk to notice.

"Did your grandma ever find out what happened?" she asked, peering up at me with eyes brimming with trouble.

I shook my head. "Hell no, that would've sent her to an early grave. What happened that night stayed between me, Laura Ann, and Preacher Winslow." I scratched the rough stubble along my chin. "I think this may have been the first time I've told the story to someone else."

She placed her hand on her chest and gasped. "Are you telling me I have custody of one of your dirty little secrets?"

Bringing the bottle of beer to my lips, I smirked. "Oh, darlin', if dirty secrets are what you're after, all you had to do was ask. I could make those pretty cheeks blush."

"Oh yeah?" she asked, leaning toward me. Her fingers slowly inched forward, stopping just shy of my own. "I bet you'd like that, wouldn't you?"

"I'd like your name a lot more," I said, setting down the beer. "Why won't you tell me?"

She groaned, dropping her head. "Because if I tell you my name, this becomes a *thing*." Her hand waved awkwardly between us. "I mean, it'll get awkward. Do we exchange phone numbers? Do we call one another? Do we plan a date?" She was fucking adorable, especially as her nose scrunched up. "Can't we just be two strangers in a bar sharing embarrassing stories?"

"We *are* two strangers in a bar, and so far, I've been the only one to divulge the memories I swore I'd take to my grave." I raised my brows. "In fact, I just realized I don't know a damn thing about you other than how goddamn gorgeous you are."

We'd towed the line all night between playful banter and lust-filled stares, careful not to cross a boundary we couldn't take back. But I was getting sick of dancing around what I wanted, and what I wanted was her.

I wanted to kiss her stupid, to know what it felt like to knead her body in my hands. I wanted to know what sounds she made as I dragged my tongue over her skin and if she tasted nearly as good as she looked.

It'd been too damn long since I'd had a woman in my bed, and I wanted to change that. Tonight.

She pointed the bottle in my direction, smirking in a way that made my dick twitch. "You think I'm gorgeous?"

Despite seemingly weak inhibitions, she spoke it like a question. If I hadn't been staring at her all night, I might've thought the blush creeping across her cheeks was from the alcohol. For some goddamn reason, this beautiful woman had no idea how sexy she was. Or, and this thought made me damn near homicidal, some dipshit had made her think otherwise.

I lifted one shoulder in a shrug. "I think you own a mirror and know exactly how pretty you are. I see the same thing you do." I let my gaze drop down her body with reckless abandon, taking in the way her nipples pebbled against her tight cotton t-shirt. "You're perfect."

Her lips parted in surprise, but this was it. I was done. Fuck the line and fuck polite conversation.

I stood up, walking around the table in two strides until she tilted her head back to stare at me with wide, grey eyes. Her legs parted as I stepped between them, and I loved the feeling of heat radiating from her body.

"What're you doing?" she breathed. I didn't care that she smelled like expensive whiskey and cheap beer, I wanted to know what she tasted like.

The bottle of Johnny Walker Blue remained on the table next to us, its contents nearly gone. I wasn't thinking clearly, driven entirely by my need for the woman before me.

She protested as I gripped the bottle, draining the last few drops, but those protests died on her lips as I placed my hand behind her neck and kissed her. Her mouth moved greedily against my own, tongue sweeping in to taste the remnants of liquor.

I was a simple man with simple beliefs. I'd never held much stock in that lovey-dovey bullshit people clung to, talking about soulmates and destinies. It was just a way for folks to feel better about their lives.

But this woman?

Something told me she could make me a believer.

josie

. . .

AT TWENTY-NINE, I thought I knew what it felt like to be kissed, but apparently, I was wrong. The man standing in front of me had just turned my world upside down in a single moment.

I wasn't too proud to admit that there was something about Lincoln that caught me off guard. I'd been trying to figure him out the entire time we'd laughed away the hours.

Growing up on a ranch, I'd been around my fair share of hardworking hands and wanna-be cowboys to tell the difference between the two, but this man? There was something different beneath the layers of bravado and sarcasm he donned.

He was authentically rugged and timelessly handsome, the type of man who commanded your attention when he walked into a room. Given the callouses lining his palms, bartending wasn't his only job, but it was the only one he'd claimed. I'd spent the better part of the night trying to get the truth out of him, but each time I asked, he changed the subject and turned it back to me.

He said I'd have to give him my name if I wanted his story.

I wasn't ready for that, though. After all, I didn't escape

Texas to land myself in a relationship with the first man I saw. I came for the mountains—for fresh air and silence. To be able to lick my wounds in the calm of Tennessee before I returned to the storm back home.

But when Lincoln stepped between my jean-clad thighs without hesitation?

I was a goner.

To hell with what I thought I wanted, the only thing that mattered was *him*. I eagerly drowned in the taste of him as his hands tangled in my hair, tugging my head back and tearing his mouth from mine.

I blinked, ready to ask a million questions that all centered around why he'd stopped kissing me. Instead, I was struck silent, unable to do anything but stare up at the darkest eyes I'd ever seen.

I'd stared at them all night, enjoying the sweet caramel shade that seemed to bleed into a soft brown, but this was different. His heated gaze turned the once warm tones into something much more sensual and promising. It reminded me of melted chocolate—the dark, bitter kind you'd dip strawberries into before letting the combination land on your tongue like a sinful invitation.

"See something you like, darlin'?" Lincoln asked, tightening his hold on my hair. He lowered his chin, drawing my attention to the smirk playing across his lips.

His impeccably soft, kissable lips.

Everything about this man seemed perfect—too good to be true. I should've taken one look at him before rolling my eyes and taking my miserable ass back to my car, but no. I decided to flirt with danger itself, and now I was going to get burned.

What a way to go, eh? Death by chocolate.

I nodded my head, unable to form words, while he stared down at me like I was his favorite meal when, in reality, I thought he was mine. One hand remained tangled in my hair while the other moved along my jaw. He ran his thumb over my mouth reverently, gaze dropping to my bottom lip as he applied pressure and swiped.

I knew my lipstick was long gone, but I couldn't stop myself from repeating his question.

"See something you like, cowboy?"

Lincoln's throaty laugh caught me by surprise, but he didn't break his gaze. "Yeah, actually... I'm thinking about what it would be like to fuck this pretty mouth. How I'd want to see it dressed in some pretty color only to fucking destroy it and then proudly wear the remnants around my cock so I could see precisely where you'd been."

Holy fuck.

I was no virgin, but I'd never been with a partner who'd unabashedly talked so filthy before, nor had I ever considered myself someone who wanted that. Sure, I'd fawned over this very scenario in books or movies when the main characters got together and, you know, indulged. I even remember thinking how exciting it must've been to be with someone who whispered dirty promises in my ear.

Reality, however, was never as good as fiction. Over the years, there'd been a handful of times when one of my exes would say something in the heat of the moment. He'd thought he sounded panty-melting hot when he actually sounded ridiculously cringeworthy and ruined the moment.

Then again, most of my sexual experiences ended in much the same way: Unfulfilled and disappointing.

Lincoln didn't have that problem. He had heat blooming at my core and my cheeks turning bright red as he openly talked about what he wanted. He said it with such ease, like he'd just asked me about the weather.

It was sexy and confident, and well... I fucking loved it.

Involuntarily, I tried to clench my thighs, realizing too little, too late, that he stood between them. He looked down, grinning like a fiend, when he realized I'd been trying to self-soothe the ache he'd so effortlessly created.

"Problem, darlin'? That pussy feeling needy?" he asked, tightening his grip on my hair. It was painful, but not in a way that made me want to tell him to stop. In fact, it made me want more.

I didn't understand it, didn't know who this new, brazen Josie Hayes was, but I liked her.

"Yes," I whimpered. I didn't care how pathetic it may have sounded, especially when his tongue darted across his lips. "Yes, I am. I mean, it is—"

Lincoln chuckled and stepped closer, raising his knee so it rested on the small section of the chair between my thighs. He leaned forward, lowering his voice so that it was nothing more than a purr in my ear. "Want me to kiss it better?"

I nodded again, not trusting myself to speak so soon. This was crazy and reckless and totally not me. I mean, I'd had my fair share of wild nights in my past—but I'd never felt so out of control.

This man had me at his mercy in what seemed like a handful of moments. He could've said or asked for anything, and I would've willingly given it to him. Which, come to think of it, should've been terrifying because I didn't know this man from a stranger on the street.

The moment Lincoln loosened his grip, I surged forward and captured his bottom lip between my teeth. My hands sought for purchase as I lifted the hem of his shirt, needing to feel the warmth of his skin on my palms. He didn't move for a moment, and I worried I'd gone too far. Did I misinterpret what he wanted? What he liked? Just as I moved to pull away, he met my frantic movements with ones of his own.

He straightened up, following my lead, and quickly removed his shirt. It landed on the floor somewhere behind us, immediately forgotten as he bared himself. I leaned back in my seat, chest heaving as I slowly scanned his body.

Lincoln had a smattering of dark hair across his chest, leading down his stomach and disappearing beneath his jeans. I ran my fingers along his chest as my gaze snagged on a long, jagged scar. It began just below his underarm and ran along the left side of his abdomen near his belly button.

I'd always thought scars were fascinating. They told a story, even if the story they were telling was one filled with pain. Growing up, I'd seen my fair share of horrific accidents, both on the circuit and on our ranch. Blood didn't bother me, and I'd been on the receiving end of more broken bones than I cared to admit.

Which was why I didn't think twice when I reached out and ran my fingertips gingerly over the soft, raised flesh.

"Does it hurt?" I asked, quickly jerking my arm back as he let out a low hiss.

Beneath furrowed brows, Lincoln's dark eyes clouded with a distant memory. "Not anymore," he said, shaking his head and leaning forward. I opened my mouth to ask more questions, to apologize for my brazen touch, but he placed a finger on my lips. "Do you want to talk, or do you want to let me see that pretty pussy, darlin'? Because I know which option I'd prefer."

Without waiting for my answer, he pulled me from the chair and lifted me in his arms. I squealed as he spun us around and placed me on top of the table. My legs hung off the side, dangling as he hooked his fingers into my belt loops. "This is your last chance to walk away," he said, slowly perusing my body. "If you don't want this, tell me now. I'll walk you to your car, kiss you goodnight, and ask for your number before watching you drive off."

The rational part of my brain told me that was exactly what I should do. I should tell Lincoln I had a good time tonight, thank him for keeping me company and for taking my mind off how shitty the past forty-eight hours had been.

Then I'd walk away.

There was no future between us. No late-night calls or lovesick texts. Absolutely no date nights. After all, I was only going to be in town for a few days before tucking tail right on back to Texas.

And yet, I couldn't make myself move. I couldn't make myself get off that table and walk out the door and his life in a matter of minutes.

I wasn't ready.

"I thought you wanted to know my name," I said, leaning back on my palms and quirking a brow.

Lincoln smiled and nodded. His tone was soft, hopeful, and full of curiosity. Somehow, he seemed younger than he had only moments ago when he thought I'd walk away. "I do, but I was hoping you'd tell me when you gave me your number."

"When?" I scoffed and rolled my eyes. "You seem awfully sure of yourself, cowboy."

He shook his head. "Call me optimistic, I guess. Can't help it when I'm standing between your pretty thighs."

"Ah," I said. His words only stoked the fire, a reminder that we were so close to crossing a line we couldn't come back from. "Well, my daddy always told me I needed to work hard for the things I want..." I drawled out the words, teasing him as I raised my hand and unclipped my hair, letting it fall around my shoulders. He tracked my movements greedily. "So, I think you should earn it, cowboy. Show me how badly you want it."

"Is that so?" he asked, bringing one hand up to rub his jaw. Anticipation coiled like a snake in my belly, forcing me to hold my breath until he spoke once more. "And how do you expect me to do that, darlin'?"

I shrugged one shoulder. "You seem like a smart enough man. I'm sure you can find a way to *incentivize* me." I sat up straighter, running my hands up the broad expanse of his chest. His skin was hot to the touch, and though he hadn't looked nervous all night, the erratic thundering of his heart gave away his trepidation.

Lincoln laughed, his breath scattering across my neck as he leaned forward and pressed a single kiss to my pulse point. Slowly, so slowly, his hands crawled up my legs, kneading my muscles with measured, deliberate strokes. "You want me to show you how badly I want you?"

I let my head fall back as he peppered open-mouthed kisses along my neck. Good god, I was putty in his damn hands, ready to be molded to his liking. "Yes," I breathed, wrapping my hands around his neck. "That might do the trick."

He pulled back, placing a hand in the center of my chest before gently pushing me back. I went without question, watching with rapt attention as his fingers found the button of my jeans. As he tugged down the zipper, he sank into the chair before me. "Lift your hips, darlin'. Let me see what's mine."

"What's yours?" I asked, raising a brow but complying anyway.

He paused, lips pursing before he answered. "For tonight. You're mine for tonight."

"It's technically the morning—"

But my words cut off as he threw my pants on the ground and placed an achingly tender kiss along my panty-clad pussy. "You're soaked, darlin'," he groaned, meeting my gaze. "This all because of me?"

I nodded, unable to speak as he let his tongue run across the saturated fabric. Usually, I would've been embarrassed. I'd been on the road all day and had to settle for an 'essentials only' bath in the bar restroom hours ago.

And no, I didn't do it for him or because I thought anything would happen between us—that would've been crazy.

At least, that's what I tried to convince myself of.

Lincoln pulled the fabric aside, pausing only for a moment to gauge my reaction. When I didn't object, he dove forward like a man on a mission. He licked and sucked and devoured my pussy, rarely coming up for air until I thought he may suffocate himself.

My hands raked through his hair, discarding the backward baseball cap on the floor with the rest of our clothes. I'd never had anyone taste me so reverently, so full of passion. This man didn't know me, and I didn't know him, but our bodies acted of their own accord. Somehow, they understood what the other needed before we could register it ourselves.

I knew only one thing for sure: I never wanted him to stop.

lincoln

. . .

I'D NEVER CONSIDERED myself a smart man. I'd made a lot of mistakes and fucked up more times than I could count, but the smartest thing I'd ever done was kiss the beautiful dark-haired tornado that swept into my bar.

Not only had it been the best kiss I'd ever experienced, but I'd be playing the sound of her sweet little whimpers on repeat for the rest of my life. I wanted to record them, to memorize the feel of her skin. I wanted to immortalize her beauty and capture our moment of need. One day, years from now, I could replay it when I was nothing more than an aging man with a fading memory and my hand wrapped around my cock.

And as I stared up at her stormcloud eyes from between her parted legs, I silently thanked whatever universal force drove her into my arms.

She tasted like liquor and temptation, like sin wrapped in a perfect silky bow. My fingers dug into her thighs, reveling in the way she gripped my hair and tugged as I drug the pad of my tongue over the seam of her pussy.

"Lincoln," she breathed, tightening her hold as I brought my finger up and played with her entrance. I liked when she said my

name. Liked it even more that she was begging for pleasure only I could give. "More."

I chuckled, pressing a kiss to her thigh as I pulled back. "Greedy girl. Give me a letter first."

She lifted her head, staring at me like I'd suddenly grown two heads. "The fuck do you mean?"

I shrugged. She'd made it clear she didn't want to just give me her name. I may not have known her reasoning, but I'd play her games so long as I got what I wanted. "You told me to get creative, so give me the first letter of your name, and I'll give you what you want." Without waiting, I slowly slipped my finger inside of her, relishing in the way she gasped as I pushed inside.

The sounds she made... God, they were fucking addicting. If I hadn't already been sporting an erection, hearing the noises that left her lips would have done it.

"J," she said without hesitation, laying back against the old wooden table with a thud. She let me play her body like an instrument, and I, like the bastard I was, greedily took anything she gave me. I could've pushed for more, but I liked the idea of withholding her orgasm the way she'd withheld her name.

Tit for tat, right?

"Let's go for letter two, then," I said, pressing my thumb against her clit. My other arm remained firmly in place— wrapped around her soft thigh with my hand resting atop her belly.

She didn't say anything as I dipped my head between her legs once more. I'd gone easy on her before, not knowing what she liked or how rough she wanted me to be, but I was done waiting.

I dipped my head back to her center, sucking her clit into my mouth and curling my finger inside her. As she cried out, I let my tongue roam across her pussy, making a mental note of every little sound she made and what I did to cause it.

It didn't take long before her hands found their way back into my hair, pulling me closer and wrapping her shaking legs firmly around my head so I could barely breathe. I didn't care. I'd gladly die with my head between her thighs.

The moment I felt her body tighten, barreling toward release, I pulled back.

"No, no, no," she pleaded, raising her head to stare down at me. "I was so close."

"Give me your name, and this can all be over," I said, a crooked smile on my lips.

I shouldn't have liked torturing her as much as I did. I'd never been with someone as mouthy as she was, but goddammit, there was something about her that had me toying with every line I'd ever set.

She glared, balling her hands into fists as she said, "O."

"How many letters are we going for, darlin'?" I asked, slowly working in and out of her wet heat.

She blew out a breath, and I watched in glee as her patience began to wane. "Well, I'm sure as hell not going with my full name if this is the game we're playing…"

Her words ended with a sigh as I leaned forward and blew on her clit. Her eyes met mine with a challenge I relished.

"I can do this all day and night, darlin'. I can wind you up so tight you'll be begging and pleading for me to fuck you, but I won't. Not until you give me your name."

Her defiant gaze didn't waver, didn't break for a second.

I sighed, trying and likely failing to hide how giddy her choice not to give in had made me. "I guess we'll have to do this my way…"

Over and over again, I brought her to the brink with my tongue, earning every bit of her ire as she bit out the remaining three letters.

S.

I.

E.

Josie.

Her name was Josie, and I'd never heard a name so sweet—almost as sweet as her perfect pussy.

It was on the last letter that I dove back in, fucking her fast and hard with my fingers. I stood, pulling her up and pressing my mouth to hers as she ground against my hand, chasing the orgasm that came only seconds later.

I'd never kissed anyone with my eyes open, but I couldn't help myself. I wanted to watch every beautiful, euphoric moment of her pleasure. She screamed and thrashed in my arms, clinging to my body like I was the sole thing in this world keeping her from floating away until, finally, she slumped forward and rested her head on my shoulder.

"Josie, huh?" I asked, feeling the curve of her smile on my skin. "Was that so hard?"

She pulled back, revealing the full flush of her cheeks. "No, but it was fun."

I quirked a brow. "Really? Because at one point, I was getting flashbacks to the Exorcist and thought I was close to losing my life."

Josie rolled her eyes, readying to volley back the same smart-ass comments we'd been trading, but I was done playing. I was done with the games.

I wanted this woman, and I wanted her now.

She let out a breathy gasp as I removed my fingers and gripped her bare ass, and brought her closer, dragging her drenched cunt along the rough denim covering my erection. "Please tell me you have a condom," she pleaded, looking down between our bodies.

"In my truck," I said, kissing her forehead. "You okay with staying right here?"

Josie nodded, but I sensed apprehension on her part. "There aren't, like, cameras in here, right?" she asked, looking around.

I shook my head, stifling a laugh. "Uh, no. Frank isn't a big fan of change and thinks the government could track him through security footage. I had to buy a card reader and computer myself so we could accommodate tourists during the summer."

That'd been one hell of a fight. For damn near a month, every day when I came in, the computer had been unplugged and the charging cord hidden. Only when I threatened to install the cameras he'd been so adamantly against did he come clean and show me where he'd stashed it.

I looked around, grabbing my shirt off the floor and tossing it to her. The last thing I wanted was for her to feel uncomfortable, and while she still had her top on, she was exposed from the waist down.

Josie draped it over her lap, calling out her thanks as I turned and jogged to the passenger side of my truck and rifled through the glove compartment.

"Please don't be fucking expired," I muttered, grabbing the box of condoms I'd stashed away months ago. *Or was it longer?* It'd been so long since I'd used one.

I checked the date, noting I was well within the time frame of use, and sent up a silent prayer. I remembered reading something in college about how they were technically good for three to five years, but questioning the integrity of condoms wasn't something I was willing to gamble on.

"We're all set," I said, running back inside and shaking the box for her to see.

Josie smiled, and the sight damn near took my breath away. "Thank god," she laughed. "I don't know if I could've waited for a store run."

"A store run, huh?" I leaned in, trying to steady my pulse. "You desperate for my dick, darlin'?"

She rolled her eyes, reaching for my belt loops and pulling

me closer. "Maybe I am, cowboy. Or maybe I just want to know just how well you ride."

I went willingly, settling myself between her legs as though I belonged. "Is that a challenge?"

"I'm just saying that your mouth has been writing a lot of checks, but it's time to cash them in—"

"I think you know my *mouth* can cash all the checks it's written, and believe me, darlin'," I said, leaning in close, "any other payout will be just as grand."

Josie's hands were working the button of my jeans before I could reach it. She fought against the worn fabric until it finally popped free, not waiting for my zipper to slide the denim down.

I hissed as she ran the heel of her palm along my erection, trying like hell to toe off my boots and shimmy out of my pants. All remaining effort went toward not coming in my briefs like a fucking pubescent teenager who'd never touched a woman before.

"Condom," I said through gritted teeth.

She reached toward the box as I slipped any remaining clothes off. When she turned her attention back toward me, her gaze slid slowly down my body to where I slowly stroked my cock. "See something you like?" I asked.

Josie ripped into the packet and pulled out the condom. She reached out, slowly rolling the latex over the head of my dick until it reached the base. When her gaze met mine, all pretenses were gone.

This was real. We were going to do this.

"Hold on," I told her with a wink.

"Wait, what?" she asked, squealing as I scooped her into my arms and carried her toward the pool table in the corner.

Frank had bought it brand new when he opened this place, and it'd quickly become a staple of the old bar. I'd recently refurbished the antique with brand new green felt as a birthday present, though he stopped me from sanding and restaining the oak wood. It was still scuffed and dented from the years gone by, but he'd said it'd just given it character.

I sat Josie down on the edge, but she placed her hand on my chest and pushed me back. She hopped down, and I cringed as her bare feet touched the floor. Sure, I tried to keep the place clean, but I hadn't done any of that shit yet since my focus had been entirely on her.

But as I opened my mouth to tell her to stop, Josie turned toward the pool table. With careful hands, she drew the hem of her shirt over her head and made quick work of her bra. All thoughts eddied from my mind as she looked over her shoulder, her hands sliding along the scarred wood as she bent over and waved her ass in a dangerous taunt.

I closed the distance between us in two strides, running one hand down the center of her back as I used the other to drag my cock along her drenched core. The sight of her on display for me was the most sensual thing I'd ever seen. This woman didn't know me, yet here she was, pushing back and seeking the relief she desperately craved.

Josie was at my will, my mercy, and—

"Please," she whimpered. "Fuck me."

And just like that, our roles had changed.

josie

. . .

WITH ONE HARD THRUST, all the air left my lungs as Lincoln drove his hips forward.

"Fuck," he growled, going still when all I wanted was for him to move. His cock filled me. I needed the friction, needed him to soothe the ache he'd created the moment I stepped into this nowhere bar.

He wrapped his arms around my stomach, tugging me back until our bodies were flush. His hands ran slowly up to my chest, palming my aching breasts and pinching my nipples until I cried out. It was a different sort of pain, a hurt caused by all the right attention.

I'd never put much stock in nipple play. Most of the time, either myself or a partner overlooked the importance, but I was sure as hell learning how erotic it could be now.

Judging by his hearty chuckle, Lincoln knew exactly what he was doing. He knew how wet he'd made me, how I was on the verge of truly begging to be fucked right here and now, and he loved it.

"Like that, darlin'?" he rasped, rolling my nipples between his fingers. "Like when I play with these pretty fucking tits?"

Holy shit.

"Yes," I breathed. I let my head fall against his shoulder, reveling in how his touch grew from reverential to downright desperate.

Lincoln groaned into my ear. His hips slowly began to move, hitting that special spot that had me seeing stars.

His lips skated along the length of my neck, nipping my pulse point as one of his hands snaked down my stomach. He found my clit with ease, the pressure of his touch sending tendrils of pleasure throughout my body as I teetered on the edge of an impending orgasm.

I never wanted this to end, yet I wanted to come undone.

He was so good—too good. How the fuck did he know what to do? What to say? Had I just been with inexperienced partners my whole life?

Yes.

I already knew the answer to that question.

"So fucking good," he breathed. "I can feel your tight cunt squeezing my cock, Josie, and it feels so fucking good. You're gonna make me come."

My name on his lips was a goddamn dream and my undoing.

I detonated around him, surrendering entirely to my pleasure as he chased his own with wild abandon. His fingers landed on my hips in a grip so brutal I knew it would leave marks behind. He fucked me hard and fast, not slowing even for a second as we slammed into the pool table.

"Fuck, fuck, *fuck*," Lincoln chanted. Each word escalated in volume until he found his release with a guttural cry. His movements grew choppy as our moans of pleasure mingled, reverberating off the walls of this dingy bar that had become our sanctuary.

I collapsed against the green felt, sweat-slicked and sated. I couldn't remember the last time I'd felt at peace after sex. Especially considering the man inside of me was a stranger.

It was funny how only hours ago, I was a woman who could count the number of times a partner had made her come on one hand, yet Lincoln had wrung two from me with ease.

I'd always struggled to orgasm, regardless of if I was trying to take care of myself solo or with someone else. Having been on antidepressants since I was a teenager, I didn't understand the full effects then, but I sure as hell did now.

It didn't matter how many times I told them about my struggles. The men I'd been with in the past had cared more about chasing their own high than tending to my needs. If I was with anyone else other than Lincoln, they would've likely taken me against a bathroom stall, thanked me for my time, and walked away satisfied while I drove to the cabin unfulfilled.

But Lincoln was different. He hadn't been in a rush to have sex. Hell, he'd given me an out. When I'd finally given in, he not only made sure that I got mine, but had me coming apart at his touch twice before he even thought about his own.

He leaned forward, pressing short, sweet kisses along my bare shoulder before he slipped free. I felt his loss immediately and hated how much I wanted it back.

"Where're you going?" I asked, turning around to face him.

"Taking care of the condom," he called out over his shoulder. "I don't need Frank walking into any messes in a few hours."

I couldn't help but ogle him as he disappeared from view. Lincoln was gorgeous. His body was crafted of well-defined muscle, likely honed from years of hard labor rather than sessions in a gym. And I'd never considered myself someone who had a thing for asses, but after one glance at his, I'd changed my mind. Honestly, it took every bit of effort I had not to chase after him and demand a second round, but that seemed a little crazy.

Ugh. Pull yourself together, Josie. You're just dick drunk.

As much as I didn't want to listen to the logical bitch inside my head, I knew she was right. I'd come to Tennessee to escape my broken heart and cheating ex. I sure as hell didn't intend—nor did I need—to cuff myself to the first man I met.

Even if he was the best sex I'd ever had.

I pushed off the table, reaching for my shirt and bra, which I'd thrown to the ground in my haste to get undressed. I needed to put my damn clothes on. I needed to get as far away from Lincoln as possible before I did something stupid like ask to see him again.

But first, I needed underwear.

Everything was scattered around the bar, thrown haphazardly with little care about where it had landed. Thankfully, my pink panties stood out beneath the dim lights, acting as a beacon for the rest of my clothes.

I'd just slipped them on when Lincoln walked by, bending down to sort through his own clothes. I helped, knowing I'd absolutely played a part in tearing them off—which would remain a memory I'd replay over and over again.

We worked silently, neither daring to break the strange tension in the air. It was a stark difference from the teasing banter we'd so quickly become accustomed to. Even though I'd been ready to run, to hurry out of here before I could want anything more from Lincoln, I hated the way it felt.

We knew what came next, but that didn't make walking away any easier.

Only when our hands accidentally brushed one another's did we make eye contact, both half-dressed and disheveled. His dark eyes, which had been filled with heat and longing, had since grown guarded.

Had they been like that before and I'd somehow not noticed? I couldn't remember them being that way when I walked through the door this evening, but maybe that was only because he was at work.

Lincoln broke contact first, standing tall with the remainder of his clothes in his hands. He got dressed in one corner while I occupied the other. The only sound was the soft croon of old country music from the antique jukebox and the shuffle of feet as we both slipped on our shoes.

Say something, you idiot! Say literally anything—

"Need a hand cleaning up around here?" I asked, reaching into my purse for a large claw clip to put my hair up.

Lincoln turned around, staring at me from under furrowed brows. I understood his probable confusion because truth be told, I could match it. I'd just agreed with the voice in my head that it was time to go—the voice that tried to preserve what little dignity I had left—and yet now I was volunteering to stay.

He reached up, running a hand along the back of his neck. "There isn't much to do but take out the trash and clean the floors. I took care of the rest earlier."

"Ah," I said, rocking back on my heels. God. Why was I so awkward? "Well, I could still help. I've cleaned so many floors in my life. You might even call me a professional."

Lincoln chuckled. "Josie, it's fine. I'm not under any impression this was anything more than two strangers sharing—" he blew out a breath and shook his head, "—a fucking phenomenal night together."

My heart sank. "I mean, that makes sense, but it doesn't mean I don't want to help you out. I've kept you up late, after all. If not for me, you'd be home in bed already."

"You didn't even want to give me your name."

There was something about the way he said it that made my stomach clench. While I might not have regretted the game we played, or how he forced the letters from my lips in such a deliriously wicked way, I regretted not giving him my name sooner. I could blame it on the alcohol, but it really stemmed from not wanting another broken heart so soon.

Not that I should be concerned with that since I was only here for a few days—a week, max.

I took a tentative step forward, waiting to see if he stopped me before I approached him. He leaned against the edge of the pool table with his arms crossed, watching every move I made with a cautious gaze.

Though the scent of sex hung in the air, remnants of his cologne clung to my clothing. The heady mixture of the two shouldn't have been as alluring as it was, but I didn't want to ever wash this shirt, so that I never forgot what he smelled like.

"I'm sorry I didn't tell you my name from the get-go, but to be honest..." I blew out a breath. I'd purposely steered clear of anything involving Wyatt or why I'd driven to Tennessee on a whim when Lincoln had asked. But maybe it was time for a dash of vulnerability. "I came up to the mountains because I found my boyfriend balls deep in someone else less than forty-eight hours ago. My family has a cabin up here, though we don't use it often."

Lincoln cursed, drawing his brows tight. "What kind of idiot would cheat on you?"

The question stung more than I could say. I had answers at the ready from my years of self-loathing. Those didn't even include the vicious retorts straight from the mouths of nearly all my exes. It'd never mattered if their criticisms weren't valid or warranted; they'd stuck all the same.

I laughed, though it was hollow. "Oof, we don't have enough time for me to list my many, *many* flaws or backtrack through my tragic dating history. I have a bad habit of falling fast for all the wrong people."

Lincoln uncrossed his arms, letting one knuckle rap against the oak table. "I don't believe that."

"Do you want references?" I asked, raising a brow. "I mean, I can give you a list of numbers to call—"

"No," he said, cutting me off. "I don't give a shit what some jaded asshole has to say. Of course, he'll find fault in you because he's lost the best thing he's ever had."

"You don't even know me," I said.

The overwhelming urge to run was creeping in. He didn't know me any more than I knew him. From our limited interaction, I assumed he was a good person, but not everyone showed their true colors from the start.

I knew I'd fallen prey to that trap more than once or twice.

"I know enough."

"And what if I told you I snore? Would that be a deal breaker?"

His lips twitched. "I can always buy a pair of ear plugs. They have them at the dollar store down the road. I'll even buy you a pair, too."

"Me a pair? Why? I won't need them for myself."

"Well, I don't know if I snore, but it couldn't hurt." He shrugged. "I wanna make sure you're comfortable when you're sleeping in my bed."

"You seem mighty confident," I muttered. He was so damn sure of himself. It was unreasonably attractive. I'd never been pursued like this. The guys I'd dated in the past would've run for the hills at the mere mention of a flaw.

"I am," he said, pushing off the table. He closed the distance between us, taking my chin between thumb and forefinger. Brown eyes bore into me, scanning my face in a way that felt way too personal, considering we were two passersby. "I'm mighty sure there isn't a damn thing you could say that'd put me off you."

And then he kissed me.

It was soft. Gentle. Different from the desperation of earlier. Lincoln didn't rush, letting us settle into the comfort of the intimate moment as though we'd done this a million times. As he pulled away, he rested his forehead on mine. Neither of us spoke, and I didn't want to.

"So, about that offer to help..." Lincoln said, shoving his hands in his pockets. "That still on the table?"

"I think I can stick around a little longer," I said, stepping aside. "Just point me in the right direction."

This time, when we separated, it wasn't taut with awkward tension. We settled into an easy silence, listening to the croon of the jukebox as we worked. It didn't take us long to gather the trash and sweep the floors. Though it would've been considerably shorter had he not grabbed the broom from me and sang along to Brooks and Dunn. It was off-key and, frankly, terrible, but I was wiping tears from my eyes as he sang the last lyrics to Neon Moon.

The scent of lemon cleaning solution filled the space, following us into the crisp morning air. I waited patiently as Lincoln locked up, setting a large black garbage bag on the ground between us.

I didn't know what would happen next. Would we exchange numbers like he'd suggested before he knew my name? Or would he want to keep whatever we shared limited to this moment right here?

Lincoln turned to face me, the grey light of dawn casting shadows from under his baseball cap. "So..." he said, rocking back on his heels. "Your place or mine?"

josie

. . .

"WHERE'RE WE GOING NOW?" I asked, sliding into the passenger seat of Lincoln's old truck. A thin stream of coffee-flavored ice cream ran over my fingers, and I ran my tongue along my skin. "Shit, sorry. I'm making a mess."

"Nowhere if you keep doing that," Lincoln groaned, following suit. He ran his hands through his hair. "Seriously, woman. Why're you apologizing? You're killing me here." He pointed to where his jeans were tightening.

An apology was on the tip of my tongue, but I swallowed it down. "Sounds like a you problem. Not my fault it's so easy to get you riled up," I quipped, wiping away the sticky remnants. "Seriously, you might want to get that checked out. It's slightly alarming."

"Wasn't an issue until I met you, darlin'. Problem solved. You should prescribe me something," he said, waggling his eyebrows and turning the ignition.

I couldn't stop my smile as he rolled down the windows and cranked up the music. He put on an old playlist and let the Commodores fill the silence. It'd been years since I'd driven down Main Street in Pinecrest, but it was just as picturesque as

I remembered. Nearly every shop was locally owned, except the Dairy Queen on the edge of town.

Our family came to spend a few weeks during school breaks when I was little. Between Dad's training schedule and the packed calendars of three teenage girls, our vacations were few and far between. It was a nice change of pace to come back and experience it with someone who knew the best spots in town.

From the moment Lincoln and I left Frank's bar, we'd been glued at the hip. We counted the passing hours with languid kisses and mind-blowing orgasms. When we'd gotten back to his house, I sent a single text to my sister telling her not to worry about me—I was okay and would be home in a week or two—before turning my phone off.

And I'd never felt freer.

I'd checked on my cabin this morning while Lincoln ran inventory at the bar. Apparently, his boss had called and told him to get his ass back to work before he got fired. It was almost enough to make me feel bad about monopolizing his time. When I tried to apologize, he'd placed his hand over my mouth and forced me to ride his fingers until I saw stars.

Needless to say, I wasn't really sorry after that.

My cabin still sat empty, untouched by the world. It'd been freshly cleaned, smelling of Windex and fabric softener. My sister, Cleo, had likely called ahead to the cleaning service when I tore out of Texas. My dad had friends in the area from his rodeo days, and they came every few months to ensure everything was in working order.

Sitting in the drive, I considered staying here like I was supposed to. This whole trip was supposed to be my opportunity to get my head right. It didn't look like it was going to happen, though. Nothing was appealing about staying in that cold house alone when I could drive a few miles down the mountain and be back in Lincoln's arms.

That's precisely how I ended up sitting shotgun in his truck, licking up melting ice cream while he laughed at the mess I was making.

Lincoln was so easygoing. Nothing seemed to ruffle his feathers or get under his skin. It was one of the things I found so attractive about him. Most of the guys I'd dated had a short fuse and an even shorter attention span. I was no stranger to being chastised, especially regarding my inability to make quick decisions.

Lincoln hadn't batted an eye when I'd taken fifteen minutes to decide on an ice cream flavor. When anxiety had begun prickling my skin, I'd tried to cancel my order. I'd much rather walk out empty-handed than cause a scene. But he hadn't let me. He stepped to my side and touched my back to steady my nerves without me saying a word.

How was it possible we'd only known each other for a handful of days? I didn't put much stock into things like fate, but I could've sworn there'd been some weird magnetic pull that led me to pull into that damn bar. There hadn't been a moment of awkwardness that had me second-guessing my place by his side—no red flags that'd sent me running for the hills.

Everything was natural between us, like picking up on something we'd already started rather than discovering something new.

"What's going through that pretty head of yours?" Lincoln asked over the roar of the engine. He leaned over and turned the radio down.

I chewed on my lip, turning in my seat to face him. He wore a faded t-shirt with Frank's logo and a backward-facing cap. Dark aviators slipped down his strong nose as he glanced over.

"All of this is kind of crazy, don't you think?" I asked, tucking a strand of hair behind my ear. "I mean, I don't know you—not really. You could be an axe murderer playing the long game, and I'm just your unsuspecting victim who fell for your gruff cowboy charm."

His laugh was deep and rich, like the smell of molasses in the air. "Gruff cowboy charm? Do you think I could quote you on that? I think that'd make a great tagline to use when they talk about all my murders."

"You know what I'm saying—"

"What if *you're* the murderer?" he cut in, tapping his fingers against the steering wheel. "I've just welcomed you into my home—my bed, no less. It'd be nothing for you to off me in the middle of the night."

I covered my face with my hands, groaning. "Never mind, forget I said anything."

"Oh, no, you don't," Lincoln said, steering the truck off the road and putting it in park.

"What're you doing?" I asked, watching the cars zoom past us on the highway.

Lincoln reached over, unbuckling my seatbelt and setting me onto his lap. My protests quickly turned into nervous laughter as his hands found my hips. My body was trapped between the steering wheel and his own. "Alright, talk to me, darlin'. What's going on?"

My anxiety had reached the point of no return—where all rational thinking had left the station, and I was on a one-way train to nowhere good. My chest tightened, constricting against my frantically beating heart.

This was where I'd ruin it—this thing I was already terrified to lose. The man who'd been so gentle to a woman who'd been running from bad decisions. Why'd I have to open my big, fat mouth? I should've shoved those fears down and capped them like I'd done so many times before.

I tried to laugh, but it was hollow. "Nothing. I'm just... I don't know. I'm just being silly—"

Lincoln shook his head. "Now, why don't you try again. I know you're lying."

I leaned back against the wheel, frustration lacing every

word. "Okay, but that's my point! How do you know I'm lying? Don't you think that's weird?"

"Nope," he said without hesitation. "Why would it be?"

"Because I'm just some girl you fucked on a pool table after a four-hour conversation."

Lincoln gnawed on the inside of his cheek, letting out a huff of breath. "That really what you think, darlin'? That you're some fuck to me? Hell, if that's all this was, don't you think I'd have turned you loose by now? I sure wouldn't be taking off work and buying you ice cream, would I?"

His hand came up, cupping my jaw. "Truth be told, I don't have all the answers, Josie. I wish I could give you what you're looking for. All I know is that I don't plan to let those thoughts in your head ruin whatever this could be. We could burn out by morning. If that's the case, so be it. But why don't we just keep doing what we're doing and see where it goes?"

I threw my arms around Lincoln's neck, kissing him with all the need I struggled to put into words. He nipped at my lips and matched my fervor. The rising panic I'd felt moments ago was chased away by each pass of his lips. I rolled my neck as he trailed kisses toward my pulse.

I could feel him hardening beneath me, bucking up into my center like a man possessed. "God, Lincoln—"

The horn blared as he pushed my back into the steering wheel. "Shit," he said, laughing as he pulled me tight against his chest. "Well, if that friendly couple over there didn't know what we were doing before, they sure as shit do now."

"What?" I said, scrambling off him. I looked out of the front window, watching as a man and woman stared at us in horror from the lot across the street. "Oh, God." I sunk deeper into the seat, tucking my head into my shirt as Lincoln laughed

"Doin' that won't change a thing, darlin'."

I peeked out. "How long were they there?"

"Oh, I clocked them the moment we pulled over. Would've

moved along somewhere new if you hadn't started talking nonsense." His lips ticked up, warming me all over. His head rolled against the seat, chocolate eyes taking me in. "But there were more important things on my mind."

"Is that right, cowboy?" I asked, biting my lip.

"That's right, darlin'. Now, how about I show you my favorite spot in the mountains. There's a real pretty view, and no one around for miles."

LINCOLN STOOD BEHIND THE BAR, laughing at something Frank said as he wiped the top with an old rag. I watched their interaction with a smile from my seat beside the old man. It had quickly become one of my favorite things.

It'd been five days since I drove across the Tennessee state line.

Five days of absolute bliss at Lincoln's side, getting lost on mountain back roads and visiting his favorite spots in town.

Five days of avoiding my family's cabin, choosing instead to sleep in a stranger's bed and have the best sex of my life.

Five days of knowing all of this had an expiration date I refused to acknowledge.

We spent our days driving up and down mountain roads with the windows down in Lincoln's old Ford. He showed me the little house where he'd grown up and took me to his favorite restaurants. The rest of the time we'd spent in his bed, unable to keep our hands off one another. We talked in the quiet moments after sex. I'd learned the way he took his coffee, how he preferred chicken to steak, and the scent of his favorite candle.

This familiarity was something I'd never experienced before. If Lincoln's long, lingering touches were anything to go by, he hadn't either. We were like two magnets, our force too strong to ignore.

The night after my momentary freak out on the highway, Lincoln hadn't let me out of his sight. I'd come to work with him every night, watching him talk to strangers and friends alike. I'd tried to stay out the way of paying customers, but Frank and Lincoln were having none of that. The old bar owner welcomed me with open arms. I liked him. He was the type of gruff old bastard who didn't take any shit. Best of all, he had more dirt on Lincoln than I ever imagined possible.

Honestly, Frank reminded me a bit of my dad. He'd told me about his years spent as a bull rider. By my calculations, his time likely overlapped with Dad's. I'd almost asked him about it a time or two, but I decided against it. Family was the one line Lincoln and I hadn't crossed.

"Last call! Get your beers, pay your tabs, and then get on home." Lincoln's voice boomed out over the low buzz of conversation. Groups began gathering their belongings, meandering toward the door with glazed eyes and high spirits. I downed the rest of my beer and grabbed an empty grey tub to pick up half-drunk glasses.

As the last customer walked out, Lincoln flipped off the flashing neon 'open' sign and locked the door.

"You look good in neon, darlin'," he said, stealing a kiss and the tub of dishes. "Grab the broom for me?"

This had become our nightly routine. He always washed the dishes while I swept and mopped. Sometimes, just like the first night, he wandered over to the jukebox and picked a song. Then he'd sing into the worn brown handle, putting on a concert meant just for me.

It was my favorite time of day.

Each time, it made me want to dance along with him. I favored the slow tunes, the ones he'd croon softly as he wiped down the bar. I wanted to hear him whisper them into my ear as he swayed to the beat of the familiar song.

I'd just grabbed a hold of the broom when Frank's voice made me pause.

"You got a great girl there, Linc," he said, tapping his fingers on the bar top.

"Yeah, I do," Lincoln said, a smile in his voice.

"When's she going back?"

My grip on the handle grew tighter. I peeked around the corner, watching them even though I knew better.

I learned from an early age what eavesdropping would get you. That was how I found out dogs didn't just go to a different farm to live out the rest of their days.

"Dunno," Lincoln said. "I haven't asked her."

A pause. "Don't you think that might be a good idea?"

Lincoln shook his head as he closed the lid to the dishwasher. He braced his hands on either side of the sink, letting his head drop between his shoulders. "Probably, but I don't want to. Not yet. Besides, what if she decides to stay? She said she was looking for an escape, a place to clear her head... What if this is that?"

I closed my eyes and let my head fall against the handle. This had gone too far. No matter how much I wanted to, I couldn't stay. The thought had crossed my mind a million times since I'd walked through the front door of this bar and into Lincoln's arms. I had a life back in Texas—my family, the ranch, and a job I didn't completely hate. Dad wanted to bring me on full time at the ranch to alleviate his stress, and I was excited about the prospect of doing something worthwhile.

God, why hadn't I left earlier? There'd be no way to leave without hurting one or both of us. There'd been so many signs to go. It'd felt too good. And what was that saying about things being too good to be true?

For five days, I'd felt blissfully free from all responsibilities and burdens, letting myself be blissfully happy. But things were changing. Getting too serious too fast. I would've been a damn liar if I said I hadn't thought about staying in this state.

In this bar.

In Lincoln's arms.

But I couldn't linger any longer. I pushed open the door leading back into the bar as Frank began to speak, but he saw me and stopped. I looked toward Lincoln, who gave me a soft, tender smile that broke my heart into a million pieces.

I needed to leave Tennessee, and not look back.

Tonight.

"YES, YES, *YES*," I chanted, pulling on Lincoln's hair as he stared up at me from between my legs. I closed my eyes, giving myself over to the building pressure low in my stomach as I ground against his mouth.

"I want you to come, baby. Let that pretty cunt soak my face." His words were a deep rumble, promising pleasure as his tongue parted my lips, and he clamped down on my clit.

Oh *God*, I was done for. The force of my orgasm had me doubling over, grasping his headboard in a white-knuckled grip. I tried to raise up, but he held onto my thighs and forced me to stay right where I was as aftershocks wracked my body.

I sagged against the iron railing as he slipped from underneath me. I felt his presence at my back, lips skating along my shoulders and neck as he whispered praises in my ear. "You did so good, Josie, but can you give me another? I can't get enough of you."

If it'd been anyone else, I likely would've said no. Then again, if it'd been anyone else, I would've been faking my way through another round of subpar sex.

The clock on Lincoln's nightstand read 3:00 AM. We'd spent

the last few hours tangled in his sheets after coming home from the bar. I'd lost count of the number of times he'd taken me, though the number of condom wrappers scattered around the room said enough.

I guess we were going to add one more to the pile.

I'd vowed to talk to Lincoln once we walked through his cabin door. To tell him that no matter what we felt, there was no future for us that didn't end in heartbreak, but the words died on my lips the moment he smiled and pulled me in for a kiss.

How was I supposed to leave this man? This perfect, wonderful man.

I cursed myself for stopping at Frank's. If I'd just driven through, I'd never have met Lincoln. I would've spent the past few days stitching my pride back together before returning to Texas.

Not falling in love with a beautiful man from Tennessee in five days.

The thought was terrifying because it shouldn't have been possible. How can you love someone in such a short time?

No, this was infatuation at best. Once I was home and the immediate ache of leaving Tennessee had passed, so would this feeling.

Right?

I should get up right now and go, but that need diminished as Lincoln turned my limp body around to face him and pressed a kiss to my forehead. He laid me down on my back, letting his heady scent envelop me.

I'd never think of pine and leather the same way.

"You're so fucking gorgeous," Lincoln whispered, rolling a condom on. He stared down at me, fisting his cock before notching it at my entrance. My response came as a whimper as he slowly sank inside of me, running his hands along my back. His low groan sent goosebumps skittering across my skin.

He drew my arms up, wrapping them around his neck until we shared breaths. His body began to move with slow, skillful precision. Each thrust was met with a languid kiss, drawing me tighter until I was begging him to move faster.

This felt different than all the other times. It was slower and full of an emotion I didn't want to think about. If I did, I knew tears would follow, and I was determined not to shed a single one until I crossed the state line.

But as Lincoln coaxed the orgasm from my body before following with his own, I couldn't deny that he'd just made love to me when I was planning on breaking his heart.

lincoln

. . .

THE SOUND of my phone alarm pulled me from the best dream I'd ever had. A dream I couldn't wait to tell Josie.

It'd been five days—or technically six, now—since that little tornado had blown into my bar and my life.

Five days of countless smiles and laughter and sex.

Hell, I couldn't remember the last time I'd smiled so much. Before Josie, I hadn't had much of a reason to. My life was as dull as it was predictable. I woke up every morning and drove to Frank's ranch to help him with the handful of cattle still lingering on his land before cleaning up and heading to the bar to prepare for opening.

Even if we weren't blood related, he was the only family I had. Frank had taken me in when I'd lost everything I loved, allowing me to turn my life around when no one else had. He'd told me he knew what it was like to have your future disappear overnight and didn't want me to end up like him.

Though he'd lived a good life, it'd been lonely. He'd come close to marrying once, but that had changed when his rodeo career came to a screeching halt. The fame he'd been right on the cusp of had disappeared, along with his fiancée.

He never opened himself up to another woman again.

Being alone had never bothered me, but recently, I'd wondered what having someone by my side would be like.

Someone like Josie.

"Good morn—" I began to say, reaching out to her side of the bed.

It was cold.

Empty.

"Josie?" I called her name, but there was nothing. It was eerily silent in my home. The sky was overcast, letting in a grey gloom even though it was nine in the morning—a jarring contrast to the brilliant blue skies of yesterday.

I padded over to my door, noticing it was unlocked. I peeked my head outside, noting her car was gone. Maybe she'd just run into town. I'd taken Josie to the small coffee shop off Main Street the first morning she'd been here, and she'd demanded we go back every morning since.

But on my way back to the bedroom, I noticed a single sheet of paper on the kitchen counter. My heart thundered in my chest as I fought the overwhelming sense of dread threatening to take over.

Balling my hands into fists, I stepped closer and read the hastily written scrawl.

I'M SORRY.
- J

josie

. . .

One Year Later

"HEY, DADDY," I said, cradling my phone between my ear and shoulder. "What's wrong?"

I cringed when I'd seen my dad's name flash across my phone, knowing today was the worst day to be running late. In my defense, I hadn't known my old coffee machine would choose this morning to finally die, thereby forcing me to stop at the nearest café for my caffeine fix.

I really wanted an energy drink, but Ellis thought they were unhealthy and didn't like me drinking them.

My dad's gruff voice greeted me on the other line. "Can't an old man check up on his daughter?"

"Not today, no. Now tell me what you need." I mouthed my thanks to the barista at the counter as they handed me my order.

The Brews Brothers coffee shop was always busy, but there was a different energy this morning. It could've just been my own nerves and frazzled nature getting the best of me. Most of the seats were filled, and it'd taken me five minutes longer than I'd expected to get my order.

Five minutes I didn't have.

"Well, you're late," my father said. I heard the shuffling of something in the background, a sign that he was searching for something to keep his hands busy and mind occupied on anything other than what he had going on today. "It's not like you to be late."

"My coffee machine died, so I had to stop and get my caffeine. Rest assured, I'm in my truck and on my way."

"We have coffee here," he grumbled.

I couldn't stop the inherent gagging noise I made when thinking about the sludge my father called coffee. "That shit is swill, Daddy. You're the only person who likes it."

"That's a lie. The boys like it fine."

I didn't have the energy or the heart to tell him that the ranch hands had hidden a single-serve maker in the breakroom so they didn't have to drink the pot Dad brewed each morning.

It'd become a rite of passage anytime we had a new hire to watch them fill their cup and spew it across the concrete floor after the first sip.

But there was no arguing with Dad about his coffee. He and I'd had that conversation many, many times. "Alright, well, I'll be there shortly. Is there anything you need from town?"

"Naw. The new hands arrived last night, and Bishop's been keeping them busy with orientation while I've been shaking hands and kissing ass all morning."

Bishop Bryant was Dad's right-hand man. He'd showed up one day as nothing more than a scraggly seventeen-year-old kid severely needing a guiding hand. My dad had been too happy to take him in and show him the ropes.

Ever since, he'd become an honorary part of our family.

"If anyone can keep them in line, it's Bishop," I said, turning onto the familiar country road ahead. It'd still take me fifteen minutes to hit the looming white gate I loved and another ten until I reached the big house on the hill.

"Yeah," Dad agreed. "But now I need you to get your ass

here so that you can keep me in line. Your mother keeps me sane, but she won't be home until next week."

"Ah, now that I can do," I laughed. "I'll be there shortly, Dad. I promise."

"I'll hold you to that, sugar." He paused, then cursed under his breath. "Alright, I've got to go. People are starting to show up."

With that, he hung up. Music began playing through the speakers of my truck as I reached for my coffee in the console. But the moment the drink was in my hand, I hit a giant pothole —one I'd been on the city's ass to fix for nearly a month.

Scalding hot liquid sloshed onto my hand, and I dropped the drink on the floorboard without thinking.

"Fuck," I yelled, pulling over the best I could on the small, two-lane road. I was halfway in the ditch, but it'd have to do. I reached for my glove compartment, popping it open to grab the roll of thick napkins I kept on hand for things like this.

I was late, my coffee was gone, and I wanted to cry.

Other than the turn of bad luck I was experiencing this morning, the past year of my life had gone exceedingly well. Dad had settled me into a role at the ranch as his and Bishop's assistant, which sounded worse than it really was. The ranch's schedule was hectic, and neither of them was good at communicating, so I'd stepped in to be the go-between.

It meant that Dad could focus on hosting his training seminars without worrying if it would interfere with Bishop transporting cattle to the auction—which had happened on more than one occasion in the past few years.

And then there was Ellis.

Ellis Martin and I had gone to the same school since kindergarten. His dad was my dad's accountant, and we'd always gotten along growing up. He was primed to take over his father's business and had been given some high profile clients —including my father and Black Springs Ranch. Dad didn't much care for change, so he'd delegated a lot of meetings to me.

Ellis and I had spent months together, sorting through old files and financial records over late night dinners and weekend coffee runs. So, when he'd asked me out on an actual date three months ago, I'd said yes. The only excuse I could make was one I was trying desperately to forget.

The only fault I could find in Ellis was his absolute disdain for energy drinks and bacon.

Cleaning up the mess, I pulled back onto the road and continued toward the ranch. I said a prayer for my sanity, knowing I'd need it for a day filled with kissing asses and shaking hands.

Today marked the beginning of Dad's summer training clinic. The program ran for two months but was segmented into eight two-week sessions. People from all over the country came to stay and learn from the best. This year, there'd been so much interest that Dad hired a few more helping hands and one more trainer, so it wasn't all on his shoulders.

Try as he might to deny it, Dad couldn't keep this up forever. His health had taken a turn in the past year, his days filled with trips to the doctor instead of long rides in the saddle. Between my mom, my sisters, and me, we'd all had to sit him down and talk about the future of his career and these clinics.

He'd asked for one more summer, and that's what we'd agreed on.

As I cleared the cattle guard to my parent's house, I pulled my truck into the spot next to my older sister, Cleo's, car. I shook my head as I saw Lennox's big ass truck was crookedly parked off to the side. She and I had always been the closest, only a year apart. I knew I could turn to her for anything and it wouldn't be met with an ounce of judgment.

After all, I'd had to pull her from plenty of mishaps when we were younger. I wasn't sure what it was about barrel racers, but trouble always seemed to follow them. Lennox was no exception. It was almost fun watching people push her buttons, not realizing she was the scrapper of the family, but I also didn't need to be bailing her out of jail.

Cleo stood on the porch with her arms crossed over her chest. She looked too much like Dad, especially with that scowl across her face.

"You're late," she said, echoing Dad's words from earlier as I hopped out of my truck.

"Good morning, sunshine. I'm so glad to see you, too."

Her face broke into a smile as I ran toward her. She wrapped me in a tight hug the way she always had when I was a kid, surrounding me with a sharp cinnamon scent that reminded me of the coffee I'd spilled.

"Please tell me you have caffeine hidden somewhere," I groaned.

She pulled back. "I thought you stopped and got coffee?"

"And I spilled it," I said, grimacing as I remembered the liquid gold splashed across my floorboard. "That damn pothole still isn't fixed, and I wasn't paying attention."

Cleo pursed her lips, tilting her head for me to follow her into the garage. In the corner, there was an old, white refrigerator that was damn near as old as I was. It only housed drinks, mainly Dad and Bishop's beer and a shitload of sweet tea, but as my sister pulled on the door, I could've wept and cried.

Because there, amongst the sea of yellow beer cans, was the silver and blue energy drink I loved so much.

"Oh god, I could kiss you!" I said, surging forward and gripping it tightly between my palms.

She laughed, closing the door. "I know I shouldn't be enabling your bad habits—"

I reached out and placed my pointer finger against her lips. "Shh, we don't have to tell a soul. Our secret." I popped open the can, groaning as the first hint of sour bubbles landed on my tongue. "Oh, how I've missed you."

"Are you talking to me or the can?" my sister asked.

"Look, I'm glad you're back…"

"But I pale compared to your precious energy drink," she said, holding her hands up. "I get it."

I looked over the rim, giving her a smile. "It really is good to see you, Cleo. I'm glad you're back."

She stuck her hands in her pocket, chewing on her bottom lip. "Yeah, me too."

Cleo had been in Montana for the past few years with her husband. He'd gone up to work on a dude ranch with his brother. What was supposed to last for one summer had turned into three years, but they were finally back.

"Cleo? Lenny? Josie?" Dad's voice echoed in the small space as he wandered in from the small door off the side of the garage. "Damn girls, I swear—"

"Don't even think about finishing that sentence, old man," I said, wagging my finger in his direction. "It's been one hell of a morning, and Cleo is the only reason I haven't run for the hills yet."

He walked over and pulled me into a tight hug. "Empty promises," he whispered in my ear. "You wouldn't leave me to fend off the wolves by myself."

I pulled back, sweeping my gaze over the man before me. His face was haggard, showing more lines and dark circles that I didn't want to acknowledge.

I already felt guilty about being late this morning. I should've stayed at the ranch last night, so I was here first thing in the morning. It was bad enough that Mom wasn't here to witness his last first day at the clinic he'd dedicated his life to. She'd gone up to Tennessee to help our aunt recover from a bad car accident, and likely wouldn't be back until the beginning of July.

Today was all about him, and I decided right here and now not to let anything else cast a dark cloud over the day.

"Come on, you two. There's someone I want you to meet," my dad said, wrapping his arm around my shoulder and tugging me out of the garage with Cleo on my heels.

It was only nine in the morning, but the Texas sun beat down on us without mercy. Thankfully, we'd had a wet spring, so the grass still had some color before the summer eventually sucked the life from everything.

There was truly nothing like home. The land had been in my family for generations, and we'd made it ours in every way we could. Mom and Dad had offered us each a slice of land to build on when the time came to settle down, and two months ago, I'd taken them up on the offer.

It was a twenty-acre plot hidden away from the main house by a large grove of oak trees. A small pond was hidden beneath their canopies, just shy of the clearing where construction had begun two weeks ago. I was there the day the concrete slab had been poured, wiping tears away because it'd felt unreal.

For so long, I never thought I'd be secure enough to plant roots. I was always on the go, wandering through a series of broken hearts and dead-end jobs that did nothing but add to the minefield of my life.

"You know, Lenny is the last single daughter, Dad. You should be shoving her in the direction of hot cowboys," I teased.

My dad scrunched up his face. "As if I'd let any of you loose on these boys. You'd all eat them alive, and I'd have no help left. Besides," he said, kissing the top of my head. "No one's good enough for any of you."

"And you don't have a ring on your finger yet, Josie," Cleo called.

I turned over my shoulder, sticking my tongue out in her direction and earning a middle finger from my dear sister before Dad caught her.

"You remember how I got word that one of my buddies from my rodeo days passed during the spring?" Dad asked, and I nodded.

It'd been a somber day in the Hayes household. Dad had just gotten back from the doctor, a visit that told him the lifestyle changes he'd implemented last year weren't working as well as they'd hoped, when the phone rang informing him of the news.

Dad hadn't said a word. Just walked out the door, saddled up his horse, and spent the day riding around the ranch. When he'd gotten home, his eyes were red-rimmed, but Mom and I'd pretended not to notice.

We did a lot of pretending these days.

"Well, Frank never married or had kids, but he'd taken in a boy that was as good as his own. The kid made quite a name for himself in the training scene before quitting. He'd never said why or what happened, but…"

Frank.

I stopped hearing anything after that goddamn name because I couldn't think about it without thinking of *him*.

Of Tennessee skies and the sweet heat of summer. Of heated kisses and hours tangled in sheets that smelled of pine and leather.

Of the man I left behind with nothing more than a note with two words.

"Ah, there he is!" My dad waved at a man standing in front of us talking to Bishop. His back was toward us, but I'd have known him anywhere. And when he turned, all the air was stolen from my lungs. "Girls, meet Lincoln Carter. Lincoln, meet two of my girls—Josie and Cleo."

josie

. . .

LINCOLN CARTER.

I'd never stayed long enough to learn his last name, which seemed silly considering I'd spent five fucking days glued to his side, but it fit him. The name was strong. It reminded me of something from those old Western films my grandparents watched.

The day I left, I'd cried a river of tears until the Texas state line, but since then, I'd refused to think about him. For the most part, I'd done a good job, but occasionally, I'd cross paths with something that would remind me of him.

It was why I removed every candle containing pine or leather from my house, throwing them out or giving them to my sisters.

And other days, I spent obsessing over what could have been.

But the moments were fleeting. The hurt would lessen when I woke up the next day, and I'd move on as though he'd never crossed my mind.

How could I do that if he was here? In my home, in my sanctuary?

For the most part, Lincoln hadn't changed. His dark stubble had grown into a trimmed beard where specks of grey seemed more pronounced. When he smiled, the lines around his eyes seemed more defined, but maybe they'd always been there, and I hadn't noticed.

It was his clothes that threw me off. When we'd spent time together, he lived in a uniform of dark, fitted t-shirts and relaxed jeans. Sometimes, he'd hide his unruly black hair under a base-ball cap. But this Lincoln was different. I'd jokingly called him 'cowboy', but he looked every bit the part standing in front of me. He wore a black button-down tucked into starched jeans and a light grey felt cowboy hat on his head.

Those goddamn hats.

"Josie?" my dad asked, pulling me from my downward spiral. "You okay, sugar? You look like you've seen a ghost?"

I opened my mouth, trying and failing to form words because what the fuck could I say? *"Hi Dad, sorry I'm shocked to find the guy I spent five incredible days with standing in my front yard because I left him with nothing more than an 'I'm sorry' scribbled on a piece of paper I found on his counter?"*

But Lincoln cut in, his deep, velvet-like voice sending shivers down my spine. "We met briefly when Josie was in Tennessee last year. She stopped by Frank's bar before heading to y'all's cabin." He stared at me while he spoke, those chocolate brown eyes I'd fantasized so much about sweeping over me in a way that felt wholly inappropriate given the company. He took off his hat, reaching forward to shake my hand like he hadn't just turned my life upside down. "Nice to see you again, darlin'."

"Oh," Dad laughed. "Might want to steer away—"

"Yup, nice to see you, too." I didn't let Dad finish his sentence, and I didn't shake Lincoln's hand. Instead, I turned to my sister. "Cleo, can I talk to you for a second?"

Without waiting for her answer, I grabbed her by the elbow and dragged her to the front door of the house. Dad called out something to our backs, but I couldn't hear him over the roaring in my ears.

"Okay, okay, okay," Cleo said, digging in her heels as we stepped inside. "What the hell was that?"

I began pacing back and forth in front of her, chewing on my nails like I used to do as a child. *"That,"* I said, pointing out the front door, "is a huge fucking problem."

"Why?" she asked. "Do you have the hots for the cowboy?" When I didn't answer, responding only with a glare, she laughed. "Oh god, you do, don't you?"

"I don't have the hots for him," I snapped. "He was why I ran from Tennessee and never looked back!"

She sobered, the smile she'd been sporting dropping instantly. "Oh shit."

"What are we 'oh shitting'?" Lennox asked, strolling in from the garage with a travel mug in her hand.

"Josie's Tennessee fling is Dad's new trainer," Cleo said, sinking into our mom's worn leather armchair.

I'd briefly told my sisters about what had happened in Tennessee, safely avoiding the fact that I'd begun falling for a man I'd only known for a few days.

"Oh shit," Lennox parroted, looking between the two of us. She ran to the window and peeked outside while I hid behind my hands. "Hell yes, Josie! He is *hot.*"

"You two are not helping," I groaned, falling back onto the matching couch. "How am I supposed to face him? To be around him?"

Lennox sat down beside me. "When's the last time you talked to him?"

I blew out a breath, shame creeping in on all sides. "Oh, you know, when I snuck out of his bed and left him a note that said I was sorry."

"And he never called?" Cleo asked, leaning forward. "Seriously?"

I groaned. "No, he did. I ignored them."

It had damn near killed me. Lincoln had called a few times a day for the first week after I'd left. I always checked for a voice-mail, but they never came. It was better that way. If I'd heard his voice, I likely would've dropped everything and run back to him. But as the days flew by, his calls lessened, and I wondered if he'd moved on and forgotten about me.

"Why is he out here as a trainer when he was working as a bartender?"

"I don't know, Cleo. We didn't talk about his previous occupations before I jumped him." She opened her mouth to ask something else, but I cut in. "And before you ask, the only other things I know about him are how he takes his coffee and how good he is in bed."

My sisters were quiet for a moment before Lennox broke the silence. "*And?* How good is he?"

Nope. I didn't want to think about how good Lincoln made me feel or the sheer number of orgasms he'd given me. I didn't want to think about the way his rough, calloused hands had felt running over my body. And damn sure didn't want to think about how those memories still carried me over the edge and back again.

I grabbed the pillow beside me, burying my face in the cushion before groaning loudly.

"I guess that means he's pretty damn good…" Cleo mused, earning Lennox's chime-like laughter.

"This isn't funny, y'all. I don't know what to do."

"This is a second chance. You were miserable when you came home from Tennessee last year, moping around the house like someone had died," Lennox said.

"But I'm in a–"

"Girls?" Dad called, opening the door. I whipped the pillow from my face, momentarily scared that Lincoln would be hiding behind our father. "What the hell are you three doing? We've got work to do."

"Don't worry about it, Daddy." Cleo stood, walking toward

him. Her eyes softened as she pressed a kiss to his cheek. "Where do you need us?"

MY DAY WAS ALREADY a bust and things had barely begun. There were a number of things I needed to do in Dad's office, including a stack of bills to pay, time sheets to finalize, and files to update.

Ellis had been helping me sort out some inconsistencies I'd noticed on the bank statements. Over the past year, we'd been short about ten thousand dollars a month. When I'd showed Dad, he'd waved it off as an oversight and had asked me to get the firm involved since they oversaw most of our accounts.

But Dad's office was on the first floor of the barn, right next to Bishops. The location made my job easier overall, but that was before my father had brought in a bomb and thrown me for a loop.

Because Lincoln had been shadowing Bishop all morning. They'd gone in and out of his office countless times, and I couldn't focus on a damn thing when he was near.

Instead, I'd remained glued to my dad's hip since the moment I'd stepped back outside. He'd been annoyed at first, especially since he could run this clinic with his eyes closed. When he opened his mouth to argue, I'd told him Mom wanted me to keep an eye on him since she wasn't going to be here to do it herself.

For all their teasing earlier, my sisters backed my little white lie so Dad didn't question it. He knew our mom fussed over him, especially since his diagnosis, and would put up with my hovering if only to please her.

But the real reason was far more embarrassing. I couldn't risk turning a corner and seeing Lincoln standing there as tempting and delicious as the first night I'd met him. It felt like he was everywhere and nowhere at the same time. I was paranoid as hell, worried about what he'd do or say. Not that I cared about people knowing our history, however short it was.

I was more worried about the stupid fucking butterflies that had suckerpunched me right in the stomach when I'd come face to face with him.

You have Ellis, I reminded myself. He's good for you. He's responsible, respectable, and most importantly... local.

Not that watching Dad was a hardship. I'd always loved seeing him work. The only person who rivaled him for passion about Black Springs was Bishop, which is why the ranch ran like a well-oiled machine.

Growing up, it'd been a joke that Dad was a horse whisperer, but I never realized how true that was until I got older and knew what to watch for. It was an instantaneous connection. Somehow, he just looked into the animal's eyes and knew what they needed and how he could give it to them. It wasn't easy to pass that on to someone else, to show them how to pick up on the little signs here and there.

He'd always told me if he could give someone even a fraction of that insight, he'd have considered his life well lived.

Arrival day at the clinic was always hectic, but it was also my favorite. It was a perfect introduction to the people we were hosting for the next two weeks. Every ranch employee was on duty as my dad and I walked around and greeted the influx of trucks and trailers. My sisters showed guests to their cabins while Bishop, Lincoln, and the hands unloaded the horses and housed them in their new stalls for the next two weeks.

Tonight, there'd be a cookout for guests and workers—a chance for everyone to unwind and familiarize themselves with their surroundings. Time and time again, it proved to be entertaining. Sometimes, it'd get rowdy, and I'd enjoy watching as people would drag their feet the following day since the first class began with the rising sun.

Though, I didn't know if I'd be staying to take part.

If it were any other year, I would've moved back to my parent's house for the next two months to be nearby in case I was needed. These clinics were all-hands-on-deck kind of events. Even before I started working for Dad, I was always around to pick up on our daily chores that might have fallen by the wayside.

But Dad had specifically hired more help this year, so we didn't have to worry about that happening. The work was split evenly amongst the staff, rotating every two weeks with each new clinic.

My packed bags sat in the backseat of my truck, judging myself and the mess I'd inadvertently gotten into. Lincoln would be housed with the rest of the hired staff in one of the cabins near the barn, putting a solid stretch of land between where he'd rest his head and where I'd rest mine.

But was it enough?

The sun began its descent, and our work finished for the day. Staff moved across the empty space past the barn where the cabins sat in neat lines. Mom and Dad had built a giant fire pit outfitted with a covered patio and grills. The familiar scent of burning wood and grilled meats wafted toward the main house, making my mouth water.

I'd barely eaten all day. If not for Dad, I likely wouldn't have stopped at all. Keeping busy was the only thing stopping my mind from wandering to the stables where a handsome cowboy had been most of the day.

"It never gets old," my dad said, sidling up beside me. I was leaning over the fence post, staring at the ranch I loved so much. The grass was taller than we usually let it get for June. It'd been an unusually wet spring, so we'd held off on cutting the first batch of hay for the season, but we wouldn't be able to put it off much longer.

It didn't mean the sight wasn't damn pretty.

There were no hills or rolling mountains as our backdrop. Black Springs Ranch was damn near as flat as it could be, but it was still the most beautiful land I'd ever seen. Maybe I was biased. Maybe it was because this land was mine, and I was born with that love in my heart.

But there was something about being able to see the rising and setting sun in its entirety that I loved. My great-grandparents had planted clusters of trees along the property—perfectly hidden groves that had been our favorite places to hide growing up.

"No, it doesn't," I agreed. These quiet moments were rare, especially on days like these. It was why I had no intention of moving, not until my father broke the silence.

"I don't know what I'm gonna do when this is over. I don't know how to move on from something I dedicated my life to." When his voice broke on the last word, he tried to cover it up with a cough, but it was too late.

I heard the hurt, heavy behind every word, the hesitation and fear of the future and what lies ahead.

"Bishop is already primed to take over the ranch, Daddy," I said, gentling my voice. "You've taught him well."

"What about these clinics?" he asked, lacing his hands together. "People depend on them. Hell, the animals do, too. Half of these horses would've been sold or traded off—labeled as a problem when it's really their owners not knowing their heads from their asses."

I didn't have an answer. No one could match my dad's natural affinity for these animals or read them like he could.

"We'll figure it out," I said, leaning on his shoulder. "But until then, we'll enjoy the moments we have left."

He hummed but said nothing more about his future or career prospects. Instead, he steered the conversation toward much more precarious topics. "You haven't brought your bags into the house."

"I haven't had time," I said, lifting my foot so it rested on the lowest fence rail. "You've kept me busy."

"Bullshit," he laughed. "Is it that boyfriend of yours?"

Dad wasn't too keen on Ellis. Sure, he thought he was friendly and respectable enough, but my father was adamant that no man alive was good enough for any of his girls.

Even after five years, he still hated Cleo's husband. To be fair, I didn't much care for the man, either.

While Ellis had grown up in our little small town where you couldn't step foot in an establishment without running into a rancher, he'd never been a part of that life. He'd never ridden a horse or herded cattle. His hands were smooth and unblemished, and he had never known a day of hard labor.

Mom and Dad had both been shocked when I told them we were dating. Ellis was nothing like my past boyfriends, which is one of the reasons I'd been incentivized to say yes. Clearly, chasing cowboys wasn't doing me any favors.

"What would Ellis have anything to do with it?"

Dad shrugged. "I don't know. Two months is a long time to be apart."

I laughed. "Well, it isn't like we're an ocean away. A thirty-minute drive into town isn't a deal-breaker."

"Is he coming out here tonight, then? To the cookout?"

"I don't know. He said he'd try," I mumbled, looking down at my worn leather boots. In the beginning, Ellis had come out to the ranch all the time, but as his client list had grown, he'd had less time to spend long days in Dad's office. Since we'd started dating, he'd only been out to the ranch once.

It wasn't the best feeling, seeing how important Black Springs was to me. When my dad had invited him out for one of our weekly family dinners, Ellis had asked if we could meet in town.

Dad wasn't too happy about that.

"There're good places to hide a body on the ranch," Dad had

told me. I had laughed while his face remained stoic and unchanged.

As the silence settled, I could tell there was more he wanted to say, but mercifully, he kept quiet. I'd been listening to his lectures on relationship etiquette since he'd found out about my first kiss at thirteen.

"Doug!"

My dad and I both turned to see Bishop walking toward us. His faded grey cowboy hat had seen better days, but he didn't care. Bishop was a simple man who lived a simple life. He drove the same '99 Dodge that he had since my dad bought it for him, and his wardrobe consisted of Wranglers, square-toed boots, and plain t-shirts.

I could count on one hand the number of times I'd seen him deviate from his everyday routine in the past twenty years, and he'd bitched about it the entire time.

But my gaze snagged on the shadow behind him. A shadow I'd know anywhere.

"Bishop," my dad greeted, shaking his hand. "Everything prepped for tonight?"

Bishop nodded once. "Yup. Cook said dinner will be ready in about an hour, so I thought I'd take Lincoln into town to grab some beer."

"Probably a good idea," my dad said. "Need a hand?"

I felt Lincoln's eyes on me, burning a hole into my side profile, but I couldn't meet his gaze. How was I supposed to get through the next two months if I couldn't even look at the man? How could I stay on this ranch, walking on eggshells, until he finally packed up and went home to Tennessee?

"Why? You offering, old man?" Bishop's gaze flicked to me, and I subtly shook my head. As much as he didn't want to admit it, Dad needed to rest.

"Yeah, give me a—"

"Dad, why don't you give me a hand with my bags?" I asked,

pushing off the pipe fence. "I'm sure these boys can take care of a beer run, right?"

This time, I let my gaze travel over Bishop's shoulder, where Lincoln's eyes remained fixed on me. His jaw was set in a hard line, likely aching for how hard he held himself back.

I wasn't sure when I'd made the decision to stay. There would be no avoiding Lincoln Carter forever, but I didn't need to.

I just needed to get through the next two months.

lincoln

. . .

I BROUGHT the beer bottle to my lips, taking a long sip as I stared over the flames of the massive bonfire. Josie sat across the way, laughing at something her sister said.

It was torture. Torture to see her again, to not know why she left. She wouldn't even look at me for longer than two seconds before tearing her gaze away.

I didn't know what the fuck I was doing here. It was a fool's errand; I'd known as much when Doug Hayes had called me a month ago with condolences and a job offer. He needed help running his training clinic and had heard from Frank that I had a gift for calming a wild spirit.

Frank.

I missed the old bastard more than I cared to admit. His death, while not a complete shock, had come much sooner than either of us thought. A year and a half ago, he'd been diagnosed with lung cancer. The doc had given him a good prognosis, considering how late they'd caught it, but he refused treatment. Said he wanted to live out the rest of his days in peace and there was no use in fighting the inevitable.

The day I found him was the worst of my life, but he got the last laugh.

Ever since I'd told him that Josie had left me with nothing more than a scrap of paper holding two pathetic words, he'd spent his days trying to convince me to go get her.

Every day, at his ranch or the bar, he'd ask me if I'd reached out.

Every day, my answer had remained the same.

No.

But he hadn't given up. This job was proof of that.

Frank had given me everything in his will. His land in Tennessee, his bar, and his blessing. He'd even arranged for someone to take care of everything while I was gone because he knew I would've said no to Doug when he called if he hadn't.

He'd said life was too short not to chase after what you want.

We shared that sentiment, but now I couldn't help but wonder if I was making the biggest mistake of my life. Being near Josie Hayes, well, it was a cruel form of torture.

I'd known what awaited me in Texas, and I'd come anyway.

It wasn't like I had anyone to keep me company in Tennessee.

It'd been a surprise for both of us when he figured out who Josie's dad was. She and I had never traded last names, but Frank had sworn there was something familiar about her he couldn't place. It wasn't until he'd been up to inspect the Hayes' cabin near the peak that it clicked.

He'd walked up to the bar, slapped a picture on the table, said, "Found your girl," and then walked back to the storage closet he called an office. Smug fucker even whistled the whole ten steps, leaving me with nothing but the sound of George Strait on the jukebox.

I didn't realize what it was at the time, or how Frank even had it. When I'd questioned him about it, he'd asked me if I'd reached out to Josie yet. He wouldn't budge, refusing to tell me his secrets until the end.

I wanted to be angry at Josie, and part of me was. I'd spent more time feeling blindsided and confused. Did I have any right to be? We'd only known each other for five days, but it'd been enough to make me want more. I wanted her time. I wanted to build on that five days until it became a lifetime.

When I agreed to come to Texas, I'd made a plan. Yes, I was going to work my ass off and try to live up to the man Frank thought I could be, but it was more than that. I wanted to look her in the eye and ask her why she'd left without a goodbye.

"How was your first day?" Bishop asked, sitting beside me with two more beers. I downed the rest, trading it for the fresh one in his hand. "Ready to run for the hills yet?"

"Naw," I said, shaking my head. There was no way I would run now. Not when everything I wanted was so close. "It's a little out of my comfort zone, but I'm grateful to learn from the best, you know? Douglas Hayes is a fucking legend."

Even before I knew Frank's connection to the Hayes family, or Josie's for that matter, I knew who Doug was. As a kid, I watched him on TV, dreaming of the day I could be just like him. It was part of the reason I'd entered the equine world to begin with.

But I'd never thought I'd be sitting here on his ranch, staring at his daughter like I was. God, she was fucking beautiful. I hadn't forgot, but it was different seeing her again.

"He is," Bishop agreed. "He's a tough bastard, but I've never met a man with a bigger heart."

"What's your story with him?" I asked, screwing off the lid.

Bishop was silent, taking a long pull of his beer before he answered. "I grew up here. My mom was an alcoholic, and my dad... Well, he was never around much. He'd pop in several times a year, stay for a few weeks, then leave. Mom never talked about him, and I learned not to ask. Then, one year later, he didn't show, and Mom was distraught. She was always a mess, but this was different. She blamed me, said it was my fault he'd left in the first place. Then she kicked me out."

"Fuck, man," I said. "I'm sorry."

He shrugged, playing it off. "It was a long time ago. Can't exactly hold it against her now. Point is, Doug took me in when I had no one else. I worked at the Tractor Supply in town. We'd met a few times when he came in to buy shit for the ranch. When mom kicked me out, I packed my bags and walked out here looking for a job and a place to stay."

"You walked here?"

"Sure did. What else was I supposed to do? I had nowhere to go. Doug was my only chance to carve out a new future for myself, and I was determined to make him see how serious I was. Turns out, he was going to offer me a job the moment I turned eighteen. He said we'd just expedited the timeline a bit."

"And you've been here ever since?"

"Yeah," he said, pulling his hat down. "No reason to leave—not that I'd want to. I just want to work hard and earn an honest living. Doug gave me both of those things."

I nodded my head. "I get that. We all need someone to believe in us."

The sensation of being watched had my gaze flitting across the roaring flames. Amongst the chaos of laughter and loud music, Josie's eyes were fixed on me. The smile on her face moments ago was gone, replaced by a million questions I was sure were reflected on my own.

How many days had I thought about her? How long had I spent wondering what would happen when I saw her again for the first time?

Josie pushed to her feet, murmuring something to her sisters as they tried to follow her. It was enough to make me believe she was going to bed.

Almost.

But then the older one, Cleo, I think, looked my way, and I knew it wasn't that simple. I couldn't have her slipping away just because she didn't want to share the same space as me.

If she wanted to run away after we'd talked, fine. I'd give her all the space she wanted after she gave me the answers I was looking for.

"I'll be back," I told Bishop, rising from the log bench I'd parked my ass on for the past hour. His only response was a gruff nod before returning to his beer. I didn't know what I was doing, but I was damn sure about to find out as I set a leisurely pace behind her.

The fire pit stood in front of the main cabins, all of which were occupied by additional staff and guests attending the clinics. It was a halfway point between our lodging and the stables. Josie was already a solid thirty feet ahead of me, her head down and hands in her pockets. She dipped into the barn, not daring to look behind her.

When I rounded the corner, I saw her standing near the end. The moonlight slipped through the windows, just enough to see a dappled grey horse poke its neck out of its stall. It bobbed its head, reaching forward to nuzzle its velvet nose into Josie's open palm.

"He yours?" I asked, resting my shoulder against a rough cedar beam.

Her body stiffened at the sound of my voice, but she didn't run away. "*She*," Josie corrected. "Her name's Silver."

"Silver, huh? How'd you come up with that one, I wonder."

Josie's lips quirked, and I took it as a win. "In my defense, I was only seven when my dad brought her home. It was either Silver or Princess Unicorn Sugar Blossom."

"Well, with two absolute contenders like that, I don't know how you ever made a choice."

"Don't be a dick," she laughed. "Blame my parents for giving me free rein. I think they thought I'd name it after my favorite movie or something, but I was really into princesses and unicorns as a kid."

I pushed off the beam, making my way to her side. "What prompted the swing toward Silver?"

Josie hummed, running her hand over Silver's forelock. "I suspect my sister swayed my decision. I distinctly remember a barn cat named Mr. Stubby Butt."

"I assume he didn't have a tail?"

"Nope," Josie said, popping the p. "He had a long, bushy tail. It makes no sense, but none of us ever questioned it."

We both laughed, falling into a companionable silence. Josie ran her hands up and down Silver's nose, and I couldn't tear my gaze away.

When I was in Tennessee, it'd been easy to pretend I hadn't missed her—that she was nothing more than a temporary distraction, a fling—but standing here in her presence was entirely different.

I'd forgotten how goddamn beautiful she was or how her laughter made me smile. I'd forgotten how she chewed on her bottom lip when she was nervous—a habit that would get me in a hell of a lot of trouble, seeing as all it made me want to do was kiss her.

"Why're you here, Lincoln?" Her voice was soft, a whisper I almost hadn't caught. And there she went, pulling that damn lip between her teeth.

"Here as in—"

"As in Texas," she said, facing me for the first time. "As in my family's ranch. As in my barn."

I blew out a breath. "There's a bunch of reasons, Josie. I don't know which one you want."

"I want the truth."

The truth was complicated and messy. Did I even know what it was?

Yes.

No.

Maybe? I mean, I'd come here for Frank, to try and make sense of my life before I died an old man with a ranch, a bar, and no one I loved at my side.

But selfishly, I'd also come for Josie.

"I think you know better than anyone how complicated the truth can be," I said, looking up at her from under the brim of my baseball cap.

"What's that supposed to mean?" she asked, crossing her arms over her chest.

"Come on, Josie," I said, running my hand along the back of my neck. How did she not understand? "I'm not looking for a fight."

I wanted to talk but not like this. She was building her wall higher by the minute, and I couldn't do anything but watch as she shut me out. If I didn't do something soon, I'd have no chance of breaking through.

She blew out a breath. "I don't know what to tell you, Lincoln. We knew each other for a short time—the blink of an eye, really. What did you expect? What did I owe you?" I tried to stop her, but she barreled through me. "You knew I'd leave eventually. My life is here. My family is here."

I stepped closer, crowding her space until her scent hit me. It was faint, hidden after working in the Texas heat all day, but the sweet hint of vanilla was there all the same.

"You didn't owe me shit. That isn't what this is about." She turned her head, refusing to look my way. I could live with that if she listened to me for five seconds. "If you'd talked to me before bolting, I'd have told you I wasn't looking to take any of that away from you. Hell, I don't know what could've happened between us. Maybe we'd have burned out in half a second, but —" I paused, reaching out and grabbing her hand. She kept her gaze on the far wall but didn't pull away. "Josie, do something for me. Look me in the eye and tell me you felt nothing. Tell me it was all in my head. There was something between us last year that neither of us could explain."

"Lincoln," she began, but I cut her off.

"And I know you felt it, too. I know you felt that familiar tug, the familiarity between two strangers that neither of us could explain."

"I don't want to talk about this," she said, trying to walk past me, but I was faster.

I tightened my hold on her hand, pulling her back to face me. All I could do now was lay it on the line. "Look, if you want nothing to do with me, tell me now. But I want to make one thing clear." My gaze dropped to her lips, and she tracked the movement. "I may have come here to honor Frank's wishes, but I also came to remind you of how good we were, of what we could be again if you let me. Is this really over?"

She looked up at me through dark, thick lashes. The barn's darkness was a protective cocoon, shielding us from the outside world as we shared breath. I let go of her hand, trailing my fingertips up the length of her arm and shoulder until I cupped her face.

We were so close. I could kiss her. I wanted to kiss her.

"Josie," I said, leaning in until there was only a fraction of space between our lips.

And then her phone rang.

Josie jumped away from me as though I'd shocked her, putting as much space as she could between us. She pulled the phone from her pocket, eyes darting between me and the screen as she pressed the green button and whispered two more words that fucking killed me.

"Hey, babe."

josie

. . .

WHEN I THOUGHT this day couldn't get worse, I saw Ellis'
name on my phone. I'd been half a second away from kissing
Lincoln Carter in my barn—a position I shouldn't have ever
even been in.

I had Ellis.

God, I was a fucking mess.

As if it hadn't been enough to put myself in such a compro-
mising position, then I went and answered the phone right in
front of the only man who'd ever made it his mission to make
me come.

And now I was thinking about those toe-curling orgasms as I
brought the phone to my ear and whispered, "Hey, babe."

Lincoln's face fell as he stared at me, his hand still
suspended in the air where he'd just tenderly cupped my jaw. It
fell to his side before he tucked it into the pocket of his snug
Wrangler jeans.

"How was the first day?" Ellis asked. I could hear the click of
a keyboard through the phone, knowing he was likely working
late, like always.

I didn't see the appeal of Ellis' job; I hated staring at

numbers. Just because I was good at math, didn't mean I enjoyed it. That had only been cemented as we'd been combing through the bank statements together. At this point, I was nearly convinced I'd imagined the mistake entirely.

"It was great," I said, turning my back on the man staring at me in shock, walking just outside the massive barn doors. I needed air; I needed to breathe, and I couldn't do that with Lincoln's crestfallen face in my view. "Dad's emotional, but our stalls and cabins are full."

"I looked over the projected totals for Black Spring's summer income, and it looks great. We'll be turning a high-end profit that should carry us into the winter."

We. Us.

I hated the words. There was no 'we' as far as I was concerned, not when it came to Black Springs. That was my parents' legacy, the business they painstakingly turned into something more than a simple cattle ranch.

Even though I knew what Ellis meant regarding the terms and how he and his father relied on this land to make money like the rest of my family did, I still hated how he used them so casually.

"Great," I said, pulling my bottom lip between my teeth. "Um, why didn't you come by tonight? It would've been nice to see you before the clinics started."

"I know, but I got caught up with work and lost myself. You know how it is. I'll come to the next one."

"Yes, but this was important to me," I said through gritted teeth, trying and failing to keep my voice below a whisper.

"There will be other cookouts, Josie," he sighed.

But would my dad be there? That was the question I didn't dare voice, too damn scared of the answer.

No one outside of the family knew about my dad's heart condition, and he was adamant it would stay that way until he was ready. I don't think he wanted to see people change toward him, acting like his grave had already been dug and he had one foot in the coffin.

"I could come over tonight. What time will you be home?"

Now, it was my turn to sigh. I may not have known earlier if I wanted to stay, but I'd told Ellis I was before ever coming out here. "I'm staying here until the clinics are over. I told you that when we had dinner last week."

Ellis paused the clicking on his keyboard suddenly stopping. "But that's two months."

"Yup, till the end of July."

"So, I won't see you for two months?" Ellis asked, tone sharpening.

I laughed, unable to help myself. He wasn't serious, was he? We didn't see each other much during the week as it was, and if we did, he was constantly on his phone or computer. "I mean, I'm at the ranch. It isn't that far of a drive, and I'll have weekends off—"

"I don't have time to drive out there whenever I want to see you. Will you be home on the weekends?"

"At this point? I don't know, Ellis. It's hard to tell what my schedule will be when clinics haven't even begun. I have a meeting with your father at the end of the week, though. Maybe I could stop by then."

"Why're you meeting with him?" he asked.

I had to stifle my groan. Sometimes, I swore he never listened to me. "We've been searching through statements and electronic transfers for over a month now and haven't come up with anything. I thought it might be worth having your father take a look at everything I've gathered to see—"

"I'm the one in charge of Black Springs' accounts, Josie. I'll find the discrepancy and sort it out."

"I know, but there's a lot of money missing. Dad may not be worried about it right now, but I am."

Suddenly, there was an all too familiar presence at my back. I didn't know how close Lincoln was, but I could feel the heat coming from his body.

"Josie—"

"I'll talk to you tomorrow," I said, quickly ending the call and turning to see Lincoln bathed in moonlight.

He was so handsome—too handsome for my own good. Like the last piece of decadent chocolate cake you know you shouldn't touch, or speeding down a deserted highway with the windows down and your favorite song on the radio.

And god, I wanted to feel the wind in my hair so badly I had to bite my tongue to keep my mouth shut.

But I had Ellis.

I had Ellis, and he was good for me. He came from a good family with a good reputation, and I didn't question where he was every night or if his words were true. I didn't question whether he was fucking another woman behind my back. Some, my sisters mainly, might have called him a safe choice, but I didn't think I would survive another relationship failure.

As it was, I was already quickly losing faith in my ability to make decisions.

"Boyfriend?" Lincoln asked, sticking his hands in his pocket and rocking back on his heels.

"It's new," I mumbled. "We've been seeing each other for a few months."

"Well, I guess that answers my question," he said, smiling sadly before nodding at the cabins in the distance. "I better get to bed. Long day tomorrow."

I let him walk past, unsure why I felt the need to apologize to him for being in a relationship. But telling him about Ellis felt wrong in a soul-deep way that made me wish the ground below my feet would open and swallow me whole.

"Lincoln, wait!" I called out, unable to stop myself. "What did you mean by answering your question?"

He paused, tipping his head back and staring at the twinkling night sky above. "It doesn't matter, Josie."

"Please?" I asked, taking a step forward. It was hypocritical to want to steal his moments, especially when I'd been trying like hell to run away from him only moments ago. "I want to know."

He turned, showing me the outline of his profile. "I was gonna ask if you'd waited for me like I'd been waiting for you."

And then he walked away, leaving me standing under the weight of his honesty and hating how it felt.

"DO YOU THINK I'M SELFISH?" I asked my sisters the next morning over breakfast.

Dad had been up before the sun, meeting with the ranch hands to delegate tasks and set expectations while the three of us huddled in the kitchen with our coffees. Lennox and I had put Cleo in charge of cooking. She was the only one who could really be trusted not to burn the food.

"Uh, context, please?" Lennox asked, raising a brow.

"Yeah," Cleo called over her shoulder. "My vote could swing either way, depending on your answer."

I rolled my eyes, setting my cup down and hoisting myself up to sit on the counter. "I dunno. Like, just in general, I guess."

I hadn't slept much last night after my talk with Lincoln. Lennox had found me not long after he left. Apparently, they'd run into one another on his way back, and he'd mentioned leaving me at the barn. She'd come running, wrapping me in a big hug before she dragged me inside and told me to go to bed.

She hadn't pushed me to talk about Lincoln, but I suspected peace was ending. "Does this have anything to do with a certain hot cowboy?" she asked, joining me on the counter.

I shrugged. It did, and it didn't. When I'd come home from

Tennessee, I'd spent weeks wondering if I'd done the right thing by leaving the way I did. There was no future for me there, but maybe Lincoln was right. We could've worked something out if I'd been honest with him about my feelings.

"I just think I should've handled things differently," I said, tucking a loose tendril of hair behind my ear.

Lennox faked a gasp. "You mean like talking to the man before bolting?"

I flipped her off, and she returned the gesture.

"What Lennox means," Cleo said, wrapping her arm around my shoulders, "is that we are your sisters and support whatever decision you make."

"But?" I asked, knowing it was coming.

"But... Yes, it probably would've been better if you hadn't spent a week shacked up with a man before leaving the state without an explanation."

My shoulders slumped forward. It was my fault for asking a stupid question to which I already had the answer. "Yeah, I know."

"But what'd he have to say last night?" Lennox asked, picking up her coffee and bringing it to her lips.

"Oh, you know, the usual conversation. *What's up? How ya been? By the way, let's get back together.*"

Lennox spewed her coffee across the kitchen. "Wait, what?"

I couldn't hide my laughter as Cleo cursed and grabbed a dishrag to wipe her arm. "Dammit, Lennox!"

"Don't blame me!" she said, jumping from the counter and ripping the rag from Cleo's hand.

"You're the one who spit it out," Cleo deadpanned. "Who else am I supposed to blame?"

"Josie's hot cowboy!"

"Hey!" I said, raising my hands in the air. "He's not *my* anything."

They both turned and stared at me, with a shared look that

said, *really bitch?* And in their defense, they might have been right. Some part of Lincoln felt like mine even when he wasn't.

Cleo switched off the stove, moving the bacon pan to the side before turning my way. "You're not selfish, Josie. Not even a little bit, okay? You made a poor decision, and you've apologized for it."

I brought my lip between my teeth, cringing because I definitely had not done that.

"You did apologize, right?" Cleo asked, placing her hands on her hips.

"Define apologize…"

My sister threw up her hands. "You haven't apologized? I thought you said you talked?"

"Well, we did," I said, crossing my arms. "Lincoln followed me into the barn and wanted me to look him in the eye and tell him what happened didn't matter, and then Ellis called."

"Oh shit," Lennox said, resting against the counter. "I'm guessing that's why I found you sitting on your ass last night?"

"I may not have handled the situation well," I agreed.

"So, what are you going to do about it?"

I tipped my head back and groaned. "I don't know, y'all. I mean, at the end of the day, nothing has really changed, has it? He still lives in Tennessee; I still live here."

"And you have a boyfriend," Lennox added.

I pointed in her direction. "Yeah, I have an Ellis. So, the point is moot."

Cleo cocked her head. "Do you realize you never say that Ellis is your boyfriend?"

"What? Yes, I do."

Surely, I did. *Right?* I mean, I thought it went without saying. We were together. Everyone else called him my boyfriend.

"No," Lennox said slowly. "You never do. You call him your Ellis, not your boyfriend."

I stared at my sisters. "What's the difference? Y'all already know we're dating."

Cleo shrugged, turning around to snag a piece of toast. "I just think it's interesting. Maybe you're holding the title for someone else."

Leaning forward, I snagged a piece of my own and plopped it into my mouth. "You, my dear sister, are reaching."

"And you," she said, booping me on my nose, "are delusional."

josie

. . .

I STARED out the kitchen window, watching the sky change from an inky blue to the soft grey of dawn. My dad was at the stove, humming a Keith Whitley song while he cooked eggs and bacon—which was turkey, much to his dismay—for a couple of breakfast sandwiches.

This was my favorite time of day. There were no people milling about, no demands, stress, or to-do lists calling my name. It was just me and my dad and the simple necessities that kept the world turning.

The first two days of the clinic had flown by in a rush. They were filled with fundamental basics so Dad could assess the attendees' current skills and needs. I stood beside the arena, taking notes as he rattled off his thoughts on each rider and horse. He liked to keep files on everyone—at the end of the clinic, he handed them over with the course certification. They detailed measurable improvement over the two weeks of training and a schedule of upcoming seminars he'd be teaching over the rest of the year.

I didn't know how he'd done it on his own before. Mom would occasionally help, but Dad had been the one to put in the work and keep things organized. It was only when his health started to decline that he brought me on board to keep him straight.

"Will you pass me the cheese?" Dad asked, reaching for the bread in the toaster.

"Dad, those are going to be too—"

"Ow, shit!" he said, placing his thumb in his mouth.

"—hot," I finished, shaking my head. "You're impatient. I don't know why you never learn."

He smiled over his shoulder. "Can't help if I'm hungry. That rabbit food you keep piling onto my plate doesn't last long."

I took a long sip of my coffee, thankful for single serve makers so that I didn't have to drink the muddy water Dad liked so much. "Well, that rabbit food is literally what the doctor ordered, so get used to it."

He used a pair of tongs to pull a piece of turkey bacon from the pan, holding it up with a grimace. "I don't know what I did to deserve a punishment like this. How's a person supposed to get used to this? It's shit."

He wasn't wrong. I hated eating it, too, but I wasn't cruel enough to make him go through it alone. "And what if that turkey bacon ends up saving your life?"

"I'd rather be sent to an early grave," he mumbled. "An old man's gotta draw the line somewhere, Josie, and this may well be mine."

I stood from my seat at the bar top, walking over to wrap my arms around my dad's shoulders. "But then, who would sign my paychecks?"

He swatted my hand away, chuckling. "Smartass. Better watch that mouth, or I'll let you walk now."

"You wouldn't do that," I said, grabbing two paper plates and setting them on the counter. "Who'd keep you in line?"

He snorted, but didn't say anything more as we assembled our sandwiches. When he reached into the fridge and grabbed the mayo, I tried to give him my stern mom look, but it didn't have much effect. Instead, he unscrewed the lid, reached for a knife, and spread a hearty layer on each side of the toast.

All while staring at me in a taunt.

I threw my hands up when he finished. "Fine, but you better change the will to give me a bigger cut because *I'm* the one who tried to save your life."

"Sure thing, sugar. I'll get right on that," he said, handing me my sandwich. He knocked his against mine and took a bite.

"What's on the docket for the day?" I asked.

He leaned back on the counter, downing the rest of his coffee. "Well, I figured we'd finish up on horsemanship before lunch—I need to know they can handle themselves in the saddle before turning them loose on the livestock. There's a couple I considered moving to the level one class. By the time we break, I'll have a better idea of where they need to be."

Movement out of the corner of my eye drew my attention as Dad continued to speak. I turned in time to see a figure walk into the barn, flipping on the overhead lights. While I couldn't see their face, I knew it was Lincoln.

He was wearing a grey Black Springs Ranch t-shirt and jeans with his stupid black cowboy hat I loved to hate. I could only imagine how he'd chat to the horses as he walked down the stalls, how his voice's deep, melodic lull would soothe them after an evening in dim lighting.

Just like I could imagine the way he'd use it on me as he whispered sinful praise in my ear if I gave him a chance. How he'd tell me I was beautiful before kissing down my neck to my chest and then lower still.

My dad stepped into my line of sight, pouring the remnants of his coffee into a travel mug. "Does Bishop have calves ready for the afternoon?"

I cleared my throat. "Uh, yeah. He does. I talked to him about it last night before closing up shop."

"Good, good," he said. His phone rang, and he pulled it from his pocket. His eyes were alight when he glanced at the screen. "I better take this."

"Tell Mom I said hi!" I called after him as he waved me off and walked into the other room.

I looked out the window, noticing Lincoln leading one of the yearlings to a round pen off the back of the barn. I chewed on my lip, drumming my fingers on the butcher-block countertop. "Fuck it," I whispered, reaching for my dad's collection of travel mugs and grabbing two.

"WHAT AM I DOING?" I muttered to myself, hugging the travel mugs close. The early morning air had an unusual bite for the beginning of summer. I hadn't thought to grab my jacket when I'd snuck out.

The clinic wouldn't start for another forty-five minutes, and Dad was still talking to Mom. The two of them had been laughing about something she'd said, and I was struck stupid at the emotion clawing its way up my throat. It'd almost been enough to make me stay and listen to them lovingly bicker at one another.

I'd never seen another love like my parents. There isn't anything either of them wouldn't do for the other. I think it was why I was such a hopeless romantic.

In a world filled with fuckboys and one-night stands, I wanted a true love—the kind that would last when looks faded and health deteriorated.

I slowed as I neared the pen, taking in the sight before me. I recognized the filly. Duchess was a beautiful sorrel Quarter Horse. Dad had found her at an auction, barely green broke and ready to run.

He knew right then and there that she belonged with us.

We quickly found out she wasn't too fond of men. She'd only been with us a week and had bucked off three hands and bit at least twice as many who dared to get too near. Lennox, Cleo, and I had been taking turns caring for her. She still didn't trust us, but at least she let us nearby.

But out here with Lincoln? There were no bared teeth in sight.

Duchess danced in one spot, nostrils flared as he stood before her with a saddle blanket. "Hey there, pretty girl," he cooed, stepping closer. "You're doing so well."

I stopped, digging my feet into the dewy ground. Hearing him talk like that was not good for my heart. He'd ditched his hat on one of the posts, giving me a full view of his face.

It looked like he hadn't shaved in a few days, but the dark shadow didn't look messy. It looked lived in. Rugged. I absent-mindedly wondered what it would feel like...

"Why don't you let me slide this over your back? I promise you'll like it."

Christ. Get a grip, Josie!

I inched closer, unable to help myself. I was drawn to him, watching in wonder as he slowly raised the blanket to her nose so she could examine the object. "See? Nothing to be afraid of. I wouldn't hurt ya."

The filly shifted on her feet but didn't spook as Lincoln dragged the material along her back. Her ears twitched, eyes growing wide as she watched with careful curiosity. She wanted to hear him speak again and hear how he praised her.

I didn't realize I'd reached the fencing until I ran into the post.

He ran his hand along her neck in gentle strokes. "Good girl," he murmured. "You remind me of someone I know. Prettiest girl in the room, scared to let anyone in..." My heart kicked up as his words trailed off. I could see the ghost of a smile on his lips. "A terrible snoop." Lincoln looked over his shoulder, zeroing in on me.

"I'm not a snoop," I said, leaning forward on the railing. I held one of the coffees out for him to take. "I come bearing gifts."

"Gifts, huh?" He scratched his stubble, looking over at Duchess. "What do you think, girl? Should we trust her?"

I reached into my jacket and pulled out the apple slices I'd snagged. "What about now?"

Lincoln smiled, and it took my breath away. "Well, now you're talking." He clicked his tongue, gently pulling on the lead rope. Duchess went with little fuss, though she glared at the blanket on her back.

I passed the coffee over to Lincoln, and he took a sip. He closed his eyes and hummed. "You remembered how I like my coffee."

"When someone uses the amount of sugar you do, it's hard to forget," I mumbled, focusing on how Duchess munched happily on the apple slices.

"The right amount," he said, correcting me. "I use the right amount. Otherwise, it just tastes like burnt water."

"It does not. It tastes exactly like it smells, which is good."

"I bet your little boyfriend loves to see you coming with a fresh cup of coffee in your hand. Does he like it black? He seems like the type."

"How would you know his type?"

He leaned in, the corner of his lips lifting. "Bishop told me all about him. Says he's a real straight-laced finance guy."

Goddamn Bishop. I'd kill him.

I held up my hand to stop Lincoln from talking. There was no way I was going to dig myself deeper into a hole with Lincoln, especially considering I had absolutely no idea how Ellis took his coffee. "Okay, well, way to ruin a nice gesture. I just thought you might want some since you're up early."

He tapped his mug against mine, smiling brighter. "Thank you, darlin'. You didn't have to do this. I could've gotten some before the first seminar."

"Yeah, well, you're welcome," I said, turning back for the house. "And stop calling me that. It's inappropriate!"

His chuckle was warm and smooth. "Whatever you say... *darlin'*."

josie

· · ·

BRINGING Lincoln coffee had turned out to be a colossal mistake because now he had it in his head that he needed to bring me one every morning.

To be fair, it'd only been two days and two coffees since our encounter on Wednesday, so it very well could've been a coincidence. At least, that's what I tried to tell myself. However, the panty-soaking smile and wink he gave me always obliterated that train of thought.

What got under my skin the most was how perfect it was.

A hazelnut roast with oat milk and brown sugar wasn't exactly something they kept in the bunkhouses. I knew I only stocked the ranch hands with the run-of-the-mill roast. One time, I'd gotten something different by accident. Bishop had spit it across the barn on his first sip and told me off about trying to make his coffee *fancy*.

Had it been anyone else, I'd have told them to shut up and drink the free coffee, but an uncaffeinated Bishop was one angry bear I didn't want to poke.

And he even brought it to me in a pink mug—my favorite color.

So, that begged the question... Where the hell was Lincoln getting his stash from? And was it horrible that I didn't want him to stop?

Thankfully, today was Friday, which meant I had two days of being Lincoln-free to look forward to. There were no classes or trainings on the weekends, which meant I was officially off the clock and could busy myself by doing anything other than crossing his path.

"Josephine! Oh, I'm so glad I caught you." I saw Ellis striding through the front door with two coffee cups.

I hated it when he called me Josephine.

Sometimes, I wondered if he realized where he lived. I understood the concept of dressing professionally, especially with his job. Still, more often than not, he looked like he had just stepped off Wall Street. He was wearing a tight button-down shirt tucked into his slacks, and his hair was perfectly combed to the side.

Even the most well-respected individuals I knew, including the mayor, considered starched jeans, boots, and a clean shirt their formal attire.

"I brought you a coffee. I'm sure that's cold by now," Ellis said, plucking the travel mug from my hand and trading it for the one he held.

I chuckled. "Well, the mug's insulated, so..."

"At least this is fresh," he said, tapping his cup against mine.

"Well, thank you," I said. His eyes bore into mine, glancing between my mouth and the cup. I brought it to my lips, taking a generous sip.

Oh god. It was horrible.

"Is this plain?" I asked, trying to school my face.

Ellis smiled. "Sure is. I know how much you love those sugary energy drinks, but honestly, babe... This is so much better for you. It's a quality roast from Ecuador, you don't even need sugar. Might as well save the calories, right?"

I raised my brows. "Why would I be worried about calories?"

"Your jeans always get a little tight after some time at the ranch," he chuckled. "I'm sure Cleo's cooking is more Paula Deen than Alton Brown. Don't worry, when you get home maybe you can join me for a run in the morning?" He looked genuinely hopeful and I couldn't tell if he even realized what he'd just said. Ellis was Ellis, I bet he thought a morning run would seem romantic."

"Miss Hayes?"

I pulled my gaze toward the blonde receptionist standing before me with a forced smile. "Yes?"

"Mr. Martin will see you now," she said, pointing a manicured finger at the mahogany door to her right. "His office is just through there."

I gave her a small smile, grateful for the interruption. "Thank you," I said, trading the cup Ellis had gotten me with the mug I'd brought. "Honestly, I've probably had too much coffee anyway."

My meeting with Ellis' dad was supposed to start at eight so that I could get back to the ranch, but I was stopped the moment I stepped into the ridiculously over-decorated reception area. A young woman told me I needed to wait, and mumbled something about international affairs and conference calls. I sipped my perfect coffee and passed the hour by trying to convince myself I wasn't attracted to the hot cowboy back home.

One who barely knew me, and yet knew exactly what I liked.

"Miss Hayes?" she called, looking at me over the top of her computer. "Mr. Martin will see you now."

I mumbled my thanks, awkwardly grabbing my bag and slinging it over my shoulder before walking inside.

I'd only gone by the Martins' office once before to drop off some documents for Dad. Still, I didn't remember it being so ostentatious. Honestly, this looked more like Ellis' decor style than the homely rustic chic I remembered from before.

The walls had gone from soft beige to blood red, complete with wainscot molding that reminded me of an old English manor. Behind the receptionist's desk was an oil painting of a fox hunt, flanked by strange landscape portraits that looked like they came from the mind of someone freshly off an acid trip.

Charles Martin sat behind a cluttered desk, peering at his computer screen with narrowed eyes. He didn't move when I stepped inside and sat in a too-stiff leather chair in front of him.

"Just one moment, Miss Hayes," he said, shuffling some papers around and gesturing for me to take a seat. His round glasses slid to the tip of his nose before he pushed them back up with one finger. "Perfect, thank you. How are you this morning? I'm sorry about that wait. This new system Ellis set up doesn't always tell me when I have conflicting meetings."

I waved him off. "It's fine. Dad has things handled. I'm just grateful you were able to see me so soon. Did you have a chance to look at the files I sent you?"

When I made the appointment, I sent over all the files I'd compiled showing the discrepancies. I'd hoped he would have time to review them beforehand and speed up the process.

"I did, and you're quite right. The figures don't match," Charles said, folding his hands on the desk. "There's only one miscalculation."

"Which would be what?"

"I want to start by ensuring I will get to the bottom of this."

"That sounds serious," I said, chuckling. It didn't match the nauseous feeling taking hold. "Surely it can't be that bad?"

"The missing total is quite a bit larger than you anticipated. I would estimate there is close to a quarter of a million dollars lost."

I wanted to throw up on his plush, beige rug. "Pardon?"

Charles sighed. "I took the totals you had and went further, trying to see if I could find the source, or maybe a trail that could explain what you'd found. Your father had wanted to diversify his portfolio a few years back. While I'd advised against any riskier investments at the time, it is ultimately his choice on how to spend his money." He pulled a file from the stack and flipped it open. "I take extensive notes on each meeting, you see. My memory isn't always what it used to be. I'd thought it possible we'd pushed an account through that I hadn't notated, but Doug had elected not to move forward. I even went through each meeting since then to see if he'd changed his mind."

"And had he?"

Charles shook his head. "I'm afraid not."

I sucked in a deep breath. "So, what does that mean?"

"That's the part I am trying to figure out. Most of the transactions lead to a few offshore shell companies. No beneficial owners are listed, and the chain to find anyone has been long. I've been putting everything I can into finding out what these might be used for."

I pinched the bridge of my nose. "So, are you telling me that your firm has misplaced over two hundred and fifty thousand dollars?" Keeping the shake from my voice was impossible. I was furious and terrified at the same time. My family was fortunate enough for this not to be a major hurdle, especially since it'd been over time. However, that was money we could've used to put back into the land or our employees. There had been several instances in which we'd discussed constructing more staff cabins. Before he'd gotten sick, Dad had wanted to take these clinics on the road, but we'd decided against it since it would've eaten the profit margin.

Charles hung his head, and I almost felt sorry for him. "I swear to you... I will find out what happened and ensure every dime is accounted for—"

"I want a formal audit done. I want the call made, and I want that money found." My hands were shaking in my lap. How was I supposed to drive home and tell Dad? And why did it feel like I was in the wrong when I'd been the one to find it?

"Of course," Charles said quickly, sliding me a card. The words were barely legible, but I could make do. "I will help in any way I can. That's a list of the top auditors in the state. I've worked with them on audits in the past."

"I don't know if I should take your recommendations," I said quietly, slipping the note into my purse.

Charles dropped his gaze. "I would understand if you didn't, but I swear, Josie, I don't know how this happened."

Somehow, I believed him.

Charles and my dad had been friends for so long. It'd been partially because of his firm that my dad had gained a stability my grandparents had never dreamed of. His firm was one of the top in the state, which was no small feat considering how small the area was. However, small towns were often ripe with ranchers who were sitting on more money than they knew how to use.

"I know you don't," My phone rang, and I saw Dad's name flash across the screen. *Shit.* "I need to take this, but I appreciate your help, Mr. Martin."

He gave me a slow nod, pushing to his feet and extending his hand. "Of course. I'll be in touch, Josie."

"Josie, baby!"

The door opened, and my head whipped to the side. Ellis strode in with a smile on his face. He put one hand on my lower back before kissing my cheek. "How'd the meeting with Dad go? Was it just a misunderstanding? We should celebrate tonight!"

"No, I didn't misunderstand anything," I gritted out, step-ping out of his touch and tightening my hold on my purse strap. "Your father informed me it's much larger than we anticipated."

I didn't even bother to remind him that I spent every Friday night with my family. It was a waste of breath if he couldn't remember after three months of dating.

"What?" he asked. "How can that be possible?"

Charles leaned forward on his desk. "That's what I'd like to know."

"How can I help? Have we done an audit?" He seemed so concerned, so genuine. It'd been easy to forget how snippy he'd been with me only days ago when I'd told him about this meeting. It was easy to forget a lot of things, actually.

"That's our next step. I'll make the call when I get back to the ranch."

I tried to step past him, but he intercepted me. "Let me take that off your plate," he said, gentling his tone. "I know you have so much going on with the clinics. Honestly, it's a miracle you could get into town for this meeting."

I opened my mouth to tell him no, that I could handle it, but Charles spoke first. "It has to come from the client, Ellis. You know that."

He turned to his father. "Of course, I know that, but sometimes these auditors try to give you the runaround. The investigations are so time-consuming, and a lot of work is involved. I wouldn't want them to take advantage of you."

"I think I'm capable of a phone call, Ellis. And isn't that their job?" I asked, feeling the skin along my palms tighten. "I don't care how long it takes. I want to know where my money is."

"Of course you do, and we'll find it." He reached out and grasped my hand, stroking the top of it lightly. I hated the sensation, especially when my anxiety was rising. Everything felt wrong against my skin; it felt like I was growing while everything else was shrinking. "Do you have time for lunch?" He checked his watch, completely unfazed. "Or brunch, I suppose. We can go to that little cafe you like. The one with the bottomless mimosas."

I stared at him with a hammering heart, wondering how someone could be so insensitive. He hated brunch, hated the bottomless mimosas. In fact, on the rare occasion he agreed to go, he'd make little comments about the kind of people who drink before noon. "Over a quarter of a million dollars is missing from my family's accounts and you want to go to *brunch?*"

"My treat," he added, as though that was a selling point.

When my phone rang again, I took it as my out. "As tempting as that is, I better get back to the ranch. After all, I have to break the news to my father that you lost a shit ton of his money."

lincoln

. . .

"YOU HEADED OUT FOR THE NIGHT?" I called, leaning over the stall door as Bishop walked by. It was Friday, and we were five days into the first clinic. I'd had a rough start to my morning, and spending it with yearlings who'd only been haltered a handful of times hadn't helped.

Neither had getting my ass thrown to the ground multiple times after some dipshit refused to listen when I told him to give his horse some slack on the lead rope. Instead, he'd tried to force his horse into submission, causing it to break away from him and give me one hell of a chase.

When we headed out for lunch, I'd gone straight to Bishop and told him that horse was one to watch. He had too much spirit to be stuck with someone who didn't appreciate it.

He nodded but pulled a beer from the small cooler. He'd removed his chaps and spurs, leaving only a dusty t-shirt and Wranglers. "Got dinner waiting on me, but I saw your little bronc shower earlier," he said, chuckling. "Thought you might need it more than I do."

"You won't find me saying no." I didn't know what it was about a beer at the end of a long day, but goddamn, I felt the

113

day's stress melt away. "What a fucking week. Is it always like this?"

"Naw, but to be fair, this is the first year Doug's divvied it up like this. He normally alternates the clinics, focusing on the newbies first and then switching to riders with more experience." He gestured around the barn. "I've never seen the stalls this full. There's a lot of excitement in the air, and the horses can sense that shit. Especially if their owners don't know what the hell they're doing."

Patience had never been my strong suit. I'd sworn that if I could just make it through the day, I'd get myself and my attitude back on track next week.

Since I was new, Doug had put me in charge of the beginners. Most of these folk didn't know their ass from their elbow, but I rated anyone willing to put their pride aside and do what was best for their animals pretty damn high.

It'd been so long since I'd trained anyone on anything that I was glad he hadn't tossed me in the deep end. The seminars Doug ran were rare. No one had done what he'd done at this scale. Ranches across the country usually held three to four-day seminars throughout the year that focused on the basics of horsemanship, while others in the business focused on boarding and training the animal rather than teaching the owners how to do it.

While Doug did all of this throughout the year on the standard industry scale, he'd also seen an opportunity for an in-depth training program that went above and beyond what could be taught in three days. He saw the importance of focusing on the connection between a horse and its rider, how they could shape one another and form a truly remarkable bond.

I shook my head. "Fucking idiots, I swear."

Bishop smiled and patted me on the back. "Yeah, but it's your job to turn those idiots into bonafide cowboys. First week's done, at least."

"Thank fuck for that. I'm out of practice."

"Don't go all sappy on me, but you've done good—much better than I'd have done."

I waggled my brows. "Bishop Bryant, is that a compliment?"

"Fuck off," he muttered. "Shouldn't have said a damn word. I take it back, you're shit."

I pointed my can in his direction. "There's the grump I've come to know over the past week."

"Yeah, yeah," he said, heading out to his truck with a wave. "Lock up when you're done, will ya?"

"Yes, sir!" I called after him. "I like a man who'll tell me what to do."

His reply came with a rev of his diesel engine and rocks kickin' up as his tires spun down the gravel road.

There was a lot I liked about Bishop. We were about the same age and had similar tastes. We both liked cold beer, horses, and being left the hell alone. And he was committed to the cowboy way of life, waking up before the sun rose and going to bed long after it set.

He lived and breathed this ranch. Everything he did seemed to revolve around the sanctity of the land, these animals, and the people who ran it all.

"Well, I guess it's just you and me, girl," I said, returning to Sundance and giving her a good pat. "Or are you ready for me to leave you alone?"

My horse, Boots, was still in Tennessee. Frank's trailer had been sitting in a field for God only knew how long. When I tried to hook it up, I discovered a whole family of rats who had apparently called it home for generations. The entire thing needed to be re-wired, and I hadn't had the time to sit around and wait. So, Bishop had assigned me a wired little filly named Sundance. Her coat was honeyed and sun-kissed, cut only by the dark chestnut stripe along her back and a white scar along her flank.

Sundance nudged my pocket, knowing damn well I kept a few peppermints on hand for her. I didn't typically resort to bribery—it didn't build the kind of relationship we were trying to foster here—but I didn't have time. I needed her to trust me for the rest of the summer.

"Alright, alright," I said, pulling out what was left and feeding them to her. "But that's all for the day. No more until next week."

She huffed and turned to face the wall. *Point taken.*

I finished my beer and cleaned up my area before heading out of the barn and locking up. My foot caught on something against the door, and I saw Bishop's small cooler, so I pulled out my phone and shot him a text.

LINCOLN:

> You forgot your cooler. Want me to bring it to you?

BISHOP:

> Naw, you need it more than I do. Plus, I have a stocked fridge, and you live with a bunch of college rejects.

Fair enough. Who was I to look a gift horse in the mouth?

It was late enough that the stars had come out, twinkling against the deep purple sky, but I was in no rush to get back to the bunkhouse.

The guys I shared with were nice enough, but Bishop was right. I had a good ten years on most of them. It'd be a rowdy shit show by the time I got back, and I didn't want to deal with that tonight.

Tonight, I wanted a fraction of the peace I'd been searching for since Josie Hayes stumbled into my life.

Grabbing the cooler, I made my way to the white iron fence surrounding the area. It allowed for a perfect view of the main back pasture against the last dregs of sunlight. I could just barely make out the silhouettes of happily grazing cattle.

"Must be nice," I muttered, reaching into the cooler and pulling out a cold can. "Y'all don't have to worry about shit."

I'd tried my best to give Josie her space. Really, I had. And I had every intention of keeping it that way until she stepped out of the house on Wednesday with two mugs of coffee when she'd been adamant about avoiding me like the damn plague.

Luckily, it'd given me one hell of an opening for a little gesture to show her I'd learned more about her than she thought. Though, it'd meant I had to bribe Bishop to pick up some essentials for me, which turned me into the laughingstock of the ranch for the remainder of the week.

Apparently, cowboys weren't supposed to drink oat milk.

It'd all been worth it when I'd seen the look of surprise on her pretty face the next morning when I brought her a steaming cup just the way she liked it. It shouldn't have made my chest ache the way it did. After all, it was just basic decency. Surely her fancy pants boyfriend did things like this, right?

For my sake, I hoped not, but for hers?

God, I hoped he did.

There were nights I still sat around and thought about how her voice wavered when she told me why she'd driven to Tennessee or how she thought she had a list of flaws a mile long.

Shit, flaws were what made a person who they were. If we were all perfect and life was cookie-cutter, would it be worth living? Besides, they were subjective. No matter how hard I'd tried over the years, the only fault I found in Josie was how she left.

I couldn't exactly blame her, though. Not after what she'd told me about her exes. And she'd been clear she hadn't been looking for anything serious. At the time, neither had I.

But sometimes, when you know, you know. And I knew Josie was it for me, even if I wasn't it for her.

I finished the remnants of my second beer when a frustrated groan and a loud whack broke the quiet summer silence. I looked around, not finding anything out of place. It could've just been one of the ranch hands screwing off. Bishop told me they liked to light a bonfire on the weekends sometimes to blow off steam.

But then it happened again, and this time, it was distinct. I heard the pain and heartbreak and frustration boil over into one angry scream before the sound of splitting wood followed.

Josie.

I didn't think before I moved, jumping down and racing across the dirt road to the large shed off the corner of the barn. The light above the shed was dim, flickering in and out like lightning bugs in June. Her face was cast in shadow, and I couldn't read her expression. She stood there, staring down at the half-cracked log like it'd done something to personally offend her before pulling the axe out and swinging it down again.

This time, it split, falling to the side. Josie kicked it over and reached for another log, this one thicker than the last. She adjusted her hands, wringing them against the worn handle before bringing it down with a harrowing cry.

"Stupid piece of shit," she mumbled, wiping at her nose. "What good are you if you can't even do your fucking job?"

I told myself she didn't need some cowboy riding in to save the day, but there were only a few times in my life I'd heard someone in that level of pain, and none of them had been good.

Maybe I would've stayed away, content to watch from the sidelines and remain in the shadows, if she hadn't dropped the weapon at her side and crumbled to her knees.

Fuck this.

I took off at a jog, startling her as I slid to a stop beside her.

"Josie, baby, what's wrong? What happened?" Her big grey eyes were wide and puffy, staring through me like she wasn't seeing me. She hiccuped as tear tracks ran down her cheeks like rivers. "Are you okay?"

Josie blinked slowly, and I saw the moment the world around her came back into focus, and her demeanor shifted. She wiped at her nose again, the sleeve of her t-shirt coming away wet. "I'm fine," she bit out. "Show's over. You can go home now."

I leaned back on my haunches, giving her only a taste of the space she thought she wanted. "I'm not going anywhere, darlin'. Not until you tell me what happened." I moved instinctually, reaching out and tucking a loose strand of hair behind her ear. "Are you okay?" I repeated the question, knowing it was dumb but asking anyway.

She laughed, but the sound was bitter. "Why do you even care, Lincoln?" Her hands dropped to her lap. "I don't deserve your kindness. I left you without so much as a goodbye. What kind of person does that?"

I had to control my temper, knowing it wouldn't do her a damn bit of good if I let it show. Not that it was aimed at her. No, it was aimed at whatever piece of shit had made her question her worth.

"Don't start that shit, Josie. Not right now. Not when I can tell you've had a rough day. I don't need a motive to make sure you're okay, and whoever the person is that made you think that deserves their fucking ass beat."

Josie blew out a long breath. "Well, it's a long list. I don't think you'll have enough time to get through it before you pack it up for Tennessee." There was a note of bitterness as she spat the word.

I wanted to tell her I didn't want to go back, that I'd give it up for her right here and now, but she didn't need me to come in with that. She needed a friend—a shoulder to cry on—and I'd be whatever she needed me to be.

"Tell me something... Why're you so dead set on keeping me at arm's length? I'm trying to be your friend. I sure as hell don't see anyone else here." Regret coursed through my veins the moment the words left my tongue. I wanted to take them back. I'd never been good with my words and hadn't ever needed to be.

"I don't have many friends," she whispered, toying with the hem of her shirt. "Not unless you count my family, but I don't think they count, do you? Because family is obligated to be there for one another." Her gaze flicked down to her hands. "People don't stay around for me often unless there's something in it for them. Every friend I've made, every boyfriend I've been with, they've only seen me as a bargaining chip—for money, for success, for my dad's fucking autograph. You name it." Her voice broke, and a new tear fell. "That's what I'm worth. Fuck all."

It was a sucker punch to my fucking gut. I couldn't breathe, couldn't speak, couldn't do a goddamn thing but stare at Josie with parted lips. The worst part was how I could tell she believed every word she said. To her, it was a fact—a way of life. There wasn't a thing I could say that would change her mind.

Not tonight, at least.

No, the only way to make Josie Hayes believe she's worth more than the land we stood on was to show up for her every day.

But she'd taken my silence as confirmation. "See? You can't even deny it."

I shook my head, inching closer until my knees brushed her own. "Baby, I'd tell you you were wrong every day if you'd let me, but that isn't what you need. You don't need me to convince you of your worth. You've got to do that shit yourself."

"I can't—"

"You can." This time, I reached out and took her hand. She watched me, chest heaving, as I intertwined our fingers. I held my breath, counting the seconds and wondering if she'd pull away. She didn't. "You can't base your own value on the words and actions of others because there are some shitty people in this world who'll take advantage of that. They'll put you down to make themselves feel in control and step on you to get what they want. You've got to remember that at the end of the day, you're the one who gives them that power."

Josie launched herself at me, settling between my knees as she hugged my neck. With each ragged exhale, I could smell the whiskey on her breath and only held her tighter.

"Break, Josie," I whispered, running my hand along her back in slow circles. She shook her head, refusing to let herself cry. Her body was rigid, holding tension in every muscle. "I've got you, darlin'. Go ahead and break so you can put yourself back together."

"I don't know how."

"I said I've got you, and I meant it. We'll pick up the pieces together. You're not alone."

She sniffled, voice shaking as she said, "I don't deserve you. As a friend, as more…"

"We're not talking about me, darlin'. This is all about you." I ran my hand up, smoothing down her hair. Josie leaned deeper into my touch. "I just wanna help *you*."

Hot tears fell against my skin within moments, her shoulders shaking with heart-crushing sobs. I pulled her closer, tightening my grip around her waist. Her body fit perfectly against my own.

We didn't talk, but I let her cry.

I let her cry until my shirt was soaked, until I felt her muscles relax when she slumped against my chest. I let her cry until her breathing returned to normal, and she softly ran her fingers against my neck.

When I loosened my grip, Josie sat back on her haunches. Her palms slid over my shoulders to my chest, lips parted. My hands fell to her hips, lingering there even though I knew they shouldn't.

The stars in the sky had nothing on her. She was a mess—a beautiful fucking mess I wanted to get lost in.

"You're a good man, Lincoln Carter." I couldn't shake the stupid grin that spread across my lips, and she tilted her head. "What?"

"It's nothing," I said."

"Tell me anyway."

My fingers hooked into her belt loops, and I gave a little tug. "I like it when you say my name."

Her storm-colored eyes dropped to my lips. "I think I like it, too." It was a soft admission, one she purposely kept low, as though she was scared of what would happen if she didn't.

Tonight wasn't about me or my feelings. It wasn't about showing Josie I was better than all the other fuckers she'd tangled with over the years. But damn, if it didn't make my hope soar to new heights, even if I knew it'd be gone by morning.

And then I was stupid. Utterly reckless.

I leaned in, brushing my lips across her forehead in a ghost of a kiss—a promise of the future and the haunting of our past crossing paths right before us.

Josie closed her eyes, letting loose a soft sigh that nearly broke my resolve. I wanted to blaze a path down her cheeks and wipe away every mascara stain with my tongue. I wanted to erase every tear she'd ever shed with promises of a future worth living.

But I didn't get the chance, not as we heard her father call her name and the sound of crunching gravel under footfall.

Josie jumped up, distancing herself as Doug walked around the corner. "Everything okay, here?" he asked.

She smiled, and it was almost convincing. I wondered how long she'd had to practice that, how long she'd been hiding her feelings from those around her. "Yeah, I saw Lincoln out here chopping wood, so I thought I'd see if he needed anything." She looked down at me. "You good?"

I dropped my head, knowing whatever we shared had already shattered. "Yeah, thanks. I'll finish up here in just a minute."

Doug said something, but I couldn't hear him. Or maybe I didn't care to. I wasn't able to put up my mask the way Josie could.

It wasn't until she stepped beside me, letting her hand linger on my shoulder, that I knew we were alone again. "Thank you, Lincoln. For everything."

And then she walked away, leaving me kneeling in the dirt and wondering what the hell I was doing in Texas.

josie

. . .

IT'D BEEN a long time since I'd let myself be as vulnerable as I was with Lincoln. I didn't know what it was about him that let my guard drop. He had this *thing* about him that made me want to divulge every secret and truth I'd ever held near my heart.

And last night, beneath the flickering yellow glow of our barn, I'd laid a few bare for him to see.

I wasn't sure when I'd decided to trust him. Letting him see that messy, anxiety-addled part of me that I'd learned to keep close from an early age. There weren't many people around here who understood it.

My parents, though, had always been my biggest support system. They listened to me without judgment or guilt, never tried to convince me that whatever I was experiencing was all in my head. It'd only taken one appointment with my local doctor before they elected to drive to the city in search of a psychiatrist who understood mental health.

I didn't think I'd ever be able to thank them enough for how they loved me. But it was because of their dedication I had the tools and medication I needed to make it through the day. My panic attacks became less frequent, and I could breathe for the first time in years.

Until last night. Until the stress of life came by and hit me so hard that I wanted to hit something back.

After meeting with Charles, I hadn't returned to the ranch. At least, not right away. Even though what happened hadn't been my fault, my mind made it feel like it was. My chest grew tight, and my pulse skyrocketed as I sat in the parking lot of Al's Liquor until they opened. Then, it'd been a mad dash toward the whiskey and a slow drive through the backroads until I got home.

But the impending conversation cast a looming shadow overhead, leaving me nauseous beyond compare. When I heard the stampede of hooves and spurs filter in from the barn, my palms were sweaty. I'd just reached for the bottle and poured myself a shot of courage when Dad walked into his office.

His face fell when he saw my own, collapsing into a leather armchair with a "What's the damage?" on his lips.

It hit me at that moment just how tired he looked. Deep wrinkles looked set in stone on his sun-kissed face. His hair, which had once been a deep brown, was peppered and worn. He'd groaned as he sat down, exhausted from a hard day running around in the arena after men who were easily half his age.

And my heart hurt.

It absolutely fucking broke because I loved this man more than I'd loved anyone else in my life. Growing up, I'd tell my friends that my dad was invincible, and there were days I still thought that. But the truth was that he wasn't.

Our family had been forced to come to terms with his mortality after the first doctor showed concerns for his heart. There had been many conversations about what life would look like when he was gone. Dad even laid out specific instructions on what he wanted to happen after he died, swearing he'd haunt us if we deviated from his plans. It was morbid and horrifying at first, but then we realized he had his own fears to manage.

I reckoned if I was in his position, I'd do the same thing.

This had been different, though. When Dad was out working, riding, or joking around with us in the kitchen, it was easy to forget his fragility. It'd been months since we had a reminder, and this one caught me off guard.

I'd tried to keep the shake from my voice as I told him everything Charles and I had discussed, focusing on the facts and our next steps. The papers in front of me were streaked with yellow highlighter marks and illegible notes from the hours I'd spent combing through each transaction.

Despite what had happened, I trusted Charles when it came to his contacts. Maybe that meant I was a fool, but his face showed genuine shock over our findings. He was as dedicated as I was to getting to the bottom of this.

So, Dad and I called the agency Charles had recommended to request a formal audit of his investment portfolio. I think it'd broken his own heart a bit to do it—he didn't want to believe a man he considered one of his best friends was capable of mismanaging his funds.

Dad looked exhausted when we returned to the house. He hardly spoke during dinner, only responding when someone prodded him for an answer. Even then, it was snappy. With his meatloaf mostly untouched, he'd shuffled to his bedroom and left us sitting in the wake of his silence.

Cleo and Lennox jumped on me, pushing me to tell them what was wrong, but I couldn't. Instead, I grabbed the bottle and stumbled outside. I'd felt the panic rising all day, but it couldn't be ignored anymore.

My clothes felt wrong against my skin, and the fabric was too itchy and tight. I felt like I was being suffocated. There was a scream rising from deep in my chest and tears that threatened to fall.

I let them.

I fell apart in the silence of the darkness and let out my frustrations with each swing of Dad's rusted axe. I cried for my dad, for the lost money, for his own heartbreak, and for my own. I cried for the guilt I felt at the heart of it all. Even if it wasn't my fault, I still believed it was.

And even though I was trying like hell not to think about it, I couldn't help but see Lincoln's crestfallen face when I walked back to the house with Dad last night.

What I needed was a distraction, and I had plenty of that to go around. Dad and I had taken Saturday off to recoup. By the time Sunday rolled around, we were ready to tackle the day.

"WHERE DO YOU WANT THESE, SUGAR?" Dad asked, peeking around the heavy boxes he held with trembling hands.

"Dad!" I rushed from behind my desk and lifted two from his grip. "I told you to bring them down one at a time, not three. These weigh a ton."

He huffed, following me to the corner behind his desk where I'd set the others. "Don't see what the fuss is, Josie. They're just boxes. I can carry 'em just fine."

I turned around, placing my hands on my hips. "I agreed to let you help on the condition you wouldn't overexert yourself."

"I'm not—"

"The beads of sweat trailing down your face say otherwise, and don't think I didn't notice how you were shaking earlier. How long has it been since you've eaten?"

Dad shifted on his feet, shoving his hands into his pockets. "All you girls are too much like your mother," he grumbled. "Stubborn, headstrong, and a pain in my ass."

I cocked my head to the side. "You just described yourself, old man. Try again."

"Don't know what you're talking about." He wiped his forehead, leaning against the wall. "I guess I am a little tired."

"Go back to the house. I've got more than enough here to get me started," I said, looking around his cluttered office.

My dad had never kept his space clean, saying he had more important things to do on the ranch. I've tried to bring some organization to his madness, but it hasn't been much use.

It was little more than a clustered shoebox with a too-big desk and a computer. Dad had a collection of old photographs lining the wall, most from his rodeo heydays. Still, there were a few personal touches from family vacations over the years.

"Josie, sugar… I don't want you to overwork yourself."

"I'm not, Dad. I promise. You just might see me a little less over the next week. I want to get this over to them as soon as possible." The chair creaked as I sat down and booted up the computer. I looked up, seeing my dad still hovering in the doorway.

"If you're allowed to be worried about me, then I can be worried about you. I've seen you throw yourself into this project like you've got something to prove, sugar. And I want you to know I don't give a shit about the money."

"*I* do. It's the principle of the matter. Daddy, someone—and I'm not saying it's Charles—but someone took advantage of you. It makes me sick to my stomach."

He sighed. "Your ass better be back in that house for dinner. Don't make me come looking for you, alright?"

I'd concede to that, especially since Cleo was going to make Mom's Mississippi Pot Roast. "I promise. No later than seven."

Dad narrowed his eyes. "Try no later than five. You're taking the evening off. Boss's orders."

"Whatever you say!" I called out as he walked from the office. I'd just turned back to the computer as footsteps sounded outside the doorway. "Dammit, old man, I told you a deal was a deal—"

But it wasn't Dad who strode around the corner.

josie

. . .

LINCOLN LEANED against the door jamb, smiling. His white tee was dirty, caked with what looked—and smelled—like motor oil and grease. Dirt stained fingers fiddled with a sheet of paper in his hands.

"I know I have a few years on you, but old man?" He clutched at his chest. "That's a deep wound."

"Obviously, I wasn't talking about you," I muttered, nodding at whatever he held. "What's that?"

"You know how Bishop was on my ass last week about turning in my timesheet for payroll?"

I leaned forward, crossing my arms over the desk. "Uh-huh."

"And you know how I told him time and again that I'd turn it in by Friday morning?"

"Yup."

His eyes dropped to the paper. "Well, I might've forgotten to do that."

"Shocker," I said, holding my hand out. "Give it here."

Lincoln stepped inside. "You see, in a roundabout way... This is your fault."

"My fault? How is it my fault?"

He dropped into the chair in front of me, even though I don't remember inviting him to stay. "Yeah, you were too damn distracting in those little denim shorts—"

"I know you're not about to blame *my* clothing for *your* actions," I said, sitting back in my chair.

His face fell. "No, no, no, not like that. I mean—shit. It was supposed to be a joke—"

I couldn't help but chuckle. "Honestly, those are my favorite shorts. I'd have been distracted too." I took the paper from his hands. "I can go ahead and get this in, but your check will be late. I can try to get it to you by midweek, though."

"It's fine. I've got everything I need here." Lincoln stared at me with unwavering conviction as I met his gaze. He wasn't talking about groceries or vices.

He was talking about me.

"What's got you working on a Sunday?" he asked, scanning the papers along the desk. I tried to pull them together into a pile, but he snagged the top page before I could stop him. "Financial records, huh? I hated staring at those for the bar. Frank couldn't keep the books for shit. It took me months to sort them out."

"You kept the books for the bar? I didn't know that."

Lincoln smiled, but it wasn't the one I'd grown used to. "You'd run off before I had the chance to tell you, but yeah, I did most of the day-to-day shit. Frank was more of a silent partner, which meant I told him when I needed money to fix something around the bar and he watched me while drinking his stock." He shook his head. "I don't know how the bar lasted as long as it did. Frank never tracked his expenses and was a risky investor. He was always coming to me with an opportunity some young buck pitched him."

"Did he ever move forward with them?"

"Sometimes. There were a few he was able to pull back after talking with a financial advisor, but a lot of it was a loss."

Lincoln met my gaze over the paper. "Hypothetically speaking, is that something you're dealing with?"

I tapped my fingers against the desk, wondering how much I could tell him. Anything I said would stay between us, I knew that. Lincoln was a locked vault, loyal until the end. It was a long shot, but he did have more experience looking at this than I did.

Giving him a brief rundown hadn't taken long, and Lincoln hung onto every word. He asked questions, some of which I had no answers to. By the time I was done, he glanced around the office with furrowed brows. "Mind if I take a look?"

"Be my guest," I said, tipping my chin to motion him behind the desk.

The only problem? It seemed to have slipped my mind at how little space I had. There was no way to avoid him, no way to escape the thick diesel scent that clung to his clothes. He leaned over my shoulder, taking control of the mouse and scrolling through the documents.

"Did Charles say when this began?" he asked.

I shook my head. "He wasn't clear. Just said that my father had wanted to diversify his portfolio a few years back and he'd advised against it. Dad swears he didn't do anything outside of the agency, so..." I shrugged. "All signs point to something happening along the way. Charles says he's going to get to the bottom of it."

"Do you believe him?" His breath fanned out against the back of my neck, and I fought to keep my composure.

"I do. It might be foolish, but—"

"It's not," he said, cutting me off. "Sometimes you've got to trust your gut, and if it's telling you it wasn't Charles, then you best believe it."

I turned in my chair to look at him, wondering if he would move. No matter how inappropriate the thought might be, I hoped he stayed. His presence was comforting, like a warm blanket on a cold night. I wanted to wrap myself in his arms and listen to him tell me it was going to be okay. I wanted to believe that it would be.

"I don't know what I believe anymore. Up is down and east is west. It tears me up that Dad's been affected. He feels like he can't turn to his best friend," I whispered, uttering the confession in the limited space between us.

What would it feel like to run my fingers through his hair again? It'd always been so thick, the coloring slightly lighter than my own. But there was more grey than I remembered, a smattering that started at his temples and worked its way back. It was the first time I'd seen him without a hat since I'd left Tennessee.

"Doug's lucky to have a daughter like you, you know? Don't get me wrong, your sisters are great, but you're something else. You fight for the ones you love with everything you have. It's admirable."

I couldn't help but laugh, feeling heat creep up along my neck. "No, they've done a lot more than me. I'm just trying to contribute what I can.

Lincoln scanned my face, eyes softening. "You've got to stop doing that."

"Doing what?"

He tilted his head. "Putting yourself down like that. You did it when I first met you, too. Seems like you haven't grown out of it. We've got to break that habit."

I pulled my lip between my teeth, unable to hide the crushing weight of his stare. The way he said 'we' caused goosebumps to break out along my skin. It was decadent. An ardent promise. It was yet another sign that Lincoln had no intention of leaving this ranch without putting up a fight.

Despite my weak insistence that what we had was over and done with, it wasn't. My heart still beat in that erratic, lovesick way it always did when he was around. No matter how much he pissed me off or pushed me, Lincoln had this uncanny way of soothing the horrible negative voice in my head.

It would've been so easy to tell him as much; to let him know with brutal clarity that as reckless of an idea it might be, I wanted him more than I'd ever wanted anyone in my life.

But at the end of the day, I had to remember that he *would* leave. He had a life back in Tennessee, something he seemed to enjoy. I couldn't ask him to give that up, could I? Because if our roles were reversed, I couldn't see myself leaving Black Springs behind.

Lincoln reached up, gently running the rough pad of his thumb along my bottom lip. His gaze dropped, hungrily watching as he slowly applied pressure. When it popped from between my teeth, he let out a low groan. "You're gonna get me in trouble, darlin'. I'm supposed to be a gentleman, and you've got me thinking about being everything but."

Fire, Josie… You're playing with fire.

"Like what?" I asked. My voice was unrecognizable, and I was a quivering mess. It took every effort not to rock myself forward, searching for friction. "What're you thinking about right now?"

Lincoln's eyes trailed down my body, lingering on the spot between my legs before flicking back up. He leaned in, causing my breathing to hitch as I felt the rough stubble brush along my cheek. "Break up with that piece of shit you call a boyfriend, and I'll tell you every sordid detail. Then, when you're writhing underneath me, just like you are right now, I'll make good on every word I said."

Holy. Fucking. Shit.

My mind told me I should be repulsed, that I should push him away and scold him for speaking to me like he did, but my body… My body was another thing entirely. I ached for his touch, longed to feel the punishing bruise of his kiss. It was madness, and it was taking me under.

He pulled away, smirking because when I looked straight ahead, I was eye-level with his dick. His very *hard* dick. I could see the outline of it through his jeans, suddenly struck with just how long it'd been since I'd been with anyone.

And how it'd been Lincoln.

"Lincoln…"

My words died as I heard the click of shoes against concrete in the barn alley. It didn't belong to anyone on the ranch. I knew the heavy thud of boots like I knew the sound of my own voice. Lincoln recognized it too, quickly stepping back just in time for Ellis to walk around the corner.

lincoln

· · ·

I'D NEVER HAD a nemesis before, but I think I did now. I hated Josie's little boyfriend with every fiber of my being. It wasn't just because she was his girl. That was too obvious. This was more about the fact that I'd been out here for just over a week and hadn't seen him once.

If she was mine, and she should be, there wasn't a force in the world that could've kept us apart.

I didn't know what I was expecting, but it wasn't the mousy little man in front of me. Ellis—*what a stupid fucking name*—was barely six feet with dirty blond hair. It'd been slicked back as though he was going to work. To top off his city boy prep look, he wore a pale pink polo shirt tucked into khaki slacks.

He didn't fit in around here with the dirt and grease and blood. Even if I hadn't shown up ready to sweep Josie off her feet, there was no way their relationship would last. That wasn't me thinking highly of myself. It was a fact.

Ellis stood in the doorway with a bouquet of dying grocery store wildflowers and a smile. It promptly died as he saw the two of us so close. I'd tried to step away, using the second to fix my dick so it wasn't painfully obvious I'd been moments away from breaking whatever moral code I had left and fucking Josie the way she deserved.

The way her pupils had dilated as I'd drawn in close was the stuff of fantasies. At that moment, Josie had wanted me just as much as I'd wanted her. It was undeniable, the energy between us cracking like a whip.

I'd be fucking my hand in the shower tonight at the mental image, watching my cum go to waste as it disappeared down the drain when it should've painted her skin.

"Ellis, what're you doing here?" Josie asked, shifting in her seat.

"I wanted to surprise you," he said, rattling the sad flowers in his hand. We all watched as a couple of petals drifted to the floor. "But I didn't know you'd have company."

I smiled, stepping forward and extending my hand. "Name's Lincoln. Doug hired me for the summer to help him with the clinic."

Ellis stared at it for a beat too long before he met me half-way, clamping down with what was supposed to be a firm shake. "Ah, nice to meet you. I'm Ellis." And then the fucker went a step further, trying like hell to piss all over the room. "Josephine's boyfriend."

"Josephine, huh? How romantic," I said, chuckling as Ellis dropped my hand. Who the fuck called their girlfriend by their full name?

Josie rounded the corner and took the flowers from Ellis. Her smile faltered as she studied the bouquet. "These are... lovely. Thank you."

Ellis smiled at Josie. "You're welcome. I saw them as I walked out of the store this morning and said to myself, '*My girl-friend would love these.*'"

Seriously, what did Josie see in this guy?

"What were y'all doing before I got here?"

"I was just swinging by to drop off my timesheet when I

found Josie in here, hard at work," I said. "Decided I'd stay and give her a bit of company."

"Lincoln used to run a bar in his hometown, and I was asking him questions about financial statements," Josie said, bracing her hands over the desk. "Dad and I called the auditors on Friday, and I have to hand everything in by the end of the week."

Ellis shifted his gaze between us. "If you needed help, you should've asked me. I understand this better than anyone and know exactly what they want. Besides, should you really be telling our business to a stranger?" he asked, turning to me with a fake smile. I'm sure he'd perfected it over the years. "No offense, of course. We just don't know you."

I couldn't help but notice the way he said 'our' business when talking about the ranch. Fighting the urge to roll my eyes and send this self-important douche packing, I leaned against the corner of the desk. One little jab couldn't hurt, after all.

"Actually, Josie *does* know me. Very well, in fact. We're practically like this." I crossed my middle and pointer fingers before showing them to him.

"Either way, I don't see how the financial records of a bar could compare to the ranch's. They're totally different establishments." His laugh was cutting, likely meant to be cruel. I'd seen his type many times before, how they loved to put men like me in our place where we belong: in the dirt and beneath their foot.

"Lincoln actually had a lot of great advice," Josie cut in, eyes narrowing.

Her words like a balm, soothing the anxious beast refusing to settle in my chest. How could she not see how wrong he was for her? And what drew her to him in the first place?

Ellis' face showed a faint hint of annoyance, as though he couldn't believe Josie dared to go against his lowly opinion of me. "I'm sure he does. Again, I meant no offense."

I held my hands up. "None taken. I'm sure you see more money in a day than I will in my life."

Ellis straightened at my words. "Yes, well, I have high-profile clients with net worths in the millions, including the Black Springs Ranch portfolio."

"I thought your father handled that?" I asked, looking toward Josie.

"Charles did, but he's retiring at the end of the year. Ellis will be taking over the firm, including his dad's list of clients," Josie explained. "I wanted to get more familiar with our finances. It's one of the reasons I found the discrepancy."

"I guess it's a good thing you're so nosy," Ellis said with a condescending smile.

If I knew it wouldn't utterly obliterate the shaky truce Josie and I have come to, I'd gladly lay his ass out. He was rude and disrespectful, contemptuous of everything around him. This prick wouldn't have a job if it wasn't for Josie and her family. And I'd bet Josie didn't even see it.

"Guess it's a good thing she looked so carefully," I said, flattening my tone. "Or else your firm would've gotten away with making one hell of a mistake. I mean, a quarter of a million dollars is a lot of money. Surely, you can agree."

I expected Josie to intervene and tell me I was overstepping, but she didn't. She peered at Ellis, waiting for his answer.

"We would've found it eventually," he said, crossing his arms.

"Oh, I'm sure you would've," I agreed.

Ellis checked his watch. "Josephine, could I get a moment alone with you? I drove all this way to see you." He spared me a glance before pushing forward. "I know things were tense on Friday. Let me help you find what you need. It's the least I could do."

"Sure," Josie said before turning toward me. "Thanks for everything, Lincoln. I'll ensure we push your check through as soon as possible." She was using her business tone, which meant she was done with our conversation.

I was just grateful my dick wasn't straining against my jeans anymore as I pushed off the desk. "I'm not worried. Like I told you earlier, I have everything I need here on this ranch."

Without so much as a goodbye to the man stewing in the doorway, I brushed past him and out of the barn.

josie

· · ·

"WHAT THE HELL WAS THAT ABOUT?" I asked as Ellis quickly shut the door. His face had grown red when Lincoln brushed past him, and I'd known him long enough to know his ticks and tells. I wasn't sure what had set him off—seeing the two of us so close together or how Lincoln constantly challenged him.

He placed his hands on the desk, glowering down at me. "You're asking *me* that? Are you serious?"

I crossed my arms. "You were rude. There was no need to act like that. Lincoln's been a huge help around the ranch and to my dad. I can't risk you pissing him off and forcing him to pack his bags."

"No need?" he echoed, laughing. The room suddenly felt smaller, like the space was closing on us. "I drove all the way out here to bring you flowers, only to find the two of you cuddling close on the other side of your desk."

Flowers that were likely on discount because they were preparing to throw them away, I thought. Ellis wasn't one for gifts. He'd told me once that he valued acts of service, and maybe that's what he was trying to do by offering to help me with the audit. I guess it had been nice for him to try to be romantic.

"We were not cuddling, Ellis," I replied. "He was looking over the statements on the computer. He's well aware of you."

It wasn't a lie. It wasn't exactly the truth, either. I didn't even know if I'd have ever mentioned Ellis if he hadn't called when Lincoln and I were in the barn. Maybe I should feel a little guilty knowing I would've done a hell of a lot more than cuddle if Lincoln hadn't dropped the reminder of Ellis.

But I didn't.

As Ellis stepped closer, I braced myself for an argument that never came. Instead, his face morphed into one I recognized— the charming, helpful man who had helped me when I didn't know what I was doing.

Anxiety eased as Ellis sat down in the chair in front of me. "I'm sorry, baby. It's just been a rough weekend. After you left the office, I felt terrible. I spent the rest of my time chained to my desk, reviewing files and trying to figure this out." He reached out his hand, intertwining our fingers.

I stared down at the point where we connected, barely listening to the words he continued to speak. His skin against my own felt wrong, like it didn't belong. When he'd touched me, it'd taken every ounce of willpower I had not to pull back.

"Josephine? Are you listening to me?" he asked, shaking me from my stupor.

"I—I'm so sorry. I was a million miles away," I offered, trying to force a smile that wouldn't come.

Ellis pouted. "You've been working yourself too hard. You need some help."

He was right, as much as I didn't want to admit it. Taking all this on while pushing away everyone who offered wasn't doing me any favors. What if I made a mistake, one that could've solved everything, because I was too stubborn to say yes? Help didn't mean I was doing anything wrong. It meant I was doing what was best for my father, our family, and the legacy he'd built.

So, why wasn't it easy to take Ellis up on his offer? Why couldn't I say yes and show him what I'd gathered already? Better yet, why did the thought of being secluded with him feel like I was being untrue to my heart?

The answer left a bitter taste lingering on my tongue because I wouldn't dare voice that out loud. Not right now.

He bent his head. "I can see the wheels turning in your head. What're you thinking about?"

And there was that guilt I thought I'd escaped, coming back and gripping my throat in a vise. "I know you're right. It's just hard to ask," I said, shaking my head.

"I'm not asking," Ellis said, reaching forward and grabbing the nearest stack of records. "I'm telling."

ELLIS PUSHED BACK HIS SEAT, pinching the bridge of his nose as my stomach growled for the fifth time in the past thirty minutes. "Alright, I think we should call it. We've gotten a lot done."

I looked around at Dad's office, noticing the piles of papers we'd combed through in the past three hours. We'd devised a system: I would scan the documents while he would sort them into the correct files. He had shared access to the program and could keep up the search from home. Overall, we'd found most of the things we'd needed.

"Good idea," I said, stretching my arms. I'd been sitting still far too long.

Ellis stood, pocketing his phone. He twirled his keys around his finger. I hated them, the constant jingle equivalent to nails on a chalkboard. "How about I kidnap you for a night?" he asked.

"What?"

"Yeah, it'll be fun. We can grab a bite, and then you can come over..." Ellis trailed off, smirking as he rounded the desk. "We can forget about the numbers. Maybe share a couple of glasses of wine? And then we can have dessert..." My heart was pounding as he leaned in and kissed my cheek. He moved closer, aiming again for my mouth, but I turned my head.

Ellis had always respected my wishes to take things slow. He'd never pushed before, never demanded more than I wanted to give, but the way he was talking made me wonder if that understanding had an expiry date.

"I can't tonight. Cleo is making dinner, and I promised Dad I'd be walking through the door no later than five." I tried to smile, but it fell flat. I wondered if he could tell.

Ellis shifted, once again taking my hand in his. "How about next weekend? The first clinic will be done, right? We can celebrate."

"I'll celebrate once this is done," I said, nodding toward the computer.

He ran his tongue across his teeth, dropping my hand. "Sure. Whatever you say."

He was halfway out the door before I closed my eyes and called out, "That sounds great, though."

Those damn keys twirled once more as he smiled. "I'll make reservations. Maybe we can go into the city instead. Have a weekend away."

I should want that, right? A weekend away was normal. Especially if it'd been months since we started seeing each other. "Maybe after summer? Mom won't be back until the end of the month."

"Alright," he said, raising his hands in surrender. "I'll concede. But we will take that trip when all these trailers pack up, and the cowboys go home."

The very thought made me sick to my stomach.

I loved summers at Black Springs and watching my dad work the clinic. The fact that it could be his last one only made the thought of missing a single day that much more bitter. Try as I might to convince myself that was the only reason I suddenly felt the urge to throw up, it didn't work.

Instead, it was the thought of watching a certain bunkhouse empty out and my cowboy ride away.

I walked toward Ellis' car, watching him climb inside and drive away. His tires kicked up a cloud of dust, swallowing him whole. I stayed like that, waiting until he was nothing more than a black dot disappearing through the gates.

And then I stayed like that a little longer, wrapping my arms around myself as though it could hold me together. For the first time since Ellis had shown up, I felt like I could breathe again. His absence wasn't an ache I missed, but a reprieve I welcomed.

"What's wrong with you, Josie?" I muttered to myself, welcoming the fresh air. A sweet summer breeze blew my hair from my face, tickling the back of my neck.

"Only one thing, far as I can tell." I turned over my shoulder, watching Lincoln leave the barn. He still wore his dirty shirt and jeans from earlier.

"Huh?"

He stepped up beside me, staring at the spot Ellis' car had just been. "You asked what was wrong with you, and I said there was only one thing."

"And what would that be?" I asked.

Lincoln didn't answer immediately, letting my question hang between us. "You're not mine."

I closed my eyes, tightening my arms around my middle as though it could stop my heart from beating out of my chest. "You can't say shit like that, Lincoln. It isn't right. I have—"

He shook his head. "You don't love him, and you know it, Josie. Hell, do you even like the guy? I've seen more chemistry between Bishop and a bottle of beer."

"That's because Bishop and Coors Banquet are a love story for the ages," I muttered. "They're inseparable. Like this." I crossed my middle and pointer fingers like Lincoln had earlier when he'd met Ellis for the first time.

"Fair enough," Lincoln laughed, kicking a rock beneath his boot. He turned to me, gently unwrapping and holding my hands in his. This time, it felt right. I don't have the urge to pull away or cower and hide. "Tell me something, darlin'... does being with him feel like being with me? I mean, am I completely off the mark here?"

"I—I don't know. It's different."

I bit my lip, peering up at him through my lashes. I expected to be met with frustration, but his face remained unchanged. His eyes had softened, settling the hint of anxiety that threatened to crop up at his questions. "A good different?"

Why *was* I with Ellis? I was exhausted from trying to convince myself every day that we had anything real. Our relationship felt more disappointing, driven only by my belief that I had to be with him to make my family happy. When I stopped to think about it, the notion was stupid. My dad didn't care, nor did he even really like Ellis. I think he'd rather see me alone than by his side.

So, what was stopping me from walking away from him?

The truth was... *nothing*. Nothing was holding me back, nothing I even wanted to hold on to. We had no wonderful memories together. No vacation trips or anniversaries that made me think twice about what I'd be giving up. He was a nice guy, and he cared about me.

The most I could offer was a simple nod in response to his question. Because, yes, Lincoln was different in every way that mattered. He lit a fire in my soul, which I didn't know had gone out. That was what terrified me the most. What would happen when he left at the end of the summer, and could I live with it?

Like earlier, he cupped one hand to my cheek tenderly. I let myself lean into his warmth. "I'm okay with waiting right now. I've done enough of it by now. Just promise me something?"

"What's that?"

Lincoln pursed his lips, rolling them together. "Just don't leave me waiting out in the cold too long, yeah? Be fair to my heart in the way I'm trying my damnedest to be to yours."

And then he leaned in, kissing my forehead before leaving me alone with my thoughts.

lincoln

. . .

THE FIRST CLINIC of the summer was done, and I was bone weary. Didn't help that I couldn't get my boss's daughter out of my fucking mind, either.

Ever since I walked away from Josie on Sunday, it seemed like she spent the next week avoiding me at all costs. As much as I hated it, maybe it was for the best. I'd already chosen her, would choose her every damn day if she let me, but she had to choose me too.

Still, I worried maybe I'd taken it too far. I might've gotten carried away with my touches, spurred on by her body's natural reaction to my proximity.

If I was a better man, maybe I would've walked away and nursed what was left of my pride. Maybe I could've been better about giving her space from the beginning, but dammit... I wasn't a better man. Josie lit up any room she walked into. I couldn't have stayed away if I'd tried—and I had tried.

I'd tried for one long fucking year to leave what we had in the past. Most would probably think being hung up on a woman you only spent five nights with was insane. Hell, maybe I was.

When I'd shown up to the ranch and found out she had a

boyfriend, I would've been fine conceding if I'd known she was happy with him. It'd only taken one look, though... One look and I knew I hadn't been making shit up in my head, and she was mine.

"You've done one hell of a good job these past two weeks, Lincoln."

I looked up from my work, noticing Doug leaning against the barn door. Sweat beaded along my neck, dripping down my back in the sweltering heat. I saw a lot of him in Josie now that I knew where to look. They had the same straight nose and storm colored eyes. Though it was now littered with streaks of grey, I was willing to bet that his hair once matched hers.

Seeing them together had been a surprise. They had something special, a bond not many people ever have. She was so attentive to his needs; it was like they shared a mind. Anytime he opened his mouth to ask for something, Josie came, item in hand, without asking.

That was just the kind of man Doug was. I'd watched how he interacted with his girls. The way he spoke was inherently different, he still showed the same love and respect to each of them.

It only furthered my respect for him. I had so much to learn, so much that wasn't taught to me growing up. Frank had done his best, but by the time he'd stumbled into my life, I wasn't much better off than he was.

I stood up and dusted my hands against my old chaps before turning down the radio. "Thank you, sir. That means a lot, especially since you didn't have much to go off when hiring me."

Doug nodded, a sad smile crossing his lips. "Well, Frank's word carries..." He trailed off, shaking his head before correcting himself. "*Carried* a lot of weight. If he said you were good, I'd be a damn fool not to listen to him."

Would Frank's death ever get easier? I wasn't sure. It'd been nearly four months. After he passed, I had to remind myself I wouldn't see his scowl greeting me the moment I walked into his barn. The bar was the same, constantly expecting to hear him call me out on whatever bullshit he disagreed with.

"He was a damn good man," I said, clearing my throat. "The world didn't deserve him."

"Got that right, but he knew what it took to run these clinics, and you've got the talent." Doug pushed off the doorway and strode to the horse I'd been working with since I arrived. "How's Sunny treating you? She's not giving you any trouble, right?"

"Naw," I said, running my hand along her dark mane. "She's just a little misunderstood."

Her nostrils flared as Doug stepped closer, reaching into his pocket and pulling out what looked like two sugar cubes. He laid his palm flat, hovering just under her mouth. "She's been through a lot. We rescued her from a real shit situation last year," he explained, chuckling as Sundance reached out and bumped her nose against his pocket in search of more treats. "Bishop had been doing a patrol near the main road one morning when he saw Sunny walking along the road. She was bleeding badly down her right flank, and he lost it. Called me down before calling down the vet and the sheriff."

My stomach turned. "What happened?"

Doug sighed. "He brought her to the barn to get cleaned up while I met the sheriff where she'd been spotted. We followed the blood back to her old home, finding three more horses standing in piles of their own filth. It was horrific. I don't know what triggered it. Hell, could've just been the drive to survive, but Sunny had broken out of the enclosure. She caught herself on a jagged piece of wood." He pulled out two more cubes and fed them to the horse. "She's got a bit of a temper and doesn't trust easily, but she's a damn fine horse."

"That she is," I agreed.

Doug stood back, much to the horse's dismay, and stuck his

hands in his now empty pockets. "Bishop's had a lot to say about you the past two weeks."

I braced my arms along Sundance's back. "Do I need to pack my bags?"

I'd come to enjoy Bishop. He was a surly bastard that didn't take much shit. But depending on what he'd told Doug, I might just change my mind.

Doug laughed. "The opposite, actually. He said that you have a damn good head on your shoulders. And I've known that boy a long time. He's not the type to blow smoke up my ass."

I smiled, trying not to let the surge of pride I felt make me cocky. It'd been a long time since I'd felt proud of my choices or work, longer still since I'd had anything to smile about. Ever since I showed up, I'd found something worth having—worth fighting to keep.

"Well, thank you, sir. That means a lot coming from you."

He waved me off. "Aw, don't start that shit. I'm just someone who got lucky. I found my passion and ran with it." He pointed at me. "That's what I want to see you do, though. I'd like to talk to you about staying on, maybe taking a permanent position here at Black Springs. I've got to slow down here, but handing over the reins isn't easy. And Bishop doesn't have the temperament to deal with the public."

Holy shit. A permanent position.

Here.

In Texas.

With Josie in reach.

When I first started training horses, I'd gotten in with a family who didn't have Doug's ideals. They ruled with fear rather than understanding, forcing their animals to submit in ways that made me sick—a stark contrast to the loving face they put on for the community.

On my last day employed, they'd told me to get my ass on the back of a horse who'd given me trouble. He was a mean son of a bitch who didn't think twice about biting your hand clean off or stomping you into the dirt.

The moment he'd seen me coming, his nostrils flared, and he'd come running. I hadn't moved fast enough, getting swept under his feet. If one of the hands hadn't seen me go down, I would've been dead.

They dropped me off at the hospital with a medical bill the size of Texas and a forced resignation.

I'd spent several years believing my working with animals was over. It'd taken six months in physical therapy to get me up and moving again. After that, I'd learned they'd blacklisted my name at every ranch. Frank had told me to hang up my hat and walk away. He could see how it was tearing me up, twisting me into someone I didn't recognize.

But that was just another reason I was destined to make this work.

"I sure as fuck don't."

Bishop rounded the corner with his horse, Titan, in tow. The name suited him perfectly. The blue roan was massive, at least seventeen hands tall, with a broad chest. He matched his rider in personality, ornery as hell with a stick up their asses.

Sundance's head shot up, her eyes wide when she saw the stallion come into view. "She's got it bad for him," I said, patting her neck.

It was taking everything I had to stop myself from jumping down Doug's throat for more information. What would he want me to do? Bishop was his second in command, and that wouldn't change. I could be another helping hand, but was it worth it?

If I said yes, I'd have to move from Tennessee to Texas. Four months ago, that wouldn't have been an issue, but with Frank's death it became a lot more complicated.

"You don't know the half of it," Bishop grunted, bringing me back to the present. "I'm just glad you're here to put her to work, or else I'd have to listen to her fuss about being left behind."

"Sundance just knows quality when she sees it," Doug added, stepping back as Bishop and I led our horses into their stall. There was a small window laid into their shared wall, letting them nuzzle the shit out of each other. "Ain't that right, girl?"

As if on cue, Sundance let out a shrill whinny we all took as agreement.

Bishop shook his head, the ghost of a smile peeking under his cowboy hat. "Lovesick fools," he muttered.

"One day, you'll meet a girl who'll get you so damn twisted inside," Doug said, clapping him on the shoulder. "And boy, I can't wait to watch you eat your damn words."

"Never gonna happen," Bishop said, shrugging out of Doug's hold. "What time's dinner?"

"Seven on the dot, just like every other Friday for the past twenty-plus years," Doug said, narrowing his eyes at a car coming up the drive.

Bishop stepped up beside him. "Expecting anyone?"

Doug didn't answer as he walked toward the approaching vehicle with Bishop and me close behind. The make was too rich for my blood, and it certainly stuck out like a sore thumb when it pulled in next to Bishop's beat-up Dodge.

Two men in suits stepped out, the older raising his hand to shield his eyes from the sun. His voice was gruff as he called out to Doug in greeting. I couldn't make out their faces from here, but they seemed strangely familiar.

"Aw, hell," Bishop said. "Fucking hate this guy."

"Why?" I asked, my voice low.

But my question was answered as the main house door opened, and Josie stepped outside. Her brows knitted together in confusion as she walked to the end of the drive. "Ellis? What're you doing here?" she asked.

"Your dad invited us," he said, kissing her cheek. "Said it'd been too long since we'd come out."

Josie met my gaze over his shoulder. I probably should have excused myself and headed back to the bunk cabin I was sharing with three other guys, but I didn't.

"Because he's a fucking tool. Comes from big money and acts like it," Bishop said, spitting at his boots. "Charles is alright, but I don't know what Josie sees in Ellis."

It's not your business, Lincoln. Not your fucking business.

"How long have they been together?" I asked, unable to stop myself. I'd never thought to ask Josie the same.

"I dunno," he said. "Couple of months, maybe? He isn't around much. Josie says his work keeps him busy, but that seems like a load of shit if you ask me. I think he doesn't like driving his fancy-as-shit car down the dirt roads."

I laughed, earning Josie's stare as we stepped up beside Doug. "Ellis, Charlie... Glad you could make it," he said, sticking his hand out in greeting.

Ellis took it. "Thank you for the invite, Doug. I'm honored to attend a legendary Hayes family dinner."

"Fuckin' brownnoser," I muttered, and Bishop laughed.

Josie gave him a half smile. "Oh, I didn't think you'd want to. You said you didn't like the drive."

Bishop snorted. "Fucking called it," he mumbled under his breath.

"Don't mention it," Doug said, waving it off. "Hope you brought your appetite, though. These girls have been cooking up a real storm all afternoon."

"Always," Ellis said, rubbing his stomach before putting his hand on Josie's lower back.

I clenched my jaw, unable to pull my gaze from the tiny spot my fingertips should be touching instead. It took everything I had not to walk over and rip his stupid hand from his body. Maybe I could crush it beneath my boot.

Ellis' gaze swept over the group, stopping when he landed on me and tucked Josie closer to his side. His dad followed suit, reaching out his hand to shake mine. "I don't think we've met before! I'm Charles—or Charlie. Whichever you prefer."

"Nice to meet you, sir," I said. "I'm just here to help out over the summer. My name's Lincoln."

"Where are you from?" he asked. His smile was genuine, unlike his son's expression.

"Tennessee. Up near the mountains."

"Really?" he asked, raising his brows. "Whereabouts?"

"Pinecrest," I said, shoving my hands in my pockets.

Ellis turned to Doug. "Don't y'all have a cabin up there?"

Before Doug could answer, I spoke up. "They do. I check in on it from time to time to make sure the maintenance is up to date."

Josie's eyes darted to me, the crease between her brows deepening. I'd never told her that, but in my defense, I didn't know it was her family's cabin until months later. All I knew was that it belonged to a buddy of Frank's, and I was doing it to help him.

"Huh," Ellis said, pulling Josie tighter. He gave me a tight smile. "That's kind of you."

I tipped my cowboy hat in his direction. "All in a day's work."

Was I stirring some shit? Yeah, a bit. The more time I spent in his company, the more I hated him. It was unreasonable. I had no real reason to dislike the guy other than out of jealousy.

When I saw the uptick of Josie's lips, it was all worth it.

"Lincoln, you have any dinner plans?" Doug asked, cutting the tension.

"No sir," I replied. "Other than going back to the bunkhouse with three other rowdy kids, my evening is wide open."

Doug only laughed. "Might do you some good to show those

young'uns how to party. But I'd love to have you at our table. We've got plenty to eat."

I glanced at Josie. She shifted on her feet, distancing herself from Ellis just a hair.

"I'd be honored, Doug," I said, throwing Ellis' words back at him with a wink.

"That's what I like to hear," he said, clapping me on the back. "Let's go, son."

As I trailed behind Ellis and Josie, I smiled as he said, "Why doesn't your dad ever call me son?"

josie

. . .

IF SOMEONE HAD TOLD me I would've been sitting around a table with Ellis and Lincoln this summer, I would have called them insane.

And yet, here I was... Sitting next to my current fling while my five-night stand from over a year ago watched me with careful consideration.

Obviously, I'd been a fluffy baby bunny murderer in my past life. That was the only possible explanation for this level of torture.

I'd spent a lot of time avoiding everyone over the past week, locking myself in Dad's office with no one to keep me company but my own thoughts. In fairness, that was likely a horrible idea. I spent most of the time mentally berating myself for digging myself into this hole.

Lennox and Cleo both stopped by frequently, pushing me to talk about the situation with Lincoln, but I didn't know what to tell either of them. I knew what I wanted, but I was still working up the courage to do it.

Family dinner was a longstanding tradition in the Hayes household: seven o'clock on the dot every Friday. It was passed down from my grandparents, something my grandma had insisted on when Dad was a kid because she said it was the only time she could bring all her rowdy boys inside at the same time.

Ranch life was hard. It kept you busy from sunup till sundown. When I was a girl, there were days I didn't see my dad until he poked his head in at bedtime, but we could always count on Friday nights.

Mom was usually in charge of Friday dinners, but since she was out of town, that commitment had fallen to Cleo, Lennox, and I. We'd spent most of the late afternoon in the kitchen making Dad's favorite meal: grilled ribeye with fully loaded baked potatoes and asparagus.

It was not on his approved eating list, but we were keeping that between us.

Ellis sat beside me, his arm resting on the back of my chair. Had I known he was coming, I would've made a salad, but a baked potato and asparagus would have to do. He'd been acting strange all week—asking to come out almost every evening to go through Dad's boxes or just to bring me dinner. I'd declined every offer, but that didn't stop him from trying.

I knew the reason was because of Lincoln. If they'd never met, Ellis never would've stepped up the way he had. But maybe he was noticing the distance between us just like I was.

Over supper, Charles had asked Lincoln more about himself and about the little mountain town he grew up in. Then, Dad had gone and dropped the bomb about my trip last summer, which gave way to a new host of questions –not that I'd told anyone other than my sisters about where I spent my time.

I'd been determined to take that tryst to the grave, keeping it a closely guarded secret that would keep me warm when my bed was cold.

The problem was that I was a shit liar, and Ellis knew that. If he asked me if there was something between Lincoln and me... Well, I didn't know what I would say.

The logical thing would be to tell him the truth, but it was far more complicated than that. My feelings for Lincoln hadn't simply vanished; they'd just lied dormant until something—or a specific someone—woke them up again.

Now, my guilty gaze was focused on the man in question sitting across from me at the dinner table. He'd been attentive all night, laughing at my dad's jokes and asking my sisters about their days. Every interaction he had with my family was genuine. He liked them, and to my quiet joy, they liked him back.

Maybe it would've been easier to hate him if his chaps didn't perfectly hug his wrangler-clad ass. How was anyone supposed to get over that? I certainly wasn't that strong.

"Thank you for dinner," Ellis said, interrupting my inappropriate train of thought. He looked down at his plate. "It was thoughtful to make a side I could actually eat."

Everyone paused, turning to look our way. He forced a smile —one I was sure he thought was polite, but really just looked like he'd swallowed something rotten.

I cleared my throat, wiping the corner of my mouth. "Well, I didn't know you were coming or I would've done something different."

"What's wrong with the steak?" Lincoln asked, gaze flitting between Ellis and his plate.

"I'm a vegetarian. I pride myself on my health, and red meat is bad for the heart."

Lennox's fork clattered against her plate as she leaned back in her chair, arms crossed tightly over her chest. She opened her mouth to say something, but Dad swooped in before she could.

"So, Ellis, how's work going?" my dad asked, passing the baked potatoes to Cleo, who was sitting next to him.

"Work is great, Doug. And we're seeing great income projection numbers for the ranch this year. Honestly, these clinics you put on? The money practically makes itself. You won't have to worry about feed in the winter."

Lincoln and Bishop both rolled their eyes, while Charles narrowed his.

He'd been quiet during dinner whenever work came up. It was more than a sore subject at the moment.

My dad smiled, but it didn't reach his eyes. "That's great to hear."

"Are you already planning one for next year? We need to keep the momentum up," Ellis said, taking a bite of his baked potato.

For more reasons than one, the fake smile vanished. The missing money was one thing, but Dad's illness was another. That was the hard truth about keeping secrets. Eventually, they'd need to come out. We'd all kept the extent of Dad's health under wraps from anyone who didn't hold a permanent position at this table.

"Well," my dad said, clearing his throat. "Let's get through this one first, and then we'll think about next year."

Ellis paused, his fork halfway to his mouth. "But why? If we start now, you could get some of these same people on the books."

Cleo and Lennox stared in my direction, willing me to do anything to intervene, but I was momentarily frozen. I didn't know what to do or say that wouldn't give away Dad's health issues. Like I said, I was a shit liar.

"But—"

"I'll have to stop you boys right there," I said, touching Ellis' shoulder. It was clammy, but I hoped he didn't notice. "Rule number two of the Hayes family dinner code says no talking business at dinner. Just because mom's out of town doesn't mean you can throw them out the window."

Okay, so it wasn't really a rule per se, but it wasn't far from the truth. My grandma had always outlawed business talk at the table because it tended to spoil her home-cooked meals. I'd never really known what that meant growing up, but now that I was old enough to recognize the awkward tension in the air, I didn't blame her.

I noticed Dad's shoulder sag from the corner of my eye. I had to force myself to keep a smile on my face.

"Sorry, sugar. You're right," Dad said, raising his hands. "Don't tattle on me."

Cleo bumped her shoulder into his. "I'll keep your secret, but only if you made those mini pies I love so much for dessert."

"Of course. Wouldn't want to disappoint my girls." He pushed up from the table and walked back into the kitchen. Those pies were another of my dad's secrets from mom and yet another thing we'd keep between us.

The room was silent as he walked away, but it didn't stay that way very long. "I don't understand what just happened," Ellis said, looking around the table. "What was wrong with asking him about the future of the clinics?"

"Let's just have a good night," I murmured, picking up my wine glass. I took a long sip, hoping my answer would be enough.

It wasn't.

Ellis turned toward me, lowering his voice. "How else am I supposed to talk to him about this shit? He rarely comes into town anymore and never returns my calls."

That was news to me. I didn't know Ellis had ever been in contact with my dad, especially not about ranch matters.

"Why are you calling him?" I asked. "He isn't even your client yet."

"But he will be. My father wants to ensure his clients have a smooth transition whenever he retires."

"I think the lady is trying to politely ask you to stop pushing the subject," Lincoln said, narrowing his eyes at Ellis.

"And I'm not retired yet," Charles said, cutting in. He shifted in his seat, offering an apologetic glance toward the table.

Ellis didn't listen, he kept pushing. "I don't see why this is an issue. Don't you handle his schedule now? Maybe you could—"

Bishop slammed his fist on the table, making everyone jump. "What part of we don't talk about business on nights like this," Bishop began, motioning toward the table, "do you not understand? This right here is family time. We come together and talk about our week and the good going on in our lives, and then we go home."

Bishop had never liked Ellis. I wasn't sure what happened between them, maybe he just hated his guts.

"The ranch making money directly affects you, doesn't it?" Ellis shot back. "It pays your salary and keeps a roof over your head. I'd say that's an important topic of conversation."

"Yeah, but we aren't concerned with money," Lennox interrupted, sitting back in her chair. "And tonight isn't about anything other than eating good food with the most important people in our lives. So, maybe you should learn some social cues before I—"

Ellis shook his head, preparing to say something else, but Dad walked in with freshly warmed pies he'd made over the weekend. "Who's ready for dessert?"

AFTER TWO HELPINGS of Dad's apple pies, it'd taken every bit of effort I had to pull myself from my seat at the table to walk Ellis out while our fathers walked around the yard.

The moment I opened the door, I was hit with a blast of Texas heat. God, it never cooled off here in the summer. Our days consisted of temperatures in the high nineties and low hundreds. In the evening, it was rare to dip into the eighties at all.

The silence between Ellis and I was awkward. I didn't know what to say that hadn't already been said. His hands were stuck in his pockets, and he only pulled out to twirl his key ring around his finger.

I hated those fucking keys.

"Thanks for coming out tonight," I said, rocking back on my heels the best I could. Before we walked out the door, I'd slipped into the boots nearest the door. They were big and worn, so they were likely Bishop's or Dad's.

"Of course," he said, his tone sharp. "Wouldn't have wanted to miss being berated by your family."

"What?" I asked, laughing. *He was joking, right?* Things had gotten tense, but berated was a far reach. If anything, he only had himself to blame for what had happened.

Ellis crossed his arms. "The security of not only your future, but the future of this ranch should matter to you."

I blinked in surprise. "I'm not sure why you think I don't care? Ellis, we just asked not to talk about it tonight. Why are you mad about that?"

He just turned his head and locked his jaw. "Maybe coming out here was a mistake."

"Maybe it was," I said, crossing my arms. "Especially if you're going to act like this."

"Don't think I didn't notice you staring at him all night," he spat. "Or the way he stepped in before Bishop's fucking outburst."

"I can't help what he does, Ellis."

"Yeah, well, you can damn well stop encouraging him, can't you?"

Glancing over his shoulder, I saw our dads walking back. "I think it's time for you to go," I said, stepping back.

He didn't say anything else as my father stepped up behind

me and wrapped his arm over my shoulder. "Thank y'all again for coming out," he said, nodding at his friend. "Charles, I'll call you on Monday."

Charles nodded, giving us a wave as he got into his car and drove away. Dad said something, but I couldn't hear him over the white nose in my mind. I didn't even notice when he walked out toward the barn and left me in the dark.

"*Men*," I mumbled, turning toward the house. I whipped open the door and stepped into the mudroom. Only, I wasn't paying attention and tripped over the stupid boots I was wearing.

I braced myself for a hard fall, throwing my hands out in an effort to stop my collision, only I didn't fall face-first on the floor.

I fell face-first into Lincoln's arms.

"Woah, there," he said, looking down at me with light in his eyes. "Watch where you're going, darlin'."

His tone was soft and playful, but I wasn't having it. "Oh, go sit on a cactus," I said, pulling my arm from his hold. "And don't call me that."

The tiny, very rational part of my brain told me I may have been overreacting, but that part was promptly squashed by the chaotic, mentally ill portion that liked to take control.

Lincoln's stupid, beautiful lips spread into a smile. "As fun as that sounds, I need my boots."

"Then what're you waiting for? Get them, and leave." I waited expectantly, watching as he dropped his gaze to my feet.

No, no, no, no.

"Well…" He blew out a breath. "If you say so."

Before I could say no, Lincoln scooped me in his arms and sat me on the table in our entryway. I was overtly aware my family was in the living room, only feet away, laughing about something.

Lincoln dropped to his knees, looking up at me as he slowly

slid each boot from my feet. Each time he moved, his fingertips lingered along my bare skin longer than was appropriate. I should've stopped it, shoved him away, and threw the shoes at his head.

But I didn't.

Instead, I gripped the table's edge as he slowly stood and slipped on his boots. My legs spread instinctively as he stepped forward, finding himself between my thighs like he had over a year ago.

What the hell were you doing, Josie?

"Not too mouthy now, are you?" he asked, keeping his voice low. My breathing hitched as he leaned forward, keeping his eyes locked on mine as he reached behind my head for his cowboy hat.

No, I wasn't. I had to keep my mouth shut so I didn't do something stupid like ask him to kiss me.

Or beg him to touch me.

"You thought anymore about what we talked about last week?" he asked.

I tilted my head. "Maybe."

Lincoln's fingertips skimmed along my hips. "Mm, I can't wait to find out what the verdict is." He stepped back, tipping his hat with a wicked smile. "Night, darlin'. Try not to dream of me."

And then he walked out the door, leaving me to walk back into a room with my family in soaked panties.

lincoln

. . .

THIS MORNING WAS BUSIER than I'd thought it was going to be. Since the first clinic was over, most patrons stayed one last night to celebrate before heading back home. Since I was technically off the clock, I had no obligation to wake my ass up and help, but honestly, it was better than the alternative.

I had nothing to do besides thinking about how close I was to Josie's body last night, how I'd stood right between those pretty thighs like I had the first time I'd tasted her. It'd taken everything in me not to say, fuck it and kiss her stupid. Especially when I heard how her breathing hitched as I drew in close to get my hat.

The "what ifs" had haunted me the entire walk back to my cabin. Thankfully, everyone had been out by the bonfire getting rip-roaring drunk, which meant I didn't have to explain why I was striding in with a hard dick. I'd spent most of the night tossing and turning with a semi before I locked myself in the small bathroom and stroked myself to the thought of the perfect little moans she made when I drove into her.

Spilling myself on the tile of a shitty shower hadn't been my proudest moment, but it'd been too long. I hadn't touched another woman since Josie. Hadn't wanted to. Frank had called me a fool, especially when a pretty woman at the bar expressed interest. No matter how much I tried to wrap my head around moving on, it was like running face-first into a brick wall that refused to budge.

So, after I watched the last trailer turn out of the gate, I tucked my earbuds in and headed to the stables. There was no use in going back to the bunk to mope. I might as well make myself useful by feeding the horses and mucking out the stalls with The White Stripes to keep me company.

Sundance stuck her head out when I rounded the corner into the barn, greeting me with a loud huff as I passed her stall and disappeared into the feed room. "I'm coming for ya, girl. Don't worry," I called out over my shoulder.

She stomped her feet when I came back with a manure fork and shovel in one hand and three carrots in the other. "This what you're after?" I asked, holding one under her nose. She reached forward and snatched it from my grip, munching happily before nudging me for the next one. "Yeah, I figured as much. You're a good girl, huh?"

I led her from her stall, securing her lead through a tie post while I worked. Occasionally, she'd grab my attention, asking where her treat was when I walked by. I was only thirty minutes into my routine before someone tapped my shoulder.

I paused my playlist, turning to find Bishop staring at me with his arms crossed. His cowboy hat was pulled low. "What the fuck are you doing?" he asked.

"What's it look like?" I shot back. "I'm working."

"Yeah, but you're taking my hand's chores." He motioned over his shoulder where a boy stood with a rake. "Didn't Doug tell you that you were off on the weekends?"

Yes, he'd told me, but what the hell was I supposed to do? Twiddle my fucking thumbs until Monday morning rolled around? As it was, I was all too aware that the woman who drove me crazy was within reach, and I didn't feel like fighting so hard to keep myself in check.

Instead of telling Bishop that, I just shrugged and stood, pulling my shirt up to wipe away the sweat rolling down my forehead. "I can't just sit around and do nothing. I'm used to working. I want to work."

He laughed, clapping me on my back and pulling me from Sundance's stall. "Yeah, but I can't have ranch hands sitting on their asses. They've got to earn their keep here." He waved the kid over to take my place as I snuck Sundance the last of her treats. "Don't you do shit for fun?"

"My only friend in Tennessee was sixty-seven years old and my boss, so no," I said.

"Man," he said, shaking his head. "Don't get me wrong, I'll work this land until the day I die if allowed, but you've got to give yourself a break sometimes."

Honestly, he caught me by surprise. I never took him as the sort to break free and cut loose. "Oh yeah?" I asked. "And what do you do for fun?"

He smirked. "Shoot the shit. Rope some steers. Chase a cowgirl now and then."

The thud of boots against concrete pulled our attention, and we both looked up to see Lennox Hayes stride into the barn.

Out of the three sisters, I'd take a guess that she looked most like her mom. I didn't see much of Doug in her. She was all bright smiles and cheer, with her tanned legs on display and blonde hair piled on top of her head.

"Hey, boys!" she called out, waving her hand to catch our attention.

It would've been impossible to miss her, but Bishop had clocked her the moment he'd heard her coming. Now his eyes were fixed on each sway of her hips and the bat of her lashes.

"Lennox," he said, dropping his eyes to take her in. "What're you up to today?"

Well, that was interesting.

"Just came in to feed Strider," she said, walking over to a brown paint horse across the aisle. He knickered as she gave his neck a pat.

"Does no one let the hands earn their pay?" Bishop mumbled, but Lennox ignored him and continued.

"But the girls and I were thinking about heading into town tonight. There's a live band playing at the Lone Star..." she trailed off, blushing. "I was thinking, especially since the first clinic is over with..."

Bishop tipped back his head and groaned. I could tell his heart wasn't in it though. I had a feeling she could've asked him to do just about anything and he would've done it. "You know I don't dance."

Lennox stepped forward with her hands outstretched. "I know, and I'm not asking you to! Well, okay... Maybe I am. But it's been a while since we've all been out, and I thought it might be fun?" She glanced my way. "Josie really wants to go out tonight. I think she and Ellis are fighting."

Well, Lennox was just full of helpful information, wasn't she? I'd known something was wrong when Josie came storming back into the house last night like a wet hen, but I'd been too busy being a shit-stirrer to say anything.

"Could be fun," I said, nudging Bishop's arm. "Weren't you just telling me I needed to get out more?"

I had a feeling Bishop would've hit me if Lennox wasn't standing in front of us, and the look he threw my way only confirmed it.

With a deep sigh, he took off his hat, running a hand through his hair. "What time are we leaving?"

Lennox let out a little squeal and clapped her hands. "We're heading out about eight."

"We'll be ready. I'll try to make him pretty for ya," I said, swinging my arm around Bishop's shoulder with a wink.

"Thanks, Lincoln. I don't care what Josie says about ya. You're pretty great!" she called over her shoulder as she sauntered toward the feed room.

"Wait, what does she say about me?" I echoed back. I looked at Bishop, who took the opportunity to slip under my arm and punch my side. "Ow, shit."

"That's for calling me pretty, jackass," Bishop said, pointing his finger at me. "Now, grab your fucking pitchfork because I'm gonna put your ass to work."

josie

. . .

"YOU DID *WHAT*?" I said, staring at my sister as she applied the finishing touches to her makeup.

When Lennox had asked if I wanted to go to the Lone Star tonight, I hadn't thought twice before saying yes. The three of us hadn't had a girls' night in so long, and I was still pissed at Ellis for what happened at family dinner last night, so it seemed like the perfect time to go dance away my frustration.

But the backstabbing little shit had failed to mention that she'd invited Lincoln and Bishop until now.

"What?" she said, rubbing her lips together. "Lincoln was with Bishop when I went to the barn. It would've been rude to invite one and not the other."

"Okay... And that matters why?" I asked, folding my arms over my chest.

Lennox shrugged. "Listen, Josie, you can't avoid him forever."

"I don't—"

Cleo and Lennox spoke at the same time. "You do."

"Two pots calling the kettle black," I muttered. "And I didn't ask either of you to meddle in my love life. Might I remind you that I have a—"

"An Ellis?" Cleo said, raising her brow as if daring me to deny it. When I didn't respond, she smiled and said, "I thought so."

Even before Lincoln had come barging back into the picture, I'd rarely called Ellis my boyfriend. I didn't know why. We were dating and had been taking all the logical steps you were supposed to take in a relationship—albeit slower than what I was used to—but I was just trying to protect my heart.

Now, I was almost glad I'd never allowed myself to make the stupid designation. The more I thought about last night, the angrier I got. Honestly, he'd been a bit of a dick a couple times, but this was different. Was it just jealousy that had him acting that way?

Or had he actually always been like this? I thought back on our relationship, if you could even call it that. He'd criticized my food choices, called me trashy for liking a mimosa with brunch, implied there was something wrong with my weight... He'd ignored all the things I cared about—he'd given me *black coffee* for fuck's sake—and I'd written it all off because why? Because I thought he was a good guy and a safe choice?

"So, if that's the case, you wouldn't mind if Lincoln looked elsewhere, right?" Cleo asked, interrupting my thought spiral.

I shifted in my seat. Of course, I minded. And I knew it didn't make sense and was a double standard, but Lincoln had always felt like mine. He was my treasured memory, firmly locked away as a favored secret. That protection shattered the moment he stepped foot on Black Springs Ranch, forcing me to share something that felt so close to my heart.

"He's free to look wherever he wants," I mumbled.

"Look, all I'm saying is that Lincoln is hot," Lennox said, pulling her t-shirt over her head. She tossed it blindly onto one of the many piles of clothes on her floor. Don't get me wrong, I wasn't a clean freak by any means—that was Cleo—but I didn't know how my younger sister found anything in here.

"And your point is?" I said, falling back onto her bed.

"Her point," Cleo said, coming over to take a seat next to me, "is that Ashwood is a small town with a limited dating pool, while Lincoln is a hot new fish that everyone will want to mate with."

"What the hell are you talking about?" Lennox called out. "Are you doing the fish talk again?"

Cleo rubbed her temples. "I teach first graders, Len. It's just instinctual."

I groaned, waving both of them off. "Okay, I get it."

The mattress dipped on my other side. "Do you, though?" Lennox's face appeared above mine. "Because I'm saying that there will be a shit ton of women tonight who will want to take home a cowboy—especially one who looks like Lincoln. And you'll have to watch that happen and be okay with it because you're stuck in a miserable relationship because you think it's what's *right*."

I bolted up, narrowly missing Lennox. "That's not true."

My sister took my hands in hers, her face going severe. "Okay, tell me something... Last time you masturbated, was it to the thought of Ellis or Lincoln?"

Shit.

"Oh my god, Len. I don't know what this has to do with anything," I huffed, pulling my hand from hers. I thought she'd been about to tell me something serious. "Don't you think it's weird that you want to know stuff like that?"

"You didn't deny it, though," Lennox sang as Cleo smacked my arm. "Answer the question, Josie. Lincoln or Ellis?"

"I plead the fifth," I said, pushing to my feet.

"Have you ever slept with Ellis?" Lennox asked. "I mean, have y'all done anything past first base?"

I closed my eyes, slowly turning around to face her. "There's been some light petting," I said, avoiding her gaze.

And by light, I meant he'd grazed my breast during a not-so-heated make out before I'd quickly said goodnight and slipped away.

Out of the corner, I saw Lennox smile like a damn cat. "So, you haven't passed first base," she said, counting off her fingers. "You won't call him your boyfriend." *Another finger.* "You think about Lincoln when you bean it."

"Oh my god, I never said that! And *bean* it? Really, Len?"

It was true, but she didn't need to know that. Lincoln had secured his spot in my mental spank bank over a year ago after the first time we'd had sex. Over the months, as the loneliness grew, so did my thoughts of him.

Since he'd come back... So had those desires.

I mean, how could they not? He was hot—too hot for his own good. What woman in their right mind could walk away from something like that without keeping a memory or two handy?

"What? There's not a good word for female masturbation, so I made one up." She shot me a severe look. "Stop deflecting and answer the question. Lincoln or Ellis, Jos."

That was what neither of my sisters understood. It wasn't a question; I think my heart would always choose Lincoln. The problem came from knowing he lived over a thousand miles away, and there would be no sustaining a relationship long-term. He had Frank's bar, and I had this ranch. I wouldn't give it up, and I knew he wouldn't ask me to.

Whether it happened now or five years in the future, someone would lose something they cared about. Without wanting to, one of us would resent the other for what we gave up, and then the love that had once felt so sacred and special would turn into something vicious and ugly.

With Ellis... I don't know. It seemed like low risk, low reward. It wasn't the most romantic notion, but neither of us would have to give up something integral to who we were to be together.

But right here, I could voice a small truth with the two people I trusted more than anything.

The truth of it was, Ellis and I seemed more like a business arrangement than a relationship. It was, yet again, another man that wanted to align himself with me because of the potential monetary value I could add to his life. For once, I wanted someone to sweep in and love me without strings or stipulations.

Like Lincoln.

My phone rang, just as it had all afternoon. I didn't even need to check to know Ellis' name would be flashing on the screen. He'd texted me this morning, apologizing for being a douche, but I was sick of half-assed apologies. Honestly, he should've thought about that before he'd opened his mouth.

It seemed like he was apologizing a lot lately. I didn't like it. There shouldn't be a reason to apologize every time we had a conversation.

I sucked in a deep breath, holding it for a few seconds before exhaling. "Lincoln. I think it'll always be Lincoln. It won't change anything. There're too many obstacles in the way."

Where I expected them to hoot and holler, I was met with silence. Cleo looked at me with a sad smile. "Don't make the same mistake I did, Josie," she said, taking me by surprise. "Don't let the person you love slip through your fingers without fighting to keep them."

I wanted to ask what she meant, but there was a knock on Lennox's door, and she called out, "Come in!" before I could stop her. It swung open, revealing a very hot cowboy on the other side.

Holy shit.

Lincoln Carter was every cowgirl's dream in a black felt hat, starched jeans that hugged his thick, muscular thighs, and a dark grey button-down. The top two buttons were undone, showing just a peek of the soft chest hair I used to trace with my fingertips.

I slid my gaze up and down his body, stopping when I was met with that cocky smirk of his. "What're you girls talking about?" he asked.

My cheeks heated as he stared straight at me. Surely, he hadn't heard me. The door was closed. Wasn't it?

Cleo grinned. "We were just talking to Josie about making difficult choices."

"Is that right?"

"Sure is," Lennox said, holding up two pairs of boots. "See, I was in town today, and I couldn't figure out if I should keep the old boots I've broken in, but these," she held up a black leather set with light grey stitching, "are clearly the better choice."

Lincoln nodded, covering his smile with his hand. "Yeah, I agree. Can't go wrong with those. They're damn good looking and dependable."

"Well, maybe they aren't," I mumbled, turning toward my sister. "And you know damn well if you wear those tonight, your feet will be covered in blisters in about two hours."

She grimaced but slid the new pair on anyway.

"You girls about ready?" Lincoln asked, raising his forearm and letting it rest on the door jamb. He was clearly enjoying the conversation too much. "Bishop's out in the truck waiting."

"We're almost done!" Lennox called out, giving Lincoln her best smile. Little shit only did it to get under my skin and prove a point.

Consider it made.

The thought of Lincoln looking at anyone else like he looked at me had my hackles rising. It was enough for me to make a promise to myself to reevaluate my decisions later. Preferably when the man of my dreams wasn't staring my way, making my heart do little flips.

josie

. . .

THE LONE STAR was packed when Bishop's old truck pulled into the crowded parking lot. "Dammit," he said, slapping the steering wheel as someone stole the spot he'd eyed near the end of the dirt lot. "Why are there so many people here tonight? Who the hell is playing?"

Lennox shrugged. "I don't know. One of my friends was talking about them, but" she said, pulling up her phone and scrolling, "according to their website, the lead singer's actually from the area."

I felt Cleo straighten beside me. "What's his name?"

"Lawson Wilde," Lennox replied. "Oh, and he's stupid hot." She thrust the phone into Cleo's hands to show us the video she'd been watching.

Lawson was standing in front of a crowd. He wore a smile as his arms were outstretched, basking in the echo of his fans screaming his words back to him. An old guitar hung in front of his body, supported by a tooled leather strap over his shoulder. Mid-length hair peeked out of a cap, sticking to the back of his neck after hours of performing under lights.

"Yeah, I'd say he's the reason for the crowd," I laughed, nudging Cleo's arm, but she didn't move. Her eyes were glued to the man on the screen. It may have just been the funky lighting of the video, but it looked like her skin had grown pale. "Hey, you okay?"

Cleo swallowed, nodding slowly. "Yeah, it's just weird," she said, forcing a laugh before handing the phone back to Lennox. "I went to high school with him. That's not his name, though. Must be some kind of stage thing I guess."

"Really?" she asked, not looking up from her phone. "What's his real name?"

"Grady," she said, drawing out the name like she hadn't said it in ages.

"Huh. Maybe you could work your charms and get us autographs," Lennox said, scrolling through his social media.

"Yeah," she said, chewing on her lip. "Maybe. I dunno. Doubt he'd remember me. Wouldn't wanna get your hopes up."

I slid my hand over and found Cleo's, giving it a squeeze. She didn't have to say anything. I knew her well enough to know there was something else on her mind. It wasn't easy for someone to show back up in your life when you least expected it —I would know—but I'd be there when she felt like talking about it.

"Well, this better be worth it," Bishop mumbled, putting the truck in park. "Because it's gonna take ages to get a beer."

"Oh no," Lennox pouted, setting her phone down to meet Bishop's gaze in the rear-view. "How will you ever survive?"

"I won't," he shot back, returning her glare. "I'll leave your ass here and find somewhere less crowded."

She narrowed her eyes. "You wouldn't dare."

"I think you know I would," he said. "Rocking Wells is right down the road."

"Ugh," she groaned. "Wells is gross and dingy. The last time I was there, my shoes stuck to the floor all night."

"Alright," Lincoln interjected, reaching over to turn the truck off. "That's enough of that."

"Hey!" Bishop called, leaning across his console, but Lincoln was already hopping out of the truck.

He stopped outside my door, opening it and offering his hand. I stared at it for a moment before placing mine on top and letting him help me.

"You know, I never got the chance to tell you how good you looked tonight, darlin'," Lincoln said, letting his gaze drop down my body.

I didn't go out much these days, so it'd taken me a while to find an outfit Cleo and Lennox deemed appropriate. They'd both opted for cute summer dresses, but that wasn't much of my style; the ones I saw in my closet were far too formal to wear to my hometown bar. Instead, I'd settled on a pair of black bell-bottom jeans with boots and a distressed, cropped t-shirt with the Black Springs Ranch logo. Cleo curled my hair in loose waves, letting it flow freely down my back.

"Well, I wanted something that'd be easy to dance in," I said, forcing a smile.

Lincoln pulled me out of the way before helping Cleo out next. "I didn't know you danced," he said.

"I grew up in a small town in Texas. There isn't much else to do on the weekends but show up here with fake IDs and learn to dance."

"Makes sense," he said. "Wish I would've known sooner." He placed his hand on the small of my back, and I relished the brush of his skin against mine.

I hated how his touch made me feel, how easy it was for him to have complete control. It took all my willpower not to curl into his arms and beg him to take me home.

Instead, like the good girl I was, I took a deep breath and let him guide me forward. Cleo and Lennox hooked their arms with mine, leaving Bishop and Lincoln behind.

The Lone Star was an Ashwood staple. I wasn't sure how long it had been around, but I knew my dad used to sneak in when he was a kid, and that was long enough for me. During the day, half the building doubled as a restaurant. Then, once the sun went down, the second half opened—that side was more in line with your typical bar decor.

Up front, there was a stage for live music. Two bars were built into the sides, allowing easy access for patrons focused on the band. The dance floor was in the middle of the room, taking up a large majority of space—which was fine with me.

Don't get me wrong, I loved listening to the music, but I mostly came to dance. It was just my luck that the two often went hand in hand.

We stepped up to the second entrance, which led us straight into the venue portion. The house band was on, playing a mix of nineties country barely audible over the hum of the crowd. I could already feel my excitement kicking in—the need to move my body to the beat of the music threatening to take over.

When we reached the front, Bishop stepped forward to shake the bouncer's hand. "Davey! How the hell are ya?"

"Busy night," Davey grumbled, slapping a wristband on each of us. He gestured toward the door without charging us the cover. "But y'all are in for one hell of a show."

Bishop thanked him, holding the door. "I'm going to get some beers. Y'all want anything?"

"I'll go with you, man," Lincoln said, turning toward me and leaning to whisper in my ear. The heady scent of leather and sandalwood filled my nose, making me dizzy. "What sounds good? Are you in for another whiskey night?" he asked, pulling back just enough to see my reaction. His eyes twinkled under the neon lights, no doubt remembering that the last time we drank together ended with us fucking on a pool table.

"Surprise me. I'm in the mood for anything," I replied, trying like hell to get the memories of Lincoln's whiskey kisses out of my mind. "We'll grab one of those tall tables by the dance floor."

He nodded, looking over my shoulder where I pointed. "Sounds good. Be right back."

I watched him go, dropping my gaze to his Wrangler clad ass. God, it really was a great ass—one that looked even better out of clothes. It was almost criminal.

Get a grip, Josephine. Don't lose your head.

It was easier said than done, especially when I was almost ready to ask him to pull me into the nearest alcove and force me to remember what being with him had been like.

Cleo and Lennox were already at the table. I sat down with a huff, running my hands through my hair. My phone vibrated in my pocket, and I groaned. Goddammit, why couldn't he take a hint? Ellis' name flashed across my screen, and I hit decline. With each call, my decision became a bit clearer.

As I slipped my phone back into my pocket, it vibrated again. I wanted to take it out, screaming at the screen to be left alone.

"Gimme that," Lennox said, reaching over the table for my phone.

"Hey!" I called. "Give that back."

She turned off the phone and tucked it into her pocket. "Nope. Not until we're home. I won't have Ellis ruining our night with his obsessive bullshit."

"This was a horrible idea," I muttered.

"Why? Because you finally realize that your feelings for Lincoln aren't gone like you've been trying to make yourself believe?" Lennox said, resting her head in her hand.

"I'm with Ellis, though. I can't be doing that shit to him when I'm with someone else."

"You don't have to be," Cleo said. "You could end it here and now with a simple text message." She glanced at Lennox. "I bet she'd give you your phone back for that."

I cocked my head to the side. "I won't break up with him

over a text message. This isn't high school. I'm almost thirty. And do you really have room to talk?" I snapped, regretting my words the moment I said them. My sister's marriage was none of my business, and I had no right to butt in where I didn't belong. "Shit, I'm sorry, Cleo. I didn't mean it like that."

Cleo looked down at her lap before clearing her throat. "You did, and you're not wrong. I'm not the person you should be taking relationship advice from." She sniffled, leaning over to place her hand over mine. "But believe me when I tell you it comes from personal experience. I don't want you to wake up in years next to a man you don't know if you've ever loved, trapped in a marriage neither of you want. Just think about it." I opened my mouth, but she pushed through. "Now, I think I'll run to the bathroom before it's ruined by the stench of stale cigarettes and bad decisions."

Lennox and I watched her walk away, my stomach churning like it always did when I felt guilty. I hung my head in my hands. "*Fuck*, I'm an asshole."

Lennox ran her hand over my back. "You are, but you aren't wrong."

I turned to the side. "I'm not?"

She shook her head. "No, but neither is she."

"I know," I sighed.

I knew it with every fiber of being that Ellis and I weren't going to last, but he was the last excuse I had not to go all in with Lincoln. After that, we'd have nothing stopping us from crossing that line and picking up where we left off. Frankly, I was terrified of getting my heart broken because I wouldn't survive if Lincoln walked away.

"Where'd Cleo go?" Bishop asked, setting down two buckets of cold beer in the middle of the table. Lincoln followed, slipping what looked like a whiskey soda in front of me with a wink.

"Bathroom," I said, bringing the glass to my lips. "She'll be right back."

Bishop nodded, taking the seat across from Lennox, while Lincoln stood at the end of the table near me. He kept his eyes on the crowd, ensuring no one came too close. The boys chatted about the ranch, going down the rabbit hole of hay cutting with other ranch hands who'd stopped by our table.

By the time Cleo came back, her eyes were red-rimmed. I hated myself in that moment, hated that I'd made her cry in a dingy bar bathroom. There was nothing I could do to excuse my behavior, but when she met my gaze, I mouthed the words, "I'm sorry."

Cleo shook her head, reaching across the table to clink her drink against mine. "Love you," she said.

"Love you, too." I forced a smile.

"Love you mostest!" Lennox called, leaning between us and doing a little cheer. "I win." I rolled my eyes, shoving her lightly. She caught herself on the table and stuck her tongue out. "Let's fucking toast to a great night!"

"Go on then. I already know you're dying to say it, so go ahead."

"What's she talking about?" Lincoln asked, bringing the glass to his lips.

Bishop shook his head, but wore a smile. "Just watch this shit."

Lennox grabbed her beer, staring each of us in the eye as she cleared her throat. "Fuck the leather, fuck the lace. Cheers to the ones who sit on our face!" And then she slammed her bottle on the table before taking a sip.

"That's sure as fuck something I could toast to," Lincoln said, following suit with a chuckle.

"Oh my god, you're the worst," Cleo groaned, but she was smiling.

"No, I'm the best," Lennox said. "It's the reason you keep me around. I'm funny, smart, and pretty as hell."

"And annoying to boot," Bishop mumbled.

Lennox leaned over the table and smirked. "Is that why you can't stop staring at me?"

"Maybe we should add delusional to the mix, too. I ain't fucking staring." He pointed the bottle in her direction. "And if I am, it's because you're too damn loud."

As Bishop and Lennox bickered, I raised my glass and savored the liquid courage as it slid down my throat. Couples turned on the dance floor, whipping around to a catchy beat. I swayed in my seat, humming to the music.

Lincoln stepped closer, and I leaned into the warmth of his body without thinking. We were magnets, drawn together by some force entirely larger than ourselves.

"You sure are wiggling in your seat," Lincoln said, flitting his gaze along my body.

I shrugged. "I like to dance."

He raised a brow. "This is considered dancing? Look, I know I'm old, but—"

"No, but it scratches the itch," I laughed. "I mean, haven't you gotten the urge to just move before? Like when a song comes on that's so good you just can't help yourself?"

Lincoln nodded. "Yeah, I suppose so." His eyes drifted to the dance floor. "Would you want to dance, Josie?"

"I don't have anyone—"

"You have me," he said. It was simple, matter-of-fact, like it was the most natural thing in the world. I had him, and he had me, and nothing else mattered.

Except, that wasn't the truth at all.

"Well, what do you say?" He held out his hand, waiting for me to take it. I stared down at it, knowing my decision would have consequences.

"She says yes," Lennox called, but Cleo smacked her arm. I couldn't make out their hushed whispers because I focused only on Lincoln's hand.

The rough and rugged hand that had once caressed my body so tenderly and full of love. The hand that had held my own and brought me pleasure I'd never known.

"Alright," I whispered, looking up into his deep brown eyes. "I'll dance with you."

lincoln

. . .

AFTER A YEAR of wondering if I'd imagined the crazy connection I shared with Josie Hayes, I had my answer.

There was no way in hell the stupid, fluttery feeling I got in the pit of my stomach was wrong. Not as she put her hand in mine and let me guide her to the dance floor.

The music was upbeat, the perfect tune to twirl the girl in my arms round and round until she had no choice but to lean on me for support. Lennox was working her charm on a cowboy at the next table, and he was so lost in her forward nature that he immediately swept her away. Bishop watched the younger Hayes sister with narrowed eyes until he pulled Cleo out after us, despite her protests.

"You okay if I touch you here?" I asked, placing my hand on her lower back. My thumb met her bare skin, soft and creamy. It took everything I had not to throw her over my shoulder and lock her in my truck, but I kept myself rooted to the spot.

Josie sucked in a small breath at the contact but nodded. "Yeah, of course. We're just dancing," she said, though it wasn't with her typical confidence. "Do you know how to dance?"

"Do you think I would've asked you if I didn't?" I gave her a little twirl, watching her eyes light up as she returned to me. "Give me some credit, darlin'."

She stood a little straighter, a little smile on her face. "Alright, then, cowboy. Let's see what you've got."

"That'll be a little hard," I admitted. "This isn't really the song to demonstrate the depth of my talent."

"No, but you can consider this a warmup. We'll figure the rest out later."

I knew she was talking about the dancing, but it felt like more. It felt like she was talking about us—how things may have been complicated now, but maybe they didn't have to be.

By the time we were halfway into the first song, we were all smiles. Bishop knocked into us several times, giggling and laughing when the bumbling young thing Lennox had pulled kept stepping on her feet.

"Oof, that's gotta fucking hurt," I laughed softly into Josie's ear. "He's stomping on her toes like he's got something to prove."

"At least it won't just be due to the brand-new boots I told her not to wear," she said, shaking her head. "I don't think she can feel much with all the liquor flowing through her system right now, though."

"Probably not."

We stayed like that for the next two songs, laughing and twirling until Josie's cheeks were tinged with pink under the bright neon lights. I couldn't remember the last time I'd enjoyed myself so much.

For the first time in years, I felt like I belonged somewhere. I didn't have much growing up. My family life had been shit. I didn't have anyone I really considered a friend. I'd only had Frank and a few of his rodeo buddies that joined him at the bar every night.

Pinecrest had always been a place I could rest my head, but Ashwood—and Black Springs Ranch—was a place I knew I could call home. In the span of a day, everything I thought I'd never have was within reach. The job, the ranch, the family... Now, all I needed was the woman, and she was nestled securely in my arms.

As the last song came to an end, the house band slowed down, playing a rendition of Keith Whitley's When You Say Nothing at All. Bishop and Cleo made their way back to the table, quickly followed by a red-faced Lennox.

"What do you think, darlin'? Are we staying or going?" I asked, pulling away slightly to gauge her reaction.

Josie hesitated only for a moment, looking over her shoulder to where her sisters were watching. They were trying to be coy, but Lennox didn't have a covert bone in her body. When she swung her gaze back to me, she slid her hand from my shoulder to my neck and ran her fingertips along my bare skin.

I took that as all the sign I needed to sweep her into a languid half-step.

"It's strange seeing you here," I said after a beat. We'd settled into a gentle silence, enjoying the other's company and the lull of the music. "I guess it's hard to see you in any bar but my own."

Josie chewed on her bottom lip, and I fought the urge to lean forward and pull it free with my teeth. God, I loved it when she did that. It was distracting and adorable and fucking everything. "Well, maybe if Frank's had a dancefloor..."

I laughed. "Was that what it would've taken to make you stay? Hell, if I would've known that—"

"What would you have done?" she asked, looking up at me with carefully guarded curiosity.

For some reason, the moment felt heavy. We weren't talking about a stupid dance floor anymore. We were talking about us, about a future, about a whole damn life.

I couldn't help it. I pulled Josie closer, eliminating the sliver of space between our bodies. She was warm in my hands, a whiskey flush creeping up her neck and coloring those pretty cheeks. "I would've cleared out every goddamn table in that place. I would've done whatever you asked. Only for you."

"Why?" Her voice was low, as though she didn't want to ask the question.

I stayed silent momentarily, trying to figure out how to say what I felt without crossing too many lines. "If I told you I didn't have a good answer, would you believe me?" She shook her head, and I laughed. "Thought not."

"It's not that I don't believe you," she quickly clarified. "I just don't really understand what this is either. I mean, I've read my fair share of romance books where the characters say they have this crazy connection, but experiencing it is different. It makes me wonder if this is real, or if you'll tuck and run when you realize being with me isn't as great as you believe."

I understood what she meant. Our connection did feel crazy when I stopped to think about it. Most guys wouldn't have thought twice if the woman they'd spent five days with had up and left. Normally, I'd have done the same—just chalked it up to a great time and went on my way.

I hadn't been able to do that with her. From the moment I'd woken up that morning, something felt wrong. It'd felt like I'd lost something, and I'd been sick to my stomach wondering if I'd ever get it back.

My thumb stroked her soft skin, enjoying the way she trembled in my arms. "I don't have much, Josie. I'm a simple man with simple needs. And for the longest time, I thought I'd be okay living alone. Frank had done it, and I thought he'd fared well, but then I met you. Something just clicked." She rolled her eyes, but I tightened my hold. "I know it sounds cliché, and maybe it feels like a cop-out, but dammit, Josie... I don't think I fully understand it either. All I know is some things are certain—the sun will set, it'll rise again, and you're it for me. That's just the truth." I took a deep breath and laid down my last card. "And I think you feel it too—otherwise, you wouldn't have told your sisters it would always be me."

Her lips fell open like she was going to protest, but she didn't say a thing. The song had come to an end, but she was still in my arms, staring up at me. And it broke me in that moment to know that she'd never been cared for in the way she'd deserved.

Some might call me crazy, and honestly, I wouldn't argue. Who falls in love after five days? But this woman had completely wrecked me, and I wasn't about to fight it.

I'd overheard her conversation with her sisters before we left for the bar. I hadn't meant to eavesdrop, but I couldn't help myself. I was damn glad I hadn't spoken up sooner.

Josie deserved so much more than a handful of meager words. I'd done my best, but I wasn't a damn poet. I hated that I couldn't explain why I felt the things I did. My love for her had become part of who I was, stitched into the fabric of my soul. It ran as deep as the oceans, as pure as freshly fallen snow. It existed and was tangible and beautiful, just like her.

And yet, she didn't see what I could. She didn't see how worthy she was. I could see it in the way she was staring at me now—the subtle way she averted her eyes and tensed beneath the weight of my words.

My god, everyone around her loved her. The amount of people who smiled and went out of their way to talk to her as she walked by was staggering. It didn't look like she'd ever met a stranger.

But I wanted to tell her. I wanted her to know my feelings without a shadow of a doubt. I wanted to run on stage and grab the microphone away from the balding man in the house band and tell this whole damn town how much I loved Josephine Hayes.

"Josie, I—"

My heart fell as she shook her head and stepped out of my arms. "No, don't," she whispered. "Not yet."

Not yet? What the hell was that supposed to mean? Was there a good time to do this sort of shit? I mean, maybe waiting until she didn't have a boyfriend would've been a good start, but I'd done my fair share of waiting.

I opened my mouth to try again, but Lennox came running up to us. She skidded to a halt next to me, and rested her hand on my shoulder. "Hey, cowboy, mind if I have this dance?"

If I wasn't so damn in love with her sister, I'd have thought she was flirting with me. Lennox wouldn't do that, though, which begged the question... What the hell was going on?

"Lennox..." I began, but she shook her head and locked eyes with Josie.

"Listen, Ellis is about to walk in, and I don't think you want him seeing what we just saw. Let me step in so that you can handle *that*."

Josie's face drained of color, obvious even in the low-lit bar. God, I hated him. I didn't have any right to—by all accounts, *I* was the asshole in the wrong, chasing after a woman who wasn't mine anymore. The thought of her having to deal with that asshole set my blood alight.

Josie quickly thanked her sister, leaving me standing in the middle of the dance floor with Lennox as dancing couples tried to maneuver their way around us.

I couldn't tear my gaze away as Josie sat on the stool and downed the rest of her drink. Then she reached for mine, whiskey dripping down her chin as she chugged it down. Cleo leaned in, saying something that had Josie's brows furrowing.

"Stop staring at her," Lennox whispered as the band said their goodbyes. They began gathering their equipment so the next act could set up. The bar kicked on one of their old playlists as Lennox took her sister's place. She wrapped my arm around her waist and forced me back into the dance.

Like her sister, Lennox was a natural. She moved with ease while I tried not to bump into every couple we encountered as I tried to catch a glance of Josie and Ellis. We were on our second pass when she squeezed my hand and brought my attention back to her. "Don't break her fucking heart."

I blinked, turning my gaze toward the petite blonde in my arms. "Pardon?"

"You heard me, cowboy. I mean it. If you break her heart, I'll kill you. There's a lot of places to hide a body on the ranch, and I won't think twice about shoving your dick back up—"

"I'm not gonna break her heart," I mumbled, glancing back at the table. "But I'm afraid she's gonna break mine."

josie

· · ·

DAMN IT.

I'd barely made it to the table in time to toss back the rest of my drink and what was left of Lincoln's, before Ellis stumbled through the crowd. The sharp stink of expensive liquor hit me before he did. He planted himself in front of me, bracing on unsteady legs, his jaw clenched tight.

It felt wrong seeing him stand where Lincoln had been just moments ago, all easy smiles and sparkling eyes.

Bishop's gaze darted toward Ellis, his body tense with silent inquiry. I shook my head. If I so much as nodded, he'd have Davey toss Ellis out on his ass. As tempting as that was, this wasn't Bishop's fight. I needed to handle it myself.

"Is this why you aren't answering my calls?" Ellis muttered. He watched Bishop and Cleo at the end of the table, ready to strike if they tried to intervene. "Because you're too busy getting drunk at a bar?"

Empty glasses and half-finished beer bottles cluttered the rickety wooden table, but I wasn't drunk. Not yet, anyway. He sure as hell was, though. His breath reeked of his father's over-priced scotch.

"I wasn't answering your calls because you were acting like a dick," I said, snatching Lennox's drink since she wasn't around to stop me.

Okay, so maybe I was a little drunk.

"And you're acting childish," he slurred. "You and I had a simple disagreement. Why are you being like this?"

"Like what?"

"Like a stuck-up bitch. Like you're too fucking good for me," he let out a bitter laugh. "Let's be real here, I'm the one doing charity work." He leaned in close. "Time to get over yourself and appreciate that you won't find better than me, Josephine."

"Maybe I'm not the one who needs to get over myself," I mumbled, taking a sip and letting the liquid courage take hold. He'd never learn, would he? God, I felt so stupid. Cleo and Lennox were right. What the hell was I doing with this jerk? "Maybe I don't want to be with someone who blatantly ignores every warning they've been given."

"Josephine…"

I slammed my hands down on the table, the sharp crack cutting through the din around us. "See? Just like that. How many times have I asked you to stop calling me that? I hate it. And I hate that I've told you how much I hate it, but you still don't listen."

He blinked at me, confusion dulling his glassy, unfocused eyes. If the crowd hadn't been so loud, I was sure I'd hear the thunder of both our hearts pounding out of sync.

"Maybe the truth is I don't want to be with you anymore. Maybe I never did. Maybe I thought you were a better man than you are. We're done, Ellis. Don't call me. Lose my number." I turned in my chair to face him fully, adrenaline fueling a bravery I didn't fully feel. "And while you're at it," I added, voice steady, "lose my father's number too. Seems like we both made a fucking mistake."

Ellis stared down like he didn't recognize me. To be honest, I hadn't been able to recognize myself in a long time. I'd spent my life so worried about the opinions of others, to the point it became to the detriment of how I thought of myself. When Dad had gotten sick, that compulsion had only grown worse.

I had this stupid, half-cocked notion that I had to settle down and get married, no matter who was waiting at the end of the aisle—that I needed to focus on stability and worldly comforts rather than the kind that nurtured my soul.

By all accounts, Ellis had fit the bill. Successful, reasonably good-looking, and well, I'd already known him. Our families had known each other since before they had kids, and most importantly... Ellis had never cheated on a girlfriend.

Believe me, I'd asked around. Not much goes on in Ashwood without someone knowing.

But I was a fool to ignore the warning signs. Everywhere I looked, little red flags popped up, waving their banners blatantly in front of my face. This had been a long time coming. I was too little too late to come to the realization that Ellis Martin was after one thing and one thing only: my connections.

Ellis surged forward, causing the glasses to rattle as he crashed into the table. He reached for my arm, jerking me off the stool and toward his body with a shattering force. "We're leaving," he growled. "You're going to sleep off whatever this fit is, and then we're going to hope you wake up in a better fucking mood."

"Like hell I am," I said, looking down at his tightening grip. "Let go of me."

"Not a chance in hell, *Josie*." He sneered my name like it was shit under his expensive heel. "Not until you start fucking acting right."

"Jesus, Ellis. You're hurting me," I hissed, trying to pry his hand from my arm to no avail. His grip was merciless, and I knew it'd bruise.

"Is it because of *him*?" he growled, pressing his forehead

against mine. His other hand traveled to my ass and squeezed. "Are you *fucking* that low-life bastard? Is that why you won't—"

Stools scraped against the concrete floor, and footsteps thundered as the crushing weight of Ellis' body was gone. I stumbled back, looking up in time to see Lincoln's fist collide with Ellis' cheek. With one blow, my ex went tumbling into the tables next to us.

Someone yelled for security, and Davey came running. Bishop held his arm out, stopping him before he could break them up.

"You will *never* touch her again, you understand me?" Lincoln followed him, grabbing his collar and forcing him upright. His eyes were wild, and he was unhinged. There was a dangerous vibe rolling off him I'd never seen before. "Don't fucking look at her. Don't call her. Don't even think about her." His voice was low and dangerous, a warning wrapped in a promise.

"You're fucking crazy," Ellis slurred, regaining his composure and breaking free from Lincoln's hold. He tried looking at me, but Lincoln grabbed his face and forced it back to him.

"What did I just say?"

"Lincoln, stop," I called, rushing forward and laying my hand on his elbow. His body shook under my touch, vibrating with barely restrained rage. "*Stop.* He isn't worth it."

Lincoln threw up his hand, letting Ellis stumble back against the table. "I'm done. It's over," he muttered as Davey barreled through to break up the fight. Lincoln wrapped his arm around my waist, tugging me close until there was no space between us.

I didn't stop to question why or think about how quickly everything seemed to go to shit. He pressed his cheek against the crown of my head, inhaling deeply to center himself.

Two men pushed Ellis toward the door, but he wasn't done. He dodged them, running right into the two of us, sending Lincoln and I crashing to the ground. Lincoln tried to break our fall, but he couldn't turn in time. I landed on the ground with a thud, the breath leaving my lungs with a whoosh.

"Hope the bitch was worth it," Ellis shouted. "You'll be hearing from my lawyers—" His words cut off in a cry as Davey and Lennox reached him at the same time.

I couldn't be sure, but I thought I heard him begging my sister for mercy as he was shoved out of the building.

"Josie," Lincoln said, taking me into his arms. He didn't so much as look back at the bastard making a scene. "Are you okay? Lemme see you, baby."

He cupped my face, sweeping it with wild eyes. "I'm okay, I promise. It was just a fall."

"I'll fucking kill him," he seethed, his gaze darting toward the door.

"No," I said quickly, placing my hand over his. He winced, and I pulled back immediately. "Let me see your hand." I tried to wiggle out of his hold, but he shook his head.

"I'm fine, Josie," he muttered through gritted teeth.

I reached around and poked the swelling skin again, causing a string of curses to fly from his mouth. "Fine, my ass. Now let me see, dammit."

Lincoln let me pull him to the small alcove near the door where it was clear. I pulled my phone out of my back pocket and turned on the light. "Really, I'm fine. I've been in plenty of fights in my life—"

"Hold this," I said, pushing my phone toward him. He didn't argue, doing as he was told while I ran my fingers over his already bruising skin.

He was right. It'd probably be fine. There was a chance of a minor fracture, given the swelling, but there was nothing to be done other than pain relievers and ice.

"Why'd you do that?" I demanded, snatching my phone back.

"Because he put his hands on you." He said it so simply that

I almost missed how his words faltered at the end. "And I'd rather risk sitting in jail than know I stood by and did nothing."

I looked down at my feet, ignoring the strange fluttering I felt. "Well, Davey wouldn't have called the cops, so you wouldn't have had to rot in a cell..."

The tips of his fingers brushed against my cheek, trailing lower until he gripped my chin and tilted my face toward his. "How are you?" he asked, eyes searching my own. "Did he hurt you?"

"I'm okay," I whispered. My gaze darted to Lincoln's lips, just for a second, but it was long enough. He tracked the movement hungrily, drawn into the desire like I was. "I'm okay, thanks to you."

I wasn't sure how long we stayed like that, trapped in a moment built by need. Oh, how I wanted to bridge that gap–to close the space between our lips and give in to the maddening temptation.

But reality came crashing down as Cleo and Lennox shouted our names above the crowd. "Are y'all okay?"

Lincoln and I jumped apart as they approached. Davey and Bishop were hot on their heels. "Yeah," I said, tucking my hair behind my ear. "I'm fine. I just wanted to check his hand."

Davey held up an ice pack before tossing it toward Lincoln. "You good, man?"

Lincoln took it with a dip of his chin in thanks, grimacing as he placed it on his knuckles. "Yeah, I'm good. No harm, no foul."

Davey nodded. "Technically, I'm supposed to ask you to leave... Bishop told me what happened. I know you were just defending your girl, but you can't go around punching the shit out of people. We wouldn't have let him get far."

Your girl. Two words had never sounded so good. I should have corrected him, but I bit my lip and stayed silent—something my sisters both clocked.

"Naw, I get it." He turned to me, giving my hand a squeeze. "I'll wait in the truck until the concert ends, okay?"

"I'll wait with you," I said without hesitation, turning toward Bishop to ask for the keys. "I don't feel like staying anyway."

And that was the truth of it. If Lincoln wasn't here, then I didn't want to be either. I'd spent more than enough time denying my feelings, but those days were long gone.

"How about y'all take the truck home?" Bishop said, tossing me his keys.

"What about you?" Lincoln asked. "We can just sit in the parking lot until the show's over."

Bishop jerked his head behind him. "There's a few hands here tonight. I'm sure I can bribe them to give us a ride home."

I looked toward my sisters. "What about y'all?"

"We'll bum a ride with Bishop," Lennox said, looping her arm with Cleo's. "You two go ahead."

I shifted my gaze to Cleo. "You sure you're okay with that?"

She nodded. "Yeah, it'll be fun. I'll be fine. There's no sense in y'all waiting around for us." She leaned in and kissed my cheek, lowering her voice. "Remember what I said, Josie. Nothing is holding you back anymore."

josie

. . .

LINCOLN LED me out to Bishop's truck with one hand on my back. The balmy air made my skin slick even in the short walk, and I was all too aware of the way his fingertips brushed my exposed skin. My palms were itchy, and it wouldn't go away no matter how much I scratched.

The adrenaline I'd felt only moments ago was fading fast, leaving room for reality to crash through the door and settle in. I'd never thought Ellis was capable of violence, and maybe in his sober state, he wouldn't have been. He'd never been much of a drinker. A glass of wine here or there, the occasional beer if the mood was right, but I'd never seen him touch liquor once.

Did he have a problem I'd never known about?

It was strange how different I felt. I'd dealt with my fair share of assholes over the years—some I dated and some who'd tried to pick me up after I'd told them no several times. None of them had ever dared lay a hand on me until now.

Bishop would've stopped Ellis, of that I had no doubt. He was ready to throw him on his ass the moment he clocked him at the end of the table. Part of me wishes I would've let him before it'd gone too far.

I hadn't realized I'd begun crying until Lincoln pulled me into his chest, resting his chin on top of my head. "It's okay, darlin'." He ran his hand in circles along my back. "I've got you."

For some reason, his words only made me cry harder. I didn't deserve this man. I didn't deserve the gentle way he showed his affection, nor how he'd fought for me every day since he arrived. He was so inherently good, and I couldn't fathom what he saw in me.

Lincoln held me like he had the night I'd broken down chopping wood, giving me a soft place to land. He was a shelter from the storm, keeping me safe in his arms. Come hell or high water, he'd make sure nothing touched me. I was allowed to break and build myself back up again without fear of condemnation.

"I—I'm sorry," I stammered, wrapping my arms around his waist. "I don't know why I'm crying. It's stupid. I'm a crier. I always cry."

He slowly shifted on his feet, rocking me back and forth in a slow, steady motion. "The reason why doesn't matter, darlin'. I'll hold you as long as you need me to."

"This is ridiculous," I whispered. "I shouldn't let him affect me like this."

He pulled back enough to press a kiss to my temple. "Now you listen to me, Josie... Don't let your mind fool you into thinking that whatever this is isn't normal. Everyone processes trauma differently. At the end of this day, the only thing that shouldn't have happened is him touching you the way he did."

Ellis' actions had set off this chain of events. None of this would've happened if he hadn't shown up to the bar drunk. However, it was so easy to push that a step further and tell myself if I'd just picked up the damn phone and spoken to him, he wouldn't have driven to the bar and did what he'd done.

"If I'd just talked to him—" I glanced back at Bishop's truck, trying to look anywhere but Lincoln's face.

This time, he curled one finger under my chin and forced me to meet his eyes. "Don't you dare pin this on yourself. He is a grown-ass adult—a fucking joke of a man—who thought it was a good idea to put his hands on you. I don't care what you said or didn't say to him. That doesn't give him the right to—"

And then I kissed him, cutting off his words and allowing myself one selfish moment as I wrapped my arms around his neck.

I didn't know why I did it. Maybe because the way he was looking at me reminded me of how my dad looked at my mom, or perhaps I wanted to wipe everything about Ellis away.

His mouth was tentative, although he clutched my waist like I was the only thing holding him here. Sparks flew as he gently moved his lips against my own, letting everything fade away momentarily.

But then he pulled away with a low groan. His chest heaved as he set his forehead against mine. "Goddammit, Josie—"

"I'm sorry," I said, quickly trying to step out of his hold. "I'm sorry, I'm—"

Lincoln didn't let me go. Instead, he backed me up until I rested against Bishop's truck. He looped his fingers in my belt loop, firmly locking me in place. "If you say you're sorry one more time, I can't be held responsible for what I do next," he growled. "I don't ever want those words to leave your lips, especially not for taking what you want."

"I don't know why I did that," I said, quickly trying to cover up the feeling of rejection clawing its way up my chest. I was thankful for the clouds that had drifted in front of the moon, blocking the light so he couldn't see how red my cheeks were.

"Josie, baby, stop," he said, pressing into me. I could feel him hardening against my body. "I've been dreaming of that kiss since you left Tennessee. I've done nothing but think of your lips on mine since the day I stepped foot on Black Springs."

"I just didn't want to make you feel uncomfortable."

He chuckled, but there was little humor in it. "The only thing uncomfortable is how tight my jeans get whenever you're this close." He lifted his hand and ran a thumb underneath my eyes. "But you've just been through something you haven't been able to process, and I'm not gonna be the asshole that takes advantage of that."

I looked up at him with watery eyes, silently hating that I hadn't come to my senses earlier. "You're a good man, Lincoln Carter. One of the best."

Lincoln gave me a soft smile. "Only for you, darlin'. Only ever for you." He leaned in to press another kiss to my temple. "You ready to go home?"

I nodded, and he moved to open the door for me. He waited until I was buckled in before jogging to the driver's side. He placed one hand on the steering wheel and the other on top of the console, palm up. Without thinking, I reached over and interlaced our fingers, and settled back into the worn seat.

We didn't speak as he drove through town, not even as he turned onto the county road toward the ranch. Instead, he turned the music on low and hummed to a Gary Stewart song.

Every now and then, he'd brush his thumb along my skin. Each time felt better than the last, sending goosebumps up and down my arms. It didn't matter that his hands were rough— calloused and worn from years of hard labor. Each swipe was a gentle promise of something I didn't quite understand yet.

All too soon, Lincoln pulled into the driveway in front of Dad's house, putting the truck in park and cutting the lights. He let his head fall back against the seat as he blew out a long breath. "Well… That wasn't how I saw the night ending."

I chuckled, unable to help myself. "Yeah, me neither." Shifting in my seat, I faced him. "How's your hand?"

He glanced down at where our fingers intertwined, a ghost of a smile dancing on his lips. "Eh, it should probably ache more than it does, but I can't dwell on that while you're holding it."

Damn, those stupid butterflies. It felt like a whole swarm of them was released in the pit of my stomach. My cheeks blazed, and I was thankful we were sitting in the dark. "You're a real smooth talker, you know that?"

"Oh, I've been told that a time or two," he laughed. It was beautiful, and I wanted to hear it again. "Guess it's that southern charm. Just comes naturally."

"You do make it look easy," I admitted. We sat in silence, staring at one another in our perfect little bubble. Nothing existed outside of this truck. Our world had hit pause, giving us a brief moment to just exist. The air was thick with things we didn't have to say.

In the back of my mind, I knew there'd need to be conversations with Dad about what happened with Ellis. After all, I'd not only broken up with him, I'd fired him too. It probably wasn't the best decision with everything going on.

As for Lincoln, well, neither of us knew what tomorrow would look like, or if the haze clouding our minds would clear come sunrise. But some part of me recognized that if I didn't let go of his hand… I'd never need to face life alone.

"What's going through that head of yours?" he whispered.

"You," I admitted, groaning as I felt the swollen skin around his knuckles. "I really would feel much better if we wrapped that hand up."

"I can do it when I get to the bunkhouse," he said, brows furrowed. "I'm sure one of the guys is up. They can help."

"Or I could do it," I said, bringing my gaze to meet his. "There's a first aid kit in the barn."

His throat bobbed as he nodded. "Well, I do think I'd like your hands on me much better."

josie

· · ·

I MOVED to open the door, but Lincoln was around the truck in a matter of seconds. He held out his good hand for me to take, closing the door quietly in case Dad was still up.

The barn was a short walk from the house, separated in the middle by a tall windmill. Lincoln's hand found mine on instinct, and I eagerly intertwined our fingers. It felt familiar. *Comfortable*. Like we'd been doing it for years and this was nothing more than a natural part of our day.

We opened the barn door, greeted by the dim night lights lining the pathway toward the offices. Most of the horses paid us no mind as we went, though Sundance and Silver stuck their nosy little heads out for pats as we walked by.

Dad's office was at the far end of the barn. He'd designed it that way so he could always hear the stomping of boots or the jingle of spurs coming. I switched on the light as we walked in and pointed toward the desk. "Take a seat over there."

Lincoln laughed. "Are you always this bossy?" I didn't answer, turning with my hands on my hips and waited until he did as I said. "Yes, ma'am," he said, holding his hands up in surrender.

"Stubborn ass," I muttered as I pulled pain relievers and a wrap from the drawer. We always kept this thing stocked since accidents occurred on a semi-regular basis. It was always one of two things that caused trouble: Cowboys getting complacent or showing off. Both were recipes for disaster.

Dad always said that was why he kept the kit in his office. He wanted to make sure no one got away with that shit without a verbal warning and he got a good laugh.

"Give me your hand," I said, holding my own out. I stepped between Lincoln's legs, feeling them close in on either side of my thighs as I worked.

I was all too aware of how similar the positioning was from the first night he kissed me, only this time, I felt in control of the situation. Lincoln's body was warm and inviting, and the scent of rich leather clung to his skin.

"You're good at this," he said. I tightened the wrap, and he winced. "Sort of."

"You're not the only one with a proclivity for fighting."

His eyes darkened, turning to near glistening black coals. "Who else have you been wrapping up then?" he bit out.

My lips twitched. It would be so fun to torture him, even if only for a second. "Well, there's Bishop. He's got a big temper. Though, he usually punches things that don't move. That angry fool has had to patch the wall in his office so many times, I've lost count. And then, surprisingly enough, there's Lennox."

His brows shot up at that. "Lennox?"

"Mmhm," I said, securing the wrap. "She's always been a little scrappy. Her teachers had mom and dad on speed dial growing up. They got plenty of calls that she'd kicked some kid's ass on the playground." I shrugged. "They almost always deserved it. And she didn't discriminate either. Whether it was a group of mean girls picking on someone or a boy who wouldn't learn to take no for an answer..." My voice faltered at the end, but I pushed through. "She always did what was right."

Lincoln laughed, tipping his head up to the ceiling. It bared his throat, and I couldn't help the thoughts I had about running my tongue along his day-old stubble. "It makes so much sense now," he said.

"What does?"

"When she and I were dancing earlier, she threatened to kill me if I broke your heart. Said there were a million places to hide a body out here." He shook his head. "Guess I might have to take her threats seriously then."

I smiled at that. Knowing Lennox's ferocity, she'd do it too. I could only imagine what Cleo and Bishop were dealing with back at the bar. "Better heed that warning then, cowboy. I'd hate to cover up such a pretty crime."

"Aw, you think I'm pretty, huh?"

I rolled my eyes and stepped out from between his legs when I finished. Lincoln flexed his fingers. "How's it feel?" I asked.

"Better than it did," he said, looking up at me from under the brim of his black hat. "Thank you, darlin'."

I hated how my heart swelled when he called me darlin', and the moment baby had left his lips, I'd been a goner. Why were those endearments so damn hot? I mean, they shouldn't be.

My dad had always called me darlin' or sugar since I was little. Whenever a man tried to do it before, I'd promptly told them it didn't sit right with me and we'd avoid it altogether. But the moment it'd come from Lincoln's lips as he poured my first shot of whiskey, it altered my brain chemistry.

With him, it felt right.

Which is why the moment I stepped foot back on Black Springs, I told Dad he couldn't call me that anymore. Every time I heard it, I thought of Lincoln. And I hadn't wanted the reminder of what I'd left.

I cleared my throat. "Thank me tomorrow when the swelling goes down," I said, tearing open the little packet and putting two pills in his hand. "This should help a little."

"I don't suppose you have something to chase these with? I've been weird about dry swallowing pills for years. Got one stuck as a kid."

"As a matter of fact, I do," I said, walking over to Dad's closet. I reached for the top shelf, letting out a whoop when I wrapped my fingers around a dusty glass bottle. The label was faded, barely legible as I held it up. "Dad's emergency stash."

"That'll do." He tossed the pills in his mouth and reached for the whiskey. He took a swig and grimaced. "Shit, this is awful."

I swiped it from him and did the same. God, it burned. That'd been a hard lesson to learn in high school. Dad didn't keep much liquor in the house. He was more of a beer drinker. He only brought out his expensive stash during holidays, and my sisters and I knew better than to break into that. So, we'd sneak out to the barn during sleepovers and crack open these instead. He had them hidden all over the barn.

"I told you it was the first night we met," I said. "I don't know why he likes this swill. It's horrible."

"But it does the job," he said, pointing the bottle toward me. "And that, darlin', is the point. Some people like the burn. It numbs whatever's got you reaching for the whiskey."

That was true. It was why I'd always done it, at least. Especially on the night Lincoln had shared his special bottle with me at the bar. I'd been running from my past, and mourning the loss of something I'd never had.

"What's got you reaching for it tonight?" I asked, holding my breath as I waited for his answer. The buzz from the alcohol from the bar and my waning adrenaline left me wanting to swipe the liquor from his grasp and down a shot of my own.

Lincoln studied the bottle, his lips pressed into a hard line. "The thought of him touching you. Of him thinking he has any claim on you, when you've been mine since the moment you walked into Frank's last summer." He raised his head, eyes shadowed. The usual warmth in them replaced by something darker, sharper. "The thought that he's had you when I—"

"I never touched him," I interrupted, the words spilling out before I could stop them. Lincoln's eyebrows lifted, his grip tightening on the bottle as I rushed to explain. "I mean, we kissed. But I've never... I couldn't..." My palms were damp, and I wiped them hastily on my jeans, hoping it was enough to still the shaking.

Come on, Josie. Fucking say it.

Lincoln sat the bottle down and reached forward, hooking his fingers in my belt loops and tugging me closer like he had earlier. "Never been able to do *what*, darlin'?"

"I haven't been able to touch another man without thinking about you," I whispered, letting my admission hang in the air between us like a taught thread.

I'd tried to move on. God, how I tried. Every time I kissed someone, desperate to forget what Lincoln's lips felt like against mine, it'd been his face I'd seen when I opened my eyes.

Just like it'd been his body I'd thought about as I touched myself on so many nights, his name I'd cried out on a ragged exhale as my toes curled and ecstasy crashed through my body.

"You haven't slept with anyone else since me?" he asked. His body trembled as his fingers squeezed my hips.

I shook my head. "I couldn't."

"Fuck, baby," he groaned, eliminating the space between our bodies with one tug.

I went willingly, placing my hands against his chest. His heart thundered under my touch, a rampant beat that matched my own.

Lincoln ran his nose up my throat and groaned. "It's taking everything in me not to give in to this temptation," he rasped. "Because I want you so badly it fucking hurts."

"Then take me," I said, baring my throat. "I want you, too."

His lips touched softly at the skin beneath my ear, and I

wanted to die. His breath fanned against me as he let out a ragged exhale, and I wanted more. It was the cruelest form of torture, and I didn't know if I could go another second without him.

He pulled back, just as he'd done when I kissed him outside the bar. "God, how I want you—don't think that I don't—but," he paused and let his hands travel from my hips to my neck, cupping it tenderly. "I wanna do this right, Josie, and that means not taking you on top of your dad's desk. I wanna show you that this is real for me. I wanna show you how you should be treated."

My eyes watered, and he wiped beneath them as the first tear fell. "I may die if you don't at least kiss me, Lincoln Carter."

His lips twitched as his molten gaze drifted lower. "Well, I'd hate for you to die before I have the chance to make good on my plans."

And then he leaned in, our mouths colliding. He tasted of whiskey and sin and every promise he'd ever made. We were greedy as we moved together, each of us taking our fill, and I couldn't get enough.

It'd been so long, and yet it almost seemed as though no time had passed—like there hadn't been a year and a thousand miles keeping us apart. We fit together like a perfect pair, and I didn't know how I'd been able to walk away the first time.

I'd been a stupid, reckless fool, but I didn't have to be. I could stay and fight for Lincoln, for us, for a future filled with laughter, passion, and *love*.

That word was flashing before my eyes like the bright neon sign that had brought me to him for the first time.

His tongue slipped in, caressing my own with a gentle touch, before he kissed me one last time and pulled back. "You're gonna kill me, woman," he whispered, curling his hands in my hair at the base of my neck. "But what a way to go."

Lincoln's smile was bright as we both laughed. I leaned in on instinct, capturing his lips once more before stepping away. If we didn't stop, I didn't know if I'd be able to. We were toeing dangerously at a line he hadn't wanted to cross.

Reaching over, I grabbed the bottle and returned it to my dad's hiding spot, considerably less full than when we'd pulled it down. Lincoln was warm behind me as he slid his hands around my waist. He dipped his hands into my pockets and pulled me back against him.

Holy shit.

I let my head fall back against his shoulder. "You're not playing fair," I groaned.

He chuckled and pressed his hips against my ass again so that I could feel his arousal. "I just didn't want you to go thinking I didn't want you," he whispered. "Because I may be a gentleman right now, but make no mistake, darlin'... When I fuck you again, you won't be able to walk straight the next morning. You'll remember exactly what it feels like to be worshipped by a man who cares about your pleasure. I'll happily spend hours with my tongue in your sweet, little cunt to prove my point."

"Are you sure you don't want that right now?" I panted, squirming against his erection.

And then he was gone, leaving me hot and desperate and squirming. I spun around to see him walking backward with a wicked grin. His cock pressed against the zipper of his jeans. I wanted to free it, to take it in my hand and stroke his delicious length. "Oh, I do, but I like this, too. Seeing you undone for me is something I'll never tire of. Hell, maybe I just wanna see you beg a little."

I'd do it right now if I thought it'd make a difference. God, how I wanted him. It was a need unlike any other.

"But—"

"No," Lincoln said, shaking his head. He held out his bandaged hand for me to take. "Now, I'm gonna walk you back to the house—probably stealing a kiss or two on the way—and say goodnight because you are way too fucking tempting."

And that's exactly what he did.

He took my hand and led me from Dad's office, kissing me five times before we'd made it to the door. Each time his lips brushed mine, I felt my walls crumble a little bit more, and for the first time in my life, I didn't mind the destruction it left in its wake.

lincoln

. . .

I WOKE the next morning feeling lighter than I had in a very long time. The weight of the past year, with all its shadows and storms, had finally begun to lift. And at the end of the tunnel, shining brighter than anything, was Josie.

Okay, so I might have gone to bed—and woke up, for that matter—with the biggest case of blue balls I'd ever experienced. Instead of having my woman in my arms, I was greeted by three snoring men. I stared up at the underside of the bunk above me, pressing down on my dick tenting in my briefs.

Every ounce of willpower I had was spent walking away last night. It'd been a goddamn nightmare, but I wanted to do things right with Josie. She deserved more than anyone had ever given her—a love so complete and unrelenting that she'd finally understand what it meant to be cared for without caveats.

Not that I knew what I was doing. Maybe I'd fuck it up before I even had the chance to try, but I'd give her everything I had.

The trill of my alarm went off, and I silenced it before looking at my notifications. I smiled at the text messages waiting for me.

JOSIE:

> I know you said I didn't have to thank you, but I
> want to try again. Thank you, Lincoln, not just
> for Ellis but for everything else.

JOSIE:

> Will you come by in the morning for breakfast?
> Dad's gonna make the works like he always
> does, and it's always way too much for us.

JOSIE:

> And then maybe we can sneak away for some
> alone time... 😏

I checked the clock. It was only eight. *Thank God.*

After a cold shower, I threw on an old T-shirt and jeans. I grabbed a hat on the way out, hoping to block the sun's warm rays. It was only a seven-minute walk to the big house, but it was already too fucking hot for my tastes. At least Tennessee cooled off some at night.

I drew a deep breath of dew-laced air, letting the crispness settle in my chest. Black Springs really was something else. Mornings here came alive with birdsong, and the sun always seemed to paint the skies gold. The pastures were sprawling, brimming with potential—flat stretches of land perfect for grazing or hay cutting, rolling on for miles just as Bishop had shown me on the maps that first day. Farther out, the land grew wilder, the forest thickening into untamed terrain. There were even a few rivers marked on those maps, and I couldn't wait to see them for myself.

Maybe Josie and I could ride out, spend the day exploring with only the responsibilities we owed ourselves.

In the back of my thoughts, I worried she might've changed her mind in the span of a few hours. Things looked different in the dark, especially when you were left alone with nothing but silence to keep you company.

I knew Josie well enough, and that woman had a damn good

track record of getting lost in her head. It hadn't mattered how many times I'd told her I was dead set on making her mine; there was always a reason she found not to believe me.

But I was here to stay—with or without Doug's job offer.

I wasn't sure when I'd decided to linger in Texas—maybe my mind was already made up before my plane landed. Now that I was here, I couldn't imagine leaving. The only way it'd happen is if Josie asked me to.

My life was filled with people who let me down in one way or the other. As painful as it was to admit it, Josie had even been among them. Now, everything I ever wanted was within reach. The thought of it being taken away from me before it'd even begun was terrifying.

At damn near thirty-seven years old, I was sick of running, chasing something that was always out of reach. Life had dealt me a shitty hand early on, and I was no longer ashamed to admit that I wanted more.

I wanted a big house with land to call my own. I wanted a job that was as exhausting as it was exhilarating, something that filled me with pride when I looked back at the end of my days. Most of all, I wanted a woman who was fiercely loyal and kind and beautiful. Someone I could settle down with, build that dream life, sit on our front porch, and watch the sun rise and set.

I wouldn't settle for anyone other than Josie Hayes—the storm-eyed cowgirl who'd knocked me off my feet the moment I laid eyes on her.

Chasing that life meant saying goodbye to things from my past. Truth be told, it was gonna be damn hard to watch the last bits of Frank I had be spread out amongst the highest bidders. I'd likely need to go back for a short time. Get things settled and a plan made. Some local folks had expressed interest in Frank's bar after he passed, and the land would sell fast.

I didn't give a shit about the money I could make; it wasn't about that. The only thing I cared about at the end of the day was making sure Frank's legacy was honored.

Sweat beaded beneath my hat as I neared Bishop's cabin. It was about a quarter of a mile from the barn. His Dodge was parked beneath a metal awning, the gravel worn beneath the tires. He'd told me to leave the keys in the truck so that he could grab them when they got home.

I'd nearly cleared the carport when his front door swung open, slamming against the outer wall. Lennox came storming out, her blonde hair streaming behind her as she ran down the porch.

She wore the same clothes she'd been in last night, only they looked rumpled. Like they'd been lying in a heap on a certain cowboy's bedroom floor.

A shirtless Bishop came out a moment later, taking the steps of his porch one by one as he called her name. Lennox didn't pay him any mind. She turned around long enough to throw two middle fingers in the air before disappearing toward the barn.

Bishop ran a hand through his hair before letting loose a string of curses and kicking the old tire planter in his yard. And then he looked up, seeing me standing on the other side of his truck.

"What the fuck are you doing here?" he mumbled before crumpling on the top step of his porch. He looked exhausted, not the same man I'd seen only hours ago at the bar.

"Well, I'd say good morning, but I don't think it is for you," I drawled, stepping around his old truck. "Rough night?"

Bishop huffed and dug into his jeans for a pack of cigarettes. It was old and falling apart, looking more like a keepsake than something he used regularly. I'd never seen him smoke before. "You could say that again."

"Wanna talk about it?"

He turned toward me with furrowed brows. "Why the fuck would I wanna talk about it?" he asked, hanging his head low.

His fingers traced the peeling plastic. "I want you to forget you saw anything."

I raised my hands in surrender and stumbled forward. "Who would I tell? I don't know anyone here."

Bishop chuckled, but it was full of resignation. "You know the people who matter." He set his elbows on his knees and looked out toward the barn. "No one can know she was here, Lincoln. I mean it."

That bit caught me off guard. "Why?"

"Because shit wouldn't end well. I can't risk this job. It's all I fucking have. And Doug treasures his girls more than he treasures this land. He'd fire me in a heartbeat if he thought I was out here breaking hearts."

"And are you?" I asked, leaning against his sun-warmed porch. "I'll admit it didn't look good—"

"I don't know what I'm doing," he interrupted, staring at his trembling hands. "I'm not blind, okay? I've known Lennox damn near her whole life, watched her grow into the fucking hurricane she is today. She is well out of my league. When she came knocking on my door last night, looking pretty as hell and tempting as sin in the moonlight..." His words trailed off, and I knew he was waging one hell of a war against himself. "I don't know. I guess I've just been lonely for too long. Like a fucking fool, I opened my door and let her in."

I stayed silent, letting him sort through his thoughts. I knew all too well what it felt like to want someone you shouldn't. Sometimes, I felt that way about Josie. She was so far out of my league that I'd almost packed it in the moment I stepped foot on the land that raised her. But I wanted her more than I wanted my pride intact.

"I don't know much about the dynamics between y'all—"

Bishop snorted. "There aren't any fucking dynamics—"

"And I don't care," I finished. "At the end of the day, I'd be willing to wager Doug doesn't either. He cares about his family, and that extends to you."

He looked down at his hands again, stuffing the cigarettes into his pocket again. "I sure as hell hope you're right, because I've got nothing if I don't have this."

I kicked my boot against the wooden porch steps. "I've got a bar in Tennessee if you fuck things up too much."

"I wouldn't make a good bar back. I'd drink your stock and flirt with pretty girls on the job," he warned, cracking a smile. "Shit, never mind. It sounds like a dream."

"Sometimes it was," I laughed. "But it sure as hell isn't this."

"Never is." Bishop pushed to his feet. "You going to the house?"

I nodded. "Sure am. You?"

He scrunched his nose, looking back toward the barn. "Naw, I think I'll stay here today. Do some shit that needs doing."

"Alright man. Let me know if you need a drinking partner." I pushed off the post and waved bye.

"Something tells me you might be too busy to drink beer with the likes of me!" he called out, followed by a series of kissing sounds.

So, I did what any other man would do. I turned around, shot him a wink, and said, "I sure as hell hope so."

lincoln

. . .

JOSIE'S melodic laughter and the scent of bacon and eggs hit me before I knocked on the front door. The window in the kitchen was cracked, giving me a peek into their picturesque Sunday morning.

Doug was singing Brooks and Dunn off-key at the stove while Josie and Cleo set the table. He danced, moved, and wiggled about, striking poses I wasn't sure a man his age should be doing.

Once upon a time, my dad had been a good man. My mom had died giving birth to me, leaving the two of us to fend for ourselves in a brand new world. He'd always said she was the light of his life, but that quickly changed as the bills began piling up. It wasn't long before he turned into a drunkard who cared more about the contents of a bottle than his own flesh and blood.

Seeing the way Doug was with his girls made my stomach churn. It was a glimpse of everything I wanted out of the past and future.

Josie's smile grew when she saw me standing there, motioning toward the door. When I stepped under the carport, she was standing barefoot at the door. She wore a t-shirt that was easily two sizes too big for her, with an old Coors Original advertisement on the front and her hair piled up on her head in a messy bun. Her face was red from laughter, and I hoped it never went away.

"Mornin' darlin'," I said, placing my hand on her waist and pulling her in for a chaste kiss. I half expected her to stop me before I got too close, but she surprised me. She wrapped her arms around my neck and held me close, deepening the kiss until she bit my lip.

My fingers dug into her soft flesh, forcing her away before I did something stupid. It would've been too easy to slide my hand into her shorts and find out just how wet she was.

Josie's eyes were glazed as I pulled back. "How was your evening in the bunkhouse with three other guys?" she asked, biting her lip. "Such a shame, really…"

"Think that's funny, huh?" I asked, grabbing her around the waist and hoisting her in my arms. She kicked and laughed and begged me to put her down, but I didn't want to. Not yet.

I turned her so that she could wrap her legs around my waist and pushed her against the rough brick exterior. She fit so perfectly, molding herself against my body like we were two halves of one puzzle.

"I bet you won't when I have you begging for my touch," I whispered, leaning in and rubbing my stubble along her exposed neck.

"Or maybe you'll be begging me," Josie breathed. "Two can play that game, and I've seen how badly you're down for me." She leaned in and took my earlobe into her mouth, letting her tongue run along my skin. "You've shown your hand, cowboy. Now, fix your dick, and let's go eat some breakfast."

My head fell back in laughter as I freed her from my hold. She wasn't wrong. My cock was straining against my jeans, and there was no way in hell I could walk into her dad's house with a hard-on.

"Alright, give me a second. I'll meet you in there."

Baseball, baseball, baseball—

She turned over her shoulder, biting her lip in the way she knew I loved. God, she was a tease. I'd have to turn her little ass red for this someday. "Maybe if you weren't dead set on being such a *gentleman*..."

Christ... What was she doing to me?

"Inside, Josie. Please," I groaned, adjusting myself.

Before I change my fucking mind.

I hadn't been with anyone since her, and it'd been a damn long time before her, too. So long, I was ready to blow in my pants if she so much as touched me. That would've been my undoing; I didn't know if I could live past the embarrassment.

It took every un-sexy thought I could muster to convince my dick to go down just so I could enter her house. The tiled entryway was messy and lived-in. There was a shoe tower that no one used, and a shit ton of hooks with more worn cowboy hats and slickers than I could count.

Their living room was huge, a big, open space for entertaining. In the middle of the room was a giant stone fireplace, and I wondered if they'd ever really needed it. Texas didn't seem like a place that saw much snow, but I supposed it was nice to have just in case.

"Lincoln!" Doug exclaimed, jerking his head in greeting. "How the hell are you? Take a seat. I'm almost finished here. Josie, sugar, will you get the man some coffee?"

"Of course, Daddy." Josie smiled as I slid into the seat at the breakfast nook across from Cleo. She was pale, clasping the cup like it was all she had.

I was going to ask her if she was okay before Josie sat down a steaming mug in front of me. "Here you go, cowboy. A cup of dark sugar water just for you."

I shrugged. "Life's too short to be denied what you really like." I let my gaze travel slowly along Josie's body. She lit up like a goddamn beacon under my attention, and damn if that didn't make my chest hurt.

"See!" Doug called, pointing at the table with his spatula. "That's how I feel too. You know these girls won't even let me have bacon?" He shook his head. "Criminal."

Cleo sighed and sat down her cup. "Daddy, we've talked about this..."

"I know, I know. It's all about my heart, but I'll tell you what... I don't think a little bacon every now and then would kill me, and if it does, then I'll go happy."

Josie and Cleo glanced at one another with wide eyes before dropping their gazes to the table. I didn't know Doug was sick, but it wasn't my place to poke around.

Was that why he'd offered me a job in the first place—because he didn't know if he'd be here next year?

"A breakfast with no bacon?" I shook my head. "Criminal. You girls run a tight ship."

Doug laughed, and it was so rich and hearty that it nearly broke my heart, especially when Cleo and Josie looked distraught. It reminded me too much of when I lost Frank.

"The man gets it! I swear, I'm gonna keep you around. Bishop and I have been outnumbered for too long. These girls are no fun."

He hummed around the kitchen, finishing setting up the food before calling on us to make our plates, but the mood had changed already. There was a heaviness in the air I couldn't place, and I suddenly felt like an intruder in what was previously a heartwarming morning.

I sought Josie's hand under the table when we all took our seats. It was clammy, but the moment I touched her, she interlaced our fingers and squeezed so hard it took an effort not to make a sound.

If this was what she needed, I'd gladly bear a little pain.

Doug prattled on about the next clinic starting like he hadn't just dropped a bomb on the table—one I wasn't meant to know about. He asked me questions about the first group I taught and how it went, and I was honest when I told him I loved it.

Frank had been the only one I'd ever told my fears to. I was worried I'd never step foot in an arena again, living out the rest of my days behind the bar instead. Which would have been fine. It'd given me a purpose and a reason to keep going, but I didn't want that to be all I had.

"You given any more thought to my offer?" he asked, stabbing his fork into a pile of eggs.

Josie's head whipped toward me. "Offer?"

Inwardly, I cringed. I hadn't gotten a chance to talk to Josie about it. There'd been too much shit going on in the past twenty-four hours, and not a damn good time to bring it up.

"I asked Lincoln if he wouldn't mind a permanent position on the ranch—depending on how the rest of the summer goes. Don't want to bring someone on who doesn't know their stuff." Doug smiled, pointing his utensil in my direction. "But I like you, Lincoln, and I'm not an easy man to please."

Cleo rolled her eyes, but hid a smile behind her coffee cup. "He's really not."

I wiped my beard with my napkin and cleared my throat. His words struck a chord of pride, and it took everything in me not to puff out my chest. "Yes, sir, I have, and I'm grateful for the consideration."

"Are you saying no?"

Josie was staring at me. I couldn't tell if she was happy or if he'd just dumped the worst news onto her plate. "No sir, not at all. There are just some things I need to consider back home. I have Frank's land and the bar. I need to make sure those fall into the right hands if your proposal turns into an offer."

He nodded. "Absolutely. The land would be no issue. It's

close to the cabin, and I've been meaning to buy something up there with ready-made stables. We have several clients from Tennessee that make the trek down here. It'd be nice to take our show on the road a few times a year. You could keep the land, and we could work out a lease agreement."

I could barely contain my excitement the more he talked, but as Josie's hand dropped from mine, my world began to crash.

"The bar's more difficult, to be sure. Frank's is a staple there, and I sure as hell don't wanna see it go. We could put out some feelers—"

"You don't have to do any of that, sir," I said quickly, anxiety rising at an alarming speed. "I appreciate the offer—more than I can say, really—but he left it to me, and it's my responsibility to sort it out. I don't want to add more to your plate."

"Nonsense!" he said, leaning back in his chair. "We're all family here, and if you're brought on, that includes you, too. I wasn't lying, Lincoln. To be frank, it'd take one hell of a fuck up to change my mind about offering you a job. It's just formalities stopping me from dragging you to my office and drawing up an employment contract."

I forced a smile. "Thank you, sir. I sure appreciate it, but can I get back to you? It's a big change, and I need to think about a few things first."

"Why? You got a girl back home?" Doug chuckled, but I didn't miss Cleo's glance at Josie. "Take the rest of the summer to get your mind right. My offer will still be on the table whenever you're ready."

My breakfast had gone cold as I murmured thanks and cleaned my plate. When Doug made a move to stand, I held up my hand. "Let me clean up since you cooked. It's the least I could do."

"Have at it, son," he chuckled, waving me off as each person passed me their plate. Josie wouldn't even look at me, and as I stared at the ranch out the window, I wondered if my time at the ranch would be coming sooner than I thought.

josie

. . .

IT WAS a good thing I'd stopped keeping track of all the times I'd made mistakes because my list seemed to grow by the day. Freezing the moment an answer to all my problems had appeared hadn't been one of my finer moments.

Neither was averting my gaze every time Lincoln looked my way afterward.

If Lincoln worked on the ranch, we wouldn't have to worry about a tearful goodbye at the end of the summer. No wondering if we'd be setting ourselves up for a disaster neither of us could come back from.

But I was so scared to hope because losing Lincoln would be more than I could bear. I wouldn't survive it again, not when I'd tasted what it could be.

There were so many things I needed to talk to Dad about. Last night's ordeal would need to be at the top of the list. Ellis was going to be a problem. He'd try to get even; his ego was far too fragile to let go of what happened. I was surprised he hadn't been out here raising hell already.

That would be tomorrow's problem once he slept over his hangover and tended to his pride.

And yet, all I could think about was rushing out to the cowboy who had my heart and telling him what I should have said from the beginning: I was damn tired of running from the good in life, and that good was him.

Was it fast? Absolutely. Crazier things had happened. Mom and Dad had met on the rodeo circuit. They'd only known each other five months before they ran off and got married without telling a soul. Both of their parents had been pissed beyond reason, but next year would be their thirty-eighth wedding anniversary, so I guess they did something right.

I was different from my parents, though. They were both sure-footed, confident people, whereas I constantly doubted every move I made. My mind played tricks on me. Overthinking was a given.

There was still the same worrisome thought in the back of my mind, reminding me of why I left in the first place. I could name a million reasons not to try. Most of them began and ended with my own fear.

For thirty years, I'd been waging a war against myself. My mind was a cruel bitch, relentless in her pursuit of my downfall. She teased and taunted me until I was left with nothing but a sea of doubts.

Today was the first day I'd tell that bitch to shut her mouth and go to hell.

I looked out the kitchen window. Lincoln and my dad strolled out of the barn, heads bent in conversation. They'd been out there for nearly half an hour, wearing a trail into the dirt.

Cleo stepped up behind me, resting her head on my shoulder as I stared off into space. "What's going on in that head of yours?"

"I don't know," I whispered. "There's a part of me that's scared."

"Scared of what?"

"Too much." I shook my head. "Cleo, you'd tell me if I was making a mistake, right? I sound like a broken record, but I'm terrified of him breaking my heart. That might finally break *me*."

When was the last time I'd felt happy? I couldn't remember. I'd been focused on everyone else's welfare and happiness that mine had gone to the wayside. This was the one thing I'd considered allowing myself.

Cleo wrapped her arms around my waist and hugged me tight. "If that cowboy breaks your heart, you know I'd be here to help put back the pieces. So would Mom and Dad and Lennox. Hell, Bishop might even lend us some glue," she chuckled, resting her chin on my shoulder. "You're not alone, Josie. You've never been alone. Opening your heart to a man so clearly head over heels in love with you isn't bad."

Love. The word filled me with dangerous excitement.

"Isn't it too soon for that? I mean, we haven't known each other that long—"

"When you know, you know," Cleo said. There was such conviction behind her words, such surety.

I pulled my lip between my teeth, glancing at the empty sink. "Is that how you felt?" I barely dared ask the question. It was dangerous. We both knew I wasn't talking about her deadbeat husband.

My sister didn't answer me at first. Part of me didn't expect her to. Cleo was a private person, even with us. "I regret losing it every day, Josie."

Cleo stepped back, and I turned to face her. "How did it feel seeing him again?" I asked, taking the risk that my assumption was right, and there was more to the story of the guy at the bar.

She pressed the heel of her hand against her chest. Her eyes were lined with unshed tears. "Like I couldn't breathe. I had no one else to blame but myself because I never chased what I wanted. Grady... He made his fair share of mistakes, don't get me wrong, but I'm far from innocent. I don't know why, but I convinced myself our relationship wasn't worth weathering the storm. Like you, I was scared of what was to come. I didn't know if I could make it through." Cleo's tears fell freely now as I swiped beneath her eyes. "But this hurts so much worse than if I would've ridden it out, Josie. Seeing him live his dreams without me is torture."

I pulled her into my arms as she wept—as she mourned a life she could've had and the emptiness of a love lost.

Could I walk away from Lincoln? Could I handle the crushing weight of disappointment that would surely come if I didn't try? I had a clear picture of the life we could have, the way he'd put everything he had into building a future by my side.

"Don't be like me, Josie," Cleo whispered. "If you love Lincoln, you go get him. You let him know without a doubt that you are his, and he is yours."

I nodded, hugging her tightly. "I love you."

She laughed, pulling back with red-rimmed eyes. "I love you, too. Now, go get your cowboy."

DAD WAS WALKING out of the barn alone by the time I'd slid into a pair of boots and ran his way. I came to a halt in front of the double doors, out of breath and already sweating.

"Woah, where's the fire?" he asked with a chuckle. "Everything okay?"

I placed my hands on my hips, sucking in a lungful of air. *Maybe I needed to start working on cardio again.* "Yeah, I was just looking for Lincoln," I said, trying to peer over his shoulder. "Is he in there?"

Dad nodded, pursing his lips. "Yup, he's in the tack room."

"Thanks, Dad—"

He held his hand out, gently touching my arm. "Josie, sugar, can I have a minute?"

Oh my god. Now was not the time for a father-daughter chat. Adrenaline was coursing through my veins, and each moment I kept my feelings bottled up was wasted time.

I shifted on my feet. "Can it wait?"

"No, sugar. I—I'm afraid it can't."

Dad hesitated, which was never a good sign. That man was as steady as a rainstorm. There were only a handful of times I'd ever seen him less than level-headed. He took off his hat, spinning it in his hands. "I got a call from Ellis this morning. Several, in fact. He had some pretty outrageous claims to make…"

Fucking dick. I thought I'd have the day before dealing with his shit. "I'm sure he did," I said, crossing my arms.

"Ellis said he saw y'all at the bar last night. That you fired him without cause, that Lincoln assaulted him, and that you've been cheating on him since the beginning of y'all's relationship. Now, I know better than to ask if that's true," he said, holding his hands up. "Quite frankly, I'd always thought he was a bit of a prick. But I did have a talk with Lincoln about what happened last night."

I tried to keep my voice even when asked, "And what did Lincoln have to say?"

He wouldn't have lied. Part of me was grateful for that. I didn't know how I was supposed to start that conversation with my dad, and Lincoln had taken that fear away from me, so I didn't have to worry about it. There'd be a time and place to go into details, but I couldn't think of that right now.

But I couldn't keep my face straight. My lip wavered and Dad's expression crumpled. I didn't have to say anything. "Oh, sugar… I'm so sorry." He drew me into a hug. "Are you okay?"

It was on my tongue to say no, but then a chocolate gaze met my own over my dad's shoulder. Lincoln was standing in the middle of the barn aisle, his hands in his pockets, watching us.

How could I not be okay with him at my side? Knowing there wasn't a damn thing anyone or anything could do to keep him away from me? My mind was the last hurdle we had to overcome, and I was going to run that bitch over with my truck so we didn't have to worry about it anymore.

Leaning forward, I squeezed my dad's hand. "I'm okay, I promise. My daddy raised me to be tough as hell, remember?"

He chuckled, putting his hat back on. "I'm not gonna let him get away with this shit, Josie. He can make threats all he wants, but—"

I couldn't do this anymore. All I could focus on was Lincoln. "Uh, Dad? Do you mind if we talk about this later?"

Dad peered over his shoulder. "Right. I'm just gonna go," he said, clearing his throat. He pressed a kiss to my temple before heading toward the house. "Y'all kids don't do anything I wouldn't."

His footsteps faded away, leaving Lincoln and I standing on either side of a line, and neither one of us was sure if we should cross. There was something significant and oddly terrifying about the moment. It was either an end or a beginning, and I didn't know if I was ready for the answer.

What if he decided I wasn't what he wanted? That I was too damaged or came with too much baggage? It'd be easier to cut his losses and get out while he still could. I wouldn't blame him for it, either.

"Fancy seeing you here, cowboy," I said, sticking my hands in my pockets to keep them from shaking. I eyed the scuffed black floor transition strip leading into the barn, wondering if I should say "fuck it" and leap into his arms.

"Oh, it ain't all that surprising, is it? You've been watching me through that kitchen window since I got here." His eyes darted down to the line before he took a step closer.

"Well, I guess I'll need to get better about that, won't I? Seeing as you'll be hanging around here for a little longer."

If he hadn't already said no.

Our relationship aside, it would've been a damn shame for Black Springs to lose Lincoln. Under my dad's supervision, he could easily be recognized as one of the best in the country. There'd be no one better to continue the Hayes legacy once Dad retired.

"I haven't said yes to anything yet, Josie." Lincoln ran his thumb over his bottom lip, staring at me warily. "Don't know if I have a reason yet."

"It's a great opportunity. Dad pays better than any other outfit you can find. We've got room and board, too. There's another cabin like Bishop's tucked away in some trees on the other side of the barn. If you stayed, you wouldn't have to worry about permanently living with three other people."

Please say you'll stay.

Lincoln shook his head. "To anyone else, it'd be a dream, but I'm not in it for the perks, darlin'. You know that. There's only one thing I'm looking for, and it's non-negotiable."

I looked down, noticing how close we'd drifted toward one another. There were only a handful of feet separating us. I could smell his musky cologne drifting through the summer breeze like a caress.

"What's that, cowboy?" I asked, tucking a strand of loose hair behind my ear. "What could possibly tip the scales one way or the other?"

"Josie..." Lincoln whispered, glancing down at his worn boots. A deep crease formed between his brows that I wanted to smooth away. "Listen, I need you to shoot straight with me here. Last night, I thought we'd come to an understanding. I thought we wanted the same things, but I saw your face when Doug mentioned a permanent position here. It sure as hell didn't seem like you were happy at the news, and I'm not gonna stay somewhere I'm not wanted."

That's where he was wrong. I'd been horrible at showing him any different, but I'd never wanted anything more.

I wanted him seated at our kitchen table every morning, sipping his coffee that'd have way too much sugar as the sun haloed his silhouette. I wanted him in our bed at night, holding me in his arms and making love until the voices in my head grew silent.

And I wanted to sit in a matching set of rocking chairs when we'd gone grey, looking out over this land and remembering the day our lives together began.

So, I closed the space between us, standing toe-to-toe with the man I'd fallen in love with a year ago. Reaching up, I gently plucked the black felt cowboy hat from his head. "Well... We can't have that."

To a cowboy, that damn hat was sacred. It symbolized pride and tradition, a nod to the one who'd come before and paved the way to where we were today. Most carried it like a badge of honor, living their life adhering to a long list of superstitions only they understood.

But there was one universal rule that went above all others.

If you wear the hat, you ride the cowboy.

His jaw ticked as he watched me set it on my head. I peeked at him beneath the brim, biting my lip the way I knew he liked. "Does this look like you aren't wanted?"

Lincoln shook his head, closing his eyes. "Don't do that, Josie."

Oh no, had I read everything wrong? "Do what?" I asked, doubt creeping in. Maybe I shouldn't have done the hat thing? Maybe I should've just come out and said what I wanted without trying to be cute and coy?

He leaned forward, bracing his hands on either side of the door. His massive body towered over me in a way that had heat pooling in my core. "You know damned well what," he bit out. "That hat on your head means you're mine, Josie. There are no takebacks, not as far as I'm concerned. So, don't do that to me and then take it away. Don't fucking tease me, baby. I can't take it."

Well, fuck.

If I wasn't already so far gone for Lincoln Carter... That declaration would've sealed the deal. This man had never wavered—not even when I'd tried like hell to push him away so I wouldn't get hurt again. I'd been burned so many times by my past mistakes that when Lincoln showed up, it felt too good to be true. I hated how I'd spent so much time doubting his intentions, but I was so glad he was as stubborn as he was.

A lesser man would've run for the hills by now, and they damn sure wouldn't have shown up at my ranch a year later to fight like hell to make me see reason.

I took a deep breath, trying to keep the shake from my voice. "Okay, I'm not good at these things. Honestly, I'm kind of surprised. You'd think that a girl who'd spent most of her life yearning for love would have something prepared for this kind of situation," I rambled, earning a laugh from Lincoln that I took as a good sign to keep going.

"I have spent years letting others dictate my worth. Every time a relationship failed, I blamed it on myself—that I loved too hard, wanted too much, or wasn't worth staying for. When I met you, I was coming out of a bad relationship and thought you'd be the same. I mean, how the hell could we fall in love in five days, you know? So, that's why I left. I was scared shitless, and at least this time, *I* was the one walking away. I thought there'd be power in that, but it felt horrible. I almost turned around fifteen times before I even made it out of Tennessee.

"Some nights, I'd lay in bed and cry, knowing, in my heart, I'd done the wrong thing. I wanted to call you, but there didn't seem to be an explanation good enough. As the months flew by, I tried to convince myself we'd both moved on and were happy."

"I never got over you, Josie," he whispered, voice breaking. "Fucking never. How could I?"

"I know," I said, choking out a laugh. My vision blurred as the tears I'd felt building began to fall. "You're too damn stubborn for that, staying when I've given you every reason to go. I've never had anyone fight for me the way you have. Somewhere along the way, you've shown me my worth, and I'm done running."

Lincoln let out a shuddering breath, surging forward and tangling his fingers in my hair. We staggered backward, falling back into the dirt as he brought his lips down harshly on my own. This kiss was branding my soul in a way that could never be undone. He was right; there'd be no going back after this.

From that moment on, I was his. Irrevocably and wholly his.

He pulled back, peppering kisses all along my face. "Josie—"

"Sometimes, you're a pain in my ass, but I love you, Lincoln Carter. I love you in a way that is terrifying because I know you could destroy me if you wanted to, but oh god, I wouldn't have it another way."

"Shit, darlin'. There ain't a damn thing you could do to get rid of me at this point. You're a part of me and have been since you ordered that double whiskey. How could I possibly let you go after that? My only mistake is not going after you earlier. I shouldn't have ever let you think I'd moved on."

"I think it needed to happen like this, though. I needed more than words to know that come hell or high water, you'd still be here. You've seen me at my worst and still loved me through it."

"You don't have to be perfect, Josie. You don't have to be a damn thing you don't want to be. Hell, you can turn into a fucking worm tomorrow, and I'll still love you. You're—*fuck*—you're it for me, baby."

"A worm?" I asked, choking on laughter. "Are there stipulations on these animals? Like, would you still love me if I turned into *any* animal?"

Lincoln smiled, resting his thumb along my pulse point. "Hm, I don't know... Those naked mole rats are pretty weird. Have you seen them? They look like someone stuck teeth on a ballsack."

"Okay, that's a fair deal breaker."

"FINALLY!" Lincoln and I turned toward the house to see my dad and sister standing in the kitchen window, cheering and clapping like they'd just won the lottery.

I groaned, letting my head fall against his shoulder. "Well, that's embarrassing."

"I don't know, it's kinda cute. And at least I've already got your dad's approval," he said, lifting his arm to wave. "But maybe we should find somewhere a little more private, huh? I don't think your family wants to see the things I want to do to you."

lincoln

· · ·

I TOSSED Josie over my shoulder and strode toward the tack room. Going somewhere a little more private would've been better, more romantic, but I couldn't hold off that long. We were both out of our minds, deliriously happy, and running on adrenaline. My cock was leaking at the thought of having her.

"What're you doing, you caveman?" Josie squealed, pounding her fists against my back in perfect rhythm with my heart. "Where're you taking me?"

I thought Josie and I were done when I left Doug's house. I was mentally preparing myself to be around her for the next six fucking weeks and act like we were strangers. There was no way I could've gone on the way we were, and it was too soon to pretend we were just friends.

My palm landed on the globes of her ass, massaging the spandex-clad flesh to soothe the hurt, turning her laughter into moans. If my dick wasn't already painfully hard, it would've been after whatever pornographic sound just left her mouth. "I'm not wasting another fucking second without being buried inside you."

I opened the door, setting Josie down on the nearest table

before kissing her. My hands landed on her waist, shoving up her shirt until her bra peeked out. "Fuck, baby…"

"Lincoln, oh my god!" she shrieked, moving back and righting her clothes.

I spun around to find two young ranch hands holding a set of bridles, looking wide-eyed and frozen in place. "I—I'm sorry, sir—"

"Out!" I bellowed, pointing toward the door. I could hear Josie's mumbled apologies as she buried her head in my chest. Their boots thudded against the concrete floor. "Get the fuck out, and don't come back until I say so. In fact, tell everyone this barn is off fucking limits until tomorrow."

I'd never seen two people move so fast. They tore out of the barn with their tails tucked firmly between their legs. One even had the decency to shut the main doors before they scurried off.

"Oh my god," Josie chuckled. "Maybe we should wait until we're alone."

"We're alone now," I said, licking the column of her neck. "And I don't give a fuck who's out there. Cry out my name, darlin'. Let them know who owns your pretty little pussy."

"Why is it so hot when you talk dirty?" Josie groaned.

"Can't get enough," I rasped. My hands roamed her body. I couldn't stop touching her. Leaning in, I nipped at her collarbone and watched her creamy skin turn pink.

"Mm, you are obsessed, cowboy."

Did she not understand what she did to me? That was adorable. I'd been dreaming of this day since I'd laid eyes on her, and now she was mine. Mine to love, mine to fuck, mine to do whatever I wanted with.

"You have no idea, Josie. Obsessed is the understatement of the fucking year when it comes to you." My fingertips danced across her thighs. For a moment, I stood there, enjoying the unobstructed view of her body as she leaned back. She was still wearing that long shirt, playing tricks, so my mind thought she was bare underneath. "You've been teasing the shit out of me, and now I'm here to get what's owed."

I reached for the fabric and pulled it over her head. Her tits were already spilling out of her frilly little pink bra, drawing my attention with each ragged intake of breath. My mouth closed around her nipple, sucking until Josie was chanting my name. I frantically tugged at her spandex shorts to get them down her thighs and my hand inside.

We both moaned as I brushed against the juncture of her thighs. There was a dark spot on her panties where she'd soaked through. Her sweet perfume filled the air, making my mouth water as I slowly peeled them off. "I want your fucking moans, Josie," I growled, sucking on her lips while I plunged three fingers into her cunt. Her back bowed, and her mouth hung open in a silent scream as I fucked her hard and fast. "That's it, darlin'. You like it rough, don't you?"

Josie frantically nodded, bringing one hand up to roll her nipples between my fingers. "Yes," she hissed, closing her eyes. "Oh my god, right there."

I kept my pace steady, massaging her clit with my thumb. "You're dripping all over my hand, Josie. Christ, baby." The sound of her arousal mixed with her moans of pleasure created the most beautiful sound I'd ever heard.

"I need you to fuck me, Lincoln. Please, please, *please*," she cried. Her hands sought out the button of my jeans, fighting to stave off her orgasm until she'd worked it free.

"Let me take care of you first," I said, applying more pressure.

"No, I'm not asking, *baby*." Josie looped one arm around my neck as the other gripped my chin. "I want you inside me when I come. So, you're going to let me take your dick out, and then you're going to fuck me."

Fuuuuuck. Well, that was new.

I'd never been dominated in bed before, never really had the chance. Most women I'd been with wanted to be told what to do, so that's what I did. But there was something about Josie bossing me around that had me panting. Goddamn, it got me so hard it was nearly painful.

She could ask for anything, and I'd give it to her. She could tell me to walk off a bridge, and I'd do it. Josie held the reins just like she had that first night when she bent over the pool table in Frank's.

"Yes, ma'am." My words whooshed out on a harsh exhale as I yanked down my zipper and freed my length.

Josie groaned at the loss of my fingers, but her eyes were locked on my heavy dick. "I forgot how big you are." She reached between us, taking it in her hands. We both hissed as she dragged it through her lips, wetness coating my head as she notched it at her entrance.

Shit. What are we doing? We can't do this.

"Baby, I don't have a condom," I rasped as Josie rocked her hips, letting me slip inside. This was so reckless, way too reckless to continue. I'd lost all sense when it came to her. This woman was going to fucking kill me. It was taking everything I had not to surge forward and claim her. "We can't—"

"We can," she said, moving once again. "I haven't been with anyone since you, and I got tested after I got home."

"So did I, but—"

"I also have an IUD, so we don't have to worry about any surprises." Josie bit her lip, looking down at where we were connected. I followed her gaze, nearly spilling myself before I'd even had the chance to fill her. "I want to feel you, Lincoln. I don't want anything else between us."

I blew out a breath, slowly notching in another inch. The view of my bare cock halfway in Josie's perfect pussy nearly did me in. She was whimpering, rotating her hips while seeking the friction both of us desperately wanted.

"I've, uh, never done this before," I whispered, meeting her soft gaze. "Just so you know."

Growing up, my dad had scared me too much to go without a condom—even when I was a wide-eyed hellion chasing skirt at the local rodeos. But the thought of marking Josie in this way was heady. Intoxicating. I wanted her to be mine in every way imaginable.

"Neither have I," Josie replied, tenderly cupping my cheek. "But it seems fitting that we're doing this together, doesn't it?"

I couldn't stop my smile, pushing her hair off her forehead and pressing a kiss there. "Yeah, darlin'. It's pretty perfect."

My girl leaned in with a smirk, hips rotating in a slow circle. I couldn't tell if it was the greatest feeling of my life or pure torture. Her hand came up, kneading her breast. "Then, fill me up, cowboy. I want to walk back in the house with your hand in mine and your cum in my pussy."

"*Christ*, Josie." I couldn't wait any longer, slamming home in one hard thrust. Our collective moans were obscene, echoing off the oak-lined walls. Holy shit, she was tight. We both stilled as she stretched around me, her cunt wrapping around my cock like a vise. "You have such a filthy fucking mouth."

Josie wrapped one arm around my neck as I began to move. Her other traveled between us, rubbing circles along her clit to the rhythm of my thrusts. My fingers dug into her skin, leaving marks behind that would surely bruise. It took everything I had to keep myself from coming within a few seconds, especially as I felt every quiver and shake of her body.

The waves of pleasure were building, and I could already feel myself reaching the point of no return. "Josie, I dunno how much longer I can last. I need to make sure you come."

"Keep going," she panted, increasing the speed of her fingers. Her pussy fluttered around me, and it was nearly the death of me. "I'm *so* close."

Each frantic piston of our hips sent us closer to the edge. We were a mess of tangled limbs and sweaty bodies. The table rattled, slamming into the wall. Whatever had been on top had fallen, littering the ground beneath us.

Her desperate whimpers spurred me on, those breathy little moans that were for me and me alone. She slid her hands beneath my shirt, clawing her nails into my back as I rutted against her. My head fell into the crook of her neck, running my tongue along her erratic pulse point.

The moment her sweet cunt tightened around my cock, I was gone. The base of my spine tingled, my balls tightened, and then Josie cried out my name as we came together. Her head fell back, mouth agape on a silent scream as I continued to fuck her through our release.

"Lincoln, oh my god." She was so beautiful like this, in the throes of ecstasy, with my name on her lips. I wanted to capture this moment forever, to burn it into my memory.

I'd spent a lot of time thinking about what our next time would be like, wondering if it could compare to those five days we spent in Tennessee, but this was better. Her sweet pussy tightened around my length, sending me careening over the edge with her. My climax was brutal. I was a damn teenager again, lasting all of ten seconds before coming.

But there was something about this moment that was different than any other. I didn't know if it was knowledge I was taking her bare, how I felt every muscle constricting around me. Or maybe it was knowing that from this moment on, we were endgame.

My hips slowed as we came down from our high. I could feel my release leaking around me, slipping between our bodies. Josie shuddered as I began to pull out, watching with glazed eyes as she saw the evidence of frantic fucking.

"That's so hot," she panted, watching as I swiped through the mess with my cock. I met her gaze as I slid my fingers deep, fucking our cum back into her. "Oh God, that's even hotter."

"Want a taste, baby?"

Josie's eyes widened, and she nodded, opening her mouth and laying her tongue flat.

Fuck. Me.

I freed my fingers and placed them on her tongue, holding her gaze. "Then, suck."

She closed her mouth around my digits, greedily cleaning them before letting me go with a wet pop. And then she smiled and hummed, licking her lips like a goddamned fiend.

"My turn," I murmured, closing the distance. Josie moaned into my mouth as I tasted us on her tongue. It was erotic and dirty and the most incredible fucking kiss of my life.

I wish I'd thought twice about this location because I only wanted to lie with her in my arms. Not that I'd let something like not having a soft spot stop me.

"Come here, you," I said, smiling as I leaned forward to scoop her up.

"Where are you taking me now?" she asked, wrapping her legs around my waist.

"Nowhere," I said, stepping around the table without breaking contact. I slid down the wall, taking a seat on the cold floor as Josie straddled my lap. She leaned forward, resting her head on my shoulder. "Just wanted to hold you in my arms for a minute."

I felt her lips curve against my skin. She was so beautiful like this, hair mussed and skin flushed from an orgasm. The room smelled like her—leather and sex and something sweet I couldn't place. "I like the sound of that."

"Hm, me too. Sorry, I couldn't wait until we got somewhere a little more private."

She pressed kisses along my collarbone. "We can be private for round two." Her bare pussy was pressed against the length of my dick, and it twitched at the thought of fucking her again so soon. "*He* seems to like it, too."

"Darlin', we don't have anywhere to go."

"Don't you remember what I said earlier?" she asked, peeking at me.

I shook my head. "Uh, no. Want to clue me in on the secret?"

"I told you. Dad's offer comes with room and board. You have your own cabin, baby."

Baby.

Something about the name warmed my chest. Josie'd never been much for those little endearments. Every now and then, she called me cowboy, but that'd been it until today.

"My own cabin, huh?" Josie nodded, squeezing her pussy around my length. "How'd you feel about christening it?"

"FOR THE LOVE OF GOD, PLEASE LEAVE!" Lennox's voice came through the wall, scaring the shit out of both of us.

"Shit, shit, shit," I cursed as Josie quickly stood and reached for her shirt. I followed suit, tucking myself away before picking up some things that'd fallen during our frenzied coupling. I didn't know where my hat had gone, likely fallen off when I'd thrown Josie over my shoulder.

"Lennox, I'm going to kill you!" Josie called out, pulling the heavy oak door open. She strode into the aisle, looking around before narrowing her eyes on Strider's stall.

The top of a blonde head peeked over the door before ducking back down again. "Let's just forget it ever happened, Jos. It's not my fault your boyfriend didn't double-check to make sure the coast was clear. I wanted to run out sooner, but it was too late, and then—"

Josie groaned. "Please don't say it."

"Oh god," Lennox said, faking a vomit sound. "I learned way too much about my sister's sex life."

"Sorry, Lennox," I said, scratching the back of my neck. I knew she'd come up here after leaving Bishop's, but I thought she'd have moved inside at some point. Apparently, I was wrong.

"Why're you hiding out here?" Josie asked, crossing her arms. "You missed breakfast."

Lennox groaned. I couldn't see her, but it sounded like she banged her head against the stall. "Can we talk about it later? Maybe when I'm not trying to forget the past twenty minutes of my life?"

Josie walked over, leaning her head into the stall. "You okay?"

"Yeah, I'm fine," Lennox sighed. "I'm gonna stay out here with Strider for a little longer."

The large horse dipped his head as if saying he'd care for his girl the way she always cared for him.

"Okay. Love you, bug," Josie said, pushing off the door. She strode up to me, wrapping her arms around my waist. "Wanna check out that cabin? I just need to grab the keys from Dad."

"Sure. Let's go."

We headed toward the house, seeing my black hat lying in the dirt outside the barn. I picked it up, dusting it on my jeans before setting it on Josie's head. She reached up, running her fingers along the brim.

"My hat looks good on you, darlin'."

Josie smiled, ducking her head. "Yeah, I think so, too."

The sound of tires on gravel drew our attention, and we both looked up to see a sleek, black car coming up the long drive. "Is that—"

Josie's grip on my hand tightened. "Ellis' dad."

josie

· · ·

LINCOLN and I stood beneath the carport, his arm wrapped protectively around my waist as we watched the car slowly approach. I shifted on my feet, keenly aware of Lincoln's release still leaking out of me.

It really shouldn't have been as hot as it was, but holy crap... Even the thought of what we did sent stupid shivers up my spine. If it wasn't for Charles' surprise arrival, I'd have dragged him off somewhere else for round two.

"You think it's really him?" Lincoln asked, narrowing his eyes at the Mercedes coming to a stop. "If it's Ellis..."

"It's not," I said, peeking up at Lincoln. I still had on his hat and did not intend to give it up. "Ellis talks a big game, but he knows better than to show up to the ranch after what happened last night."

Lincoln grunted but said nothing else as Charles stepped out of his car. He waved our way before stepping to the back and pulling his briefcase from the trunk. "Josie! Lincoln!"

Behind us, the front door opened, and my father stormed out. Cleo followed on his heels, mumbling something about keeping a level head. His face was dark and thunderous, matching in time with each stomp of his feet.

"You have some fucking nerve showing up here, Charles," he growled, stopping at the nose of his car. "After what your son did, I should have Josie press charges."

Charles' shoulders slumped as he dropped his head on a sigh. "After the information I found last night, you might be right. Mind if we go inside and talk?"

Dad's brows furrowed as he gestured toward the house. Charles thanked him, striding into the house with Cleo.

"You okay with this?" Dad asked, turning toward me. "I can tell him to leave."

I shook my head. "No, I'm fine. I want to know what this is about."

"Alright, sugar. Let's find out."

Lincoln and I followed my dad inside. We settled at the large dining room table, waiting not-so-patiently as Charles set his briefcase down. He began pulling out files, stacking them along the table, as Cleo brought everyone a glass of tea.

"Alright, Charles, you've got our attention. Tell us what's going on," my dad said, sipping from his glass.

Charles looked down at the files, running a hand through his tousled hair. He looked like he'd hardly slept a wink. Dark circles were prominent beneath his beady eyes. "I don't know where to start, but I feel like this is my own damn fault," he huffed, sitting down in the chair at the head of the table. "After all, Ellis is my son. I taught him all he knows about this job in the hopes he'd one day run my firm, but that ship has long since sailed."

Charles glanced my way. "I know it isn't right, but I want to apologize for his behavior last night. He dropped by the house yesterday afternoon—hell, it wasn't even four—mad as hell and spitting nonsense about your infidelity." Lincoln tensed beside me but relaxed as I placed my hand on his knee. "Please know that I didn't believe a word of it. Ellis is... well, I don't know anymore. I barely recognize the kid these days. If I would've known he was headed to you when he left my house, I would've stopped him."

"It's fine, Charles. It isn't your fault. I don't blame you," I said, looking down at my lap.

Lincoln stretched, laying his arm over the back of my chair. "I might, though. Seeing as you knew he was intoxicated and let him leave your house."

Charles raised his hands. "You'll get no argument from me. There are many things I'm realizing I failed at when it comes to my son."

"What is all this, Charles?" my dad said, gesturing toward the files. "I imagine this isn't about what happened last night."

He shook his head. "Ever since Josie left my office after our meeting, I've been doing some searching on my own. It's been incredibly slow. Whenever I thought I was getting somewhere, it ended up being a dead end. Until last night." He paused, grabbing his glasses from his briefcase and slipping them on. "I was doing some research when Ellis came to visit. You remember me telling you about those shell corporations?" I nodded. "Well, I found the owner."

Charles reached over and set a stack of documents in front of me. I briefly glanced over them, not understanding most of the legal terms I saw. It was only after a few pages that I saw a name that made my blood run cold. I glanced up, seeing Charles staring at me with sympathy.

"It was Ellis," I whispered, glancing back down at where my ex's name was written in bold, black letters. "Ellis stole the money. These are his companies."

"What?" Dad asked, sitting up straighter. I handed over the documents, watching his face grow redder by the second. "How could this happen?"

Charles pursed his lips before setting down the next file. "Because he did a goddamn good job of forging your signature."

He set two more documents on the table before us, and we leaned over to examine them. Both had my dad's signature, but minor differences set them apart. Ellis' attempt was too neat. It was like he took my dad's choppy scrawl and turned it into symmetrical loops and curves, a perfect copy across every document.

"Christ, how did we not catch this?" I said, rifling through the stack. "There must be at least twenty-five transfer agreements here."

"I didn't think I'd have to go over his work with a fine-tooth comb when he started. You know how Ellis is—stubborn, cocksure. Always thinking he's got something to prove. I showed him the ropes, and he was damn good at what he does. He learned things from his years at school that I didn't even know. That was why I sent him there in the first place. I didn't want my legacy to be dead before it ever had a chance to grow. Maybe that's what drove him to do what he did." Charles shook his head, voice breaking. "Maybe I did this."

"Naw, that ain't it," my dad said, scrunching his nose. "Whatever mess your boy made, he did it himself."

"Be that as it may, it slipped under my radar and has caused quite a mess."

"On that, we can agree," Dad said. "What're the next steps then?"

Charles took off his glasses, tossing them on the table. "I've sent my findings to the auditor this morning. They'll review the documents, authenticate them, and ensure I haven't missed anything. Now that they know what they're looking for, it might be easy to find patterns. These amounts, though... They match with what we'd found earlier. I don't think there's any more."

"What's the legal recourse?" My dad turned to stare at me as the question left my lips. I settled back in my chair, crossing my arms. "What? That asshole—no offense, Charles—stole over a quarter of a million dollars from you, Daddy. He's not getting away with a slap on the wrist and a measly fine."

"She's right, Doug," Charles said. "He doesn't get to walk away without consequences. I don't trust him anymore, and there's damn sure no other firm that'd take him. He'll do it again if he gets away with this now."

My dad drummed his fingers against the table. "Charles, you understand what kind of position I'm in…"

"I already told the auditor if the findings are correct," he nodded at the briefcase, "I'd recommend prosecuting, but my word isn't the one they need, Doug. It's your decision. That'll be key in getting your funds back."

I leaned back into Lincoln's chest, soaking up his warmth. Having him next to me was the only thing preventing me from panicking. Somehow, knowing he was there kept me steady.

Dad looked at me, scrunching his nose. "And this is what you want, too?"

I nodded. "It is."

How could I not when he'd not only stolen from my family for his own benefit but put his hands on me as well? No, I was done letting men like him walk over me and my family.

The relationship between Ellis and I made sense now. Whenever he saw me slipping away, he'd throw on a fake smile and turn on the charm to lure me back in. Like an idiot, I fell for it every time. When he met Lincoln, he saw that the control he'd worked so hard to secure had begun to slip away. Somehow, that bastard knew he wouldn't stand a chance against the man at my side.

Lincoln kissed my forehead, running his fingertips along the hem of my shirt sleeve. "You sure, darlin'?"

I nodded, leaning into his side. "Yeah. It isn't just about me. This is about what happened with Dad."

"I don't give a shit about myself, Josie. Money is money. We could lose everything tomorrow, and I know we'd be okay." I looked over, seeing him clasp Cleo's hand and press a kiss to it. "My family is all I care about."

"I know, Daddy," I said, giving him a genuine smile. "I love you."

Charles piled the documents in a neat stack, packing the rest of his stuff. He stood from the table. "I'm requesting an investigation on all the accounts Ellis represented. By the morning, the office will be crawling with auditors and Ellis... Well, I don't know what will happen with him."

Dad pushed to his feet. "I'm sorry about that, Charles. I really am."

Charles sighed. "So am I." He looked at me. "I thought I raised a good man, but I was wrong. A good man wouldn't have done this."

"I don't think it's your fault, Charles," I said, wiping my eyes. Seeing what this was doing to him was eating me alive. Charles was one of the kindest men I knew outside of my dad.

Charles nodded. "I hope you're right." He tapped the table, grabbing his briefcase. "I'm gonna get out of your hair. I just wanted to make sure the news came from me first. The auditors will likely be calling first thing."

The timing wasn't ideal. Tomorrow was the first day of our second round of clinics. Our time would be spent sorting out the new arrivals and their horses. As if reading my mind, Dad looked at me and said, "Don't worry, sugar. We'll figure it out. If we need to step away to handle it, we'll do that."

"Just tell me what you need from me, sir," Lincoln said, sitting up straighter. "Bishop and I can whip the hands into shape."

"I appreciate that, son, and I'll be taking you up on that." We stood up, taking turns shaking Charles's hand before Cleo walked him out. As I sat back down, I turned and stared out the big bay windows, looking over the drive, waiting until Charles' car was a blip down the road.

Dad sighed, running his hand through his hair. "This is a fucking mess."

"It is. I'm sorry, Daddy," I said, wrapping my arms around my middle.

"Why're you apologizing, sugar? I should be thanking you. If you hadn't found this shit, who knows how much more we could've lost. I hate that this has fallen on your shoulders."

I leaned over and placed my hand on his. "I'd do anything for you. You know that."

"I do, and I'm damn thankful for that." His gaze swept between Lincoln and me, smiling. "I guess congratulations are in order, then?"

I coughed. "We aren't getting married..."

"*Yet,*" Lincoln added. "I'll wear her down eventually, though."

"Oh my god," I said, turning to slap his arm. "You can't just say that shit."

"Why not?" he asked. "It's the truth. I can't wait to be Mr. Hayes."

My cheeks flushed. This was absolutely not the time to have this conversation. "Mr. Hayes?"

Lincoln shrugged. "I have no connection to Carter, but you do with Hayes. Figured you might want to keep it."

I didn't know why the thought of Lincoln taking my surname got me all emotional, but it did. I'd always assumed I'd hyphenate, seeing as most guys I knew expected their wife to take their last name.

But Lincoln wasn't just any guy. I shouldn't have even been surprised he'd do something so thoughtful. That was just who he was.

"Well, I'll be damned," my dad chuckled, covering his mouth with his hand. "That old bastard was right."

Lincoln and I both turned, staring at my dad in confusion. "Who?"

Dad's face sobered for a moment before clearing his throat. "Frank. He'd said something that didn't make much sense then, but I see it now." He stood from his seat, pulling a key from his pocket and setting it on the table before us. "We'll handle the details of your full-time employment later, but I wanted to go ahead and give that to you. The cabin's been vacant for quite a while, so it'll need a good cleaning before it's livable, but I think you'll like it."

"Wait, Frank said something about us?" Lincoln asked, his voice wavering. He looked down at me in question, but I was just as confused as he was.

I reached over and took his hand as Dad nodded. "Now, I didn't know the extent of y'all's *relationship* when I called you up and offered you the temp job, but Frank had mentioned the two of you met when Josie went up there. He thought it'd be damn good for the both of you if I gave you a job and brought your ass to Texas. I didn't get it then, but I sure as hell do now." He paused, and looked up at me. Tears lined my eyes, mimicking the ones in his own. "You know, I used to think there wasn't a soul alive who was good enough for my daughters, but I'll say this, son..." His gaze shifted to Lincoln. "I've never been so happy to be wrong before."

"Sir, I don't know what to say..." Lincoln began, but my dad held his hand up.

"Nothing to say, son. Just take care of my girl, and love her well."

"Dammit, Daddy. Way to make me cry," I said, wiping my eyes. My dad was the best man I knew, and though I didn't need it... Knowing Lincoln had his approval meant the world to me.

"Aw, sugar... As long as those are happy tears, cry all you want."

"C'mon, Dad," Cleo said, smiling at us as Dad wrapped his

arm around her waist. "Let's leave the lovebirds be." They walked into the kitchen, heads bent together in conversation, leaving us to gawk at Dad's news.

As I turned toward Lincoln, his eyes were brimming with unshed tears. "You okay, baby?"

He cleared his throat, blinking rapidly to clear them away. "I think so. It's just a lot," he whispered, giving me a shaky smile. "I'm glad I have you, though, darlin'."

I laid my head on his shoulder. "I'm glad I have you, cowboy."

epilogue

. . .

Josie

"HOW DOES IT FEEL BEING BACK?" I asked, placing my hand in Lincoln's as we walked around the front of his truck toward the entrance of Frank's bar.

He paused, looking up at the new neon sign that'd been installed this morning. The casing around it was clear and fresh, unblemished from the harsh weather and years of wear and tear.

It was the beginning of September, and there was a chill in the air from the changing seasons. Summer clinics had been over for over a month. Dad, Lincoln, and I hit the road to take a break from the hectic summer we'd had and to pack up his stuff and sort out the sale of the bar. We took him out to Frank's land, where he'd ended up staying most of our visit.

It was crazy watching Lincoln and Dad together. They were like two damn peas in a pod. Where one went, the other followed. After the day we'd gotten together, I wondered if Dad would rescind his approval and make Lincoln's life a living hell, but he was just as smitten as I was. After we got to Tennessee, they'd spent the first two days going out and exploring Frank's property, making plans to renovate the small house and barn while keeping the integrity of the structures intact. Just like he'd said, Dad laid out an offer on Frank's land, making the transfer as easy as crossing t's and dotting i's.

But the bar had taken time.

Lincoln had contacted some of Frank's old buddies, asking them to put the feeler out for someone interested in keeping Frank's legacy alive. The outpouring of interest had been staggering, but most wanted to take what was here and renovate it until it became something new.

It wasn't until the mayor's grandson threw in his offer that we knew we had a legitimate deal on the table. Duke Bennett ran the mechanic shop downtown and was a frequent patron of the bar. He reminded me a lot of Lincoln—respectful, straightforward, handsomely rugged—. Still, there was a darkness in his gaze my cowboy never had.

Negotiations went quick. Lincoln's contract was thorough. He had the right of first refusal, and the buyer agreed to never demolish or renovate the bar in a way that would alter Frank's vision. They sealed the deal over a glass of whiskey and a handshake before signing on the dotted line.

And then there was Ellis.

After further digging and investigations, it'd come to light that he'd not only forged my dad's name on a large number of financial transfers, but others as well. All in all, he'd embezzled well over one million dollars from his clients in the span of one to two years and was now sitting in jail waiting for a trial I couldn't wait to see.

It'd been a lot to handle once news broke. Ashwood had been shaken by the allegations, and Ellis had put up a fuss the entire way to the jail. He screamed his innocence until he was hoarse, but at that point, he was only further digging his grave.

Charles assisted in building the case against his son, which I knew was breaking his heart more than he let on. Everytime we saw him, he looked more haggard than the last. He'd since retired from his firm, and spent his free time out here on the ranch with my dad.

I was glad their friendship hadn't been affected for long.

"Feels weird to be a regular patron," Lincoln said, holding the door open for me. "It's like I'm waiting for that old bastard to yell at me for being late or some shit."

"I'm sure there's a line of them in there waiting to welcome you back home," I said with a wink.

He smacked my ass, ushering me toward the bar where we'd first met. I took my seat as Lincoln shook the hands of the old men sitting nearby. There was a worn, empty stool in the middle of their group. On the back was a bronze plaque emblazoned with four words.

Frank's seat. Fuck off.

There was a young woman behind the bar, pouring a round of beers for the rowdy group of cowboys near the jukebox. They hooted and hollered, trying to get her attention, but she paid them no mind.

I slid my gaze to the pool table in the corner as they grabbed their drinks and made their way over. My cheeks heated as I remembered how Lincoln had taken me there for the first time. How my hips had bruised from being slammed into the worn wood over and over again.

"Oh hell, I know that look," Lincoln said, sneaking behind me. He kissed my cheek, sliding me a beer and a shot of whiskey. "What do you say, darlin'? Wanna get drunk and shut this place down for the night? See how much of a mess you can make while bent over and screaming my name?"

"You'd like that, wouldn't you?" I asked, shifting in my seat to soothe the ache he'd created.

His eyes traveled down, smirking when he realized what I was doing. "I sure would. Something tells me you'd like it too."

I lifted my glass to my lips, hiding the smile behind it. "Too bad you don't run the place anymore. Guess we'll have to settle for memories."

Lincoln sat beside me, tossing his arm over the back of my chair. "That's where you're wrong, darlin'."

"What do you mean?"

He shrugged, looking straight ahead as he sipped his beer. "I might have cut a deal with the new owner."

"What kind of deal would that be?"

"The kind that says I don't have to turn in my keys to this place until the morning and that I'll be loading up that damn pool table on our trailer before we head out."

I turned toward him, mouth open. "Wait, what? I thought it was the first thing Frank bought when he opened the place?"

"It was, but those old fuckers down there insisted I take it." Lincoln looked down at his bottle. "I'm damn glad they did because the thought of losing everything he gave to me didn't sit right. Now it's coming home with us."

My gut churned. Lincoln and I had talked about selling the land and bar many times over the past few months. Each time, he insisted Texas was his new home, and he had no regrets about leaving Tennessee. That didn't mean I felt any better about it. Instead, I worried he'd regret it one day.

"Before that mind shifts into overdrive," he said, placing a hand on my knee, "this has nothing to do with me moving away. That's what he wanted in the end, anyhow."

"Then what's it about?" I asked, letting his touch calm me down. I didn't know how he did it or why it worked, but he was always steady. Somehow, he kept me from losing myself to the thoughts in my head.

"Frank only wanted the best for me, and I don't know if you've noticed, but darlin'… that's you." Lincoln looked around the bar before shaking his head. "You know, I used to think it only took me five days to fall in love with you, but honestly… I fell in love with you the moment you walked into this little bar tucked between the pines." His dark brown eyes turned to me, melting me and any argument I'd been preparing to make. "I may be giving up some pieces of my past, but I'm gaining a damn fine future."

I reached forward, tugging on the collar of his shirt to bring him closer. As our lips met, the bar erupted in a chorus of laughter and cheers. Lincoln's mouth curled up in a smile against my own. He raised his arm, flipping the room off as we pulled apart.

"You're quite the romantic," I said, wiping away the remnants of my lip gloss.

Lincoln smiled, tucking my hair behind my ear. "So, what do you say, baby? Feel like getting a little wild for old time's sake?"

I looked up, taking his hat from his head and setting it on my own. "Damn right, Cowboy. Let's go."

want more?

Want to see how Josie and Lincoln spent their last night in Tennessee? Fair warning: It gets HOT! 🌚 Head over to my newsletter to receive the bonus scene!

Can't wait to see what happens with Black Spring Ranch's favorite grump when he is thrown together with the one woman who can bring him to his knees? Keep reading for a sneak peek!

lennox

. . .

Through the Dust Sneak Peak

"FUCK THE LEATHER, fuck the lace. Cheers to the ones who sit on our face!" I yelled, slamming the bottle on the rickety wooden table before bringing it to my lips. The cold beer hit my tongue, calming the nervous energy fluttering in my veins.

I was met with a declaration of cheers and groans—both, sure signs that my words had done the job.

Cold beer and whiskey were the standards at the Lone Star Bar in Ashwood, Texas. Nothing could ever get better than this —bright, neon lights and music too loud to carry on conversations. Add in the hot-as-hell cowboys walking around the place, and I was set.

There was a reason I was a regular here, and it wasn't for the cheap alcohol. Tonight was different, though. Or so I told myself.

Every summer, my dad taught at an intensive training clinic that brought in rich folk with horses from around the world. Each session lasted two weeks, and they were held back-to-back over two months.

Today marked the end of the first round, and we were out to celebrate. I'd already clocked at least half of our ranch hands amongst the crowd, drinking, dancing, and laughing their fill. I couldn't wait to watch them stumble around hungover tomorrow when the next group showed up.

The Lone Star hosted live bands on the weekend. Tonight, there was a local playing who'd made a big name for himself in the music scene. I'd never seen the bar so full. The whole damn town seemed to have showed up. I hadn't ever heard of him, but I hoped he was good.

My sisters, Josie and Cleo, sat beside me, shaking their heads at my antics. Not that I cared. My toasts had become somewhat of a party trick when I went out—an icebreaker. I couldn't even remember what started it or where it came from. I grew up around too many foul-mouthed cowboys who had no business speaking the way they did when I was present. I had to do something with all the dirty anecdotes I picked up along the way. Plus, trying to top whatever I said last time was always fun.

Like a little competition with myself, which I always enjoyed.

"That's sure as fuck something I could toast to," the tall man to my left chuckled.

"Hear, hear!" I said, leaning over Josie to knock my bottle with his.

Lincoln Carter was a new addition to our little group. I didn't know him well, but I liked him so far. Dad hired him at the beginning of the summer to help with the clinics, and he'd done a great job the past two weeks. He'd come down from Tennessee and was staying in the bunkhouse with some of the temporary hires Dad had brought on.

What I enjoyed the most, though, was the way he made my sister squirm. Lincoln hovered near the end of the table, conveniently next to Josie, and was having a damn hard time keeping his eyes off her.

On his first day here, Dad had introduced the two of them,

but the universe was a funny bitch about things like that. Apparently, they'd had some sort of fling last summer before she'd run off and broken both their hearts in the process.

Ever since Lincoln had shown up, she'd been trying to convince us that there was nothing between them anymore, but anyone in a ten-foot radius saw what a lie that was.

Sure, she technically had a boyfriend, but Ellis Martin was a skeezy dickwad who cared more about making money than he ever did about her. Our whole family hated him, honestly. He had never fit in with us, always looking down on our family and what we did—even though my father was one of the biggest clients at his investment firm.

Now that Lincoln was here, though… Josie had changed. The two of them were like ducklings: where one went, the other followed. I reckoned they'd be knocking boots before the end of the week, if not the end of the night.

"Oh my god, you're the worst," Cleo groaned. She was smiling, though, so I didn't take it to heart.

"No, I'm the best," I said, pointing in her direction. "It's the reason you keep me around. I'm funny, smart, and pretty as hell."

"And annoying to boot."

I slid my gaze toward the green-eyed cowboy sitting across from me. Bishop Bryant sipped at his beer, gripping it tightly in his scarred hand. He had his black felt hat pulled down, concealing him beneath the shadows.

Like, who did he think he was? An outlaw on the run? Get over yourself.

Ugh. Everything about him got on my damn nerves. From his stupidly hot, bearded face—because *yes*, I was woman enough to admit he was attractive—to the way he always glared at me like I was in the wrong.

Bishop was the epitome of a grump. He was kind of like a mean ol' bear that'd just come out of hibernation, and I just couldn't help but poke. I'd known him almost my whole life. He'd come to work on our ranch before graduating high school and spent the past twenty-three years praying at the altar of Black Springs Ranch.

I leaned over the table, smirking as his eyes dropped to my chest. "Is that why you can't stop staring at me?"

It was dark, but I swore his cheeks heated. "Maybe we should add delusional to the mix, too. I ain't fucking staring." He pointed the bottle toward me, and I fought the urge to lick it. It'd be worth it just to see him squirm, but I decided not to for the sake of our company. "And if I am, it's because you're too damn loud."

"It's a bar, Bishop. If I wasn't loud, your old man ears wouldn't be able to hear me."

He huffed. "Yeah, that'd be *really* horrible. What a shame."

I sat back on the barstool, crossing my arms. Again, his gaze dropped to where my forearms pushed up my cleavage. It was only a second, but I saw it all the same. "You know, if you really want to keep me quiet, you could give me something to fill my mouth and shut me up. It's worked for others in the past."

Bishop coughed, choking on his beer while I grinned like the Cheshire Cat. He made it too easy to mess with him. Sometimes, my conscience would pop in and say, *"Hey girl, maybe we should take it easy on him,"* but then he'd say something stupid, and I'd throw her advice right out the window.

That mean shit was fine when we were younger. I was a chicken-legged brat running around the barn and asking a million questions, but not anymore. Now I was a twenty-seven-year-old championship barrel racer who didn't feel like taking shit from an old cowboy with a stick up his ass.

Plus, maybe I liked seeing his cheeks flush with embarrassment when I said some off-the-cuff remark that made him uncomfortable. He should've known better by now that if you give me an inch, I'm gonna turn it into a mile.

"Christ, Lennox," he said, wiping his mouth with the back of his hand. "No one needs to hear that shit."

"Is that your problem, Bish? Feeling a little pent-up? Haven't gotten laid in a while?" I pouted, reaching out to pat his hand. He pulled away quickly, shifting in his seat. *Bingo.* "You know, that always helps me when I'm feeling wrung too tight. I just go out and find someone who looks like they'll fuck me really—"

"Don't finish that fucking sentence," he growled.

I raised my brow. "Why? Are you jealous?"

Bishop opened his mouth and closed it, looking more like a fish out of water than a cowboy at a bar. I was preparing to tease him when I heard Lincoln ask Josie to dance. My head turned their way, studying how she swayed gently in her stool. If I were a betting woman, I'd say she was getting ready to turn him down for a dance.

Well... as her loving younger sister, I couldn't let that happen.

Lincoln stepped back, holding out his hand for her to take. "Well, what do you say?"

"She says yes," I called out over the music.

Cleo smacked my arm. "Len, stop meddling! She's an adult—"

"Yeah, and she's acting like she's a child. I don't see how I'm the problem for pushing her toward something she wants. Isn't that what you were doing earlier?"

My sister chewed on the inside of her cheek. "Yeah, but you can't just butt into their conversation."

I shrugged. "I can, and I did." The sound of stools scraping against the floor caught our attention, and we glanced up, watching Josie place her hand in Lincoln's. I smiled, turning back to Cleo. "And look! It worked. I don't know what this family would do without me."

"Probably stay out of everyone's business," Bishop muttered, but I paid him no mind. I didn't have to look to know his eyes were on me. His attention was hard to get and even harder to ignore.

If he wanted a show, then I'd give him one.

Reaching for my beer, I downed what little was left. Then I straightened my shoulders and pushed up my tits. The night was early, and the live music hadn't even started. I hadn't been out in far too long and was ready to let loose.

Yeah, it was going to be one hell of a night.

"What're you doing?" Cleo asked.

"Is there anything in my teeth?" She shook her head. "What about my lipstick? Is it smudged?"

"No, you're good—"

"Great," I said, not letting her finish. "I'm gonna go talk to that tall drink of whatever over there," I said, nodding to the man at the next table. "Would've been embarrassing to make a bad impression, don't you think?"

Cleo chuckled to herself. "Whatever you say, sis."

"Will I see you out on the dancefloor?"

My sister looked down at the bottle between her palms, picking at the peeling label. "I'm married, Len."

"Yeah, and I like men in Wrangler jeans and Stetsons," I deadpanned.

"What does that have to do with anything?" she asked.

"My point exactly."

My sister rolled her eyes. "Well, *my* point is that I'm not going to ask some random stranger to dance. I don't want to give them the wrong impression."

I rolled my lips together, dropping my gaze to my sister's hand, where she fidgeted with the finger where a simple gold band once sat. It seemed like I was the only one who'd notice the tan line that'd taken its place.

Cleo had recently moved back from helping her supposed husband and his brother at a dude ranch in Montana. When she'd come back alone, she'd made some comment about work keeping him there and her needing to be here, but she never spoke about him—never called him, either.

"I'll dance with you," Bishop said, downing his beer. "If you want."

We both looked at him in shock. Bishop hated dancing. In fact, I was sure he hated anything to do with fun. I could probably count the number of times I'd seen him smile on one hand —maybe two if I really tried.

I reached over the table, placing my hand on his forehead. "Are you sick?"

"What?" He swatted my hand away. "No, I'm not fucking sick. I was just being polite."

"Yeah, which is why I'm circling back to my original question."

Bishop pinched the bridge of his nose. "Why are you such a pain in the ass?"

I batted my eyelashes. "Because it drives you insane."

Cleo looked between us. "Listen, it's okay. I'm fine here, and I know it isn't your scene…"

"Oh no, you don't," he said, shaking his head. "Let's go see if I remember how to dance."

"I may be more out of practice than you are," she laughed, walking around the table. He took her hand, leading her to the floor before I could make another comment.

"Perfect!" I called out, forcing my voice to remain steady. "So, I'll see you out there then!"

There was a time when I would've given anything for Bishop Bryant to take my hand and hold me close on the dance floor, but that crush had been killed a long time ago. I wasn't the same naive little girl I was back then. Besides, I didn't even want a relationship right now. I'd taken a year off the rodeo circuit after Dad had gotten sick so that I could help around the ranch. Next year, I was hitting the ground running and wasn't planning on looking back.

Still, I couldn't deny the ache in my chest that refused to go away as I watched him pull my sister close. He said something, making her laugh as they moved around the enclosed space.

"Heya sweetheart, wanna dance?"

I slid my gaze to the cowboy standing beside me, the same one who'd been making eyes at me from across the table. Up close, he'd lost his appeal. I mean, he was cute in a boyish way —blond hair, blue eyes, and a cocky swagger that I'm sure he thought made him look cool—but there was no edge to him. There was nothing there that screamed, *"I'll fuck you into a coma."*

But I wasn't about to sit around and watch everyone else dance when I'd been the one who forced them to go out.

So, I smirked like I always did, hiding my discomfort, and said, "Let's go cowboy."

lennox

. . .

Through the Dust Sneak Peak

THE COWBOY COULDN'T DANCE for shit. He kept stepping on my toes every time we moved, and his turns were sloppy and out of control. I'd lost count of how many couples he'd bumped us into after the first song.

It didn't help that I'd worn brand-new boots. Josie had warned me not to, but I didn't listen. I never listened. At least when I showed up limping tomorrow, I could blame it on the man staring at my tits rather than my eyes.

Fortunately, after two songs, Bishop and Cleo made their way back to the table, and I had an excuse to save what was left of my toes. As the music came to an end, I forced a smile. "Thanks so much for the dances! My friends are headed back, though, so I'm gonna..." I trailed off, shooting finger guns in their direction.

Maybe Bishop's onto something. Why am I the way I am?

The cowboy laughed. "Then let's go."

He gripped my hand in his, following my sister and Bishop. It would've been fine had he not grabbed his beer and set it on our table, looking around expectantly at everyone. "'Sup? Names Case."

Case? Oh no. I had an ex-boyfriend on the circuit named Case, and he was a fuckboy supreme. Looked a lot like this guy, to be honest.

He stuck out his hand toward the others. Cleo shook it because she was polite and never wanted anyone to think anything bad about her, but Bishop stared at it like it was a hot branding iron.

And then his gaze slid to me in a *"Are you fucking kidding me?"* look.

Oops.

"I'm gonna grab some more drinks," Cleo muttered, shaking her head as she made her way to the bar. I wanted to beg her to take me.

"Ouch," Case said, pulling back and laughing. "Tough fucking crowd. You her brother or something?"

I said, "Or something," while Bishop growled, "Absolutely fucking not."

Lord, give me strength.

"He's the foreman at our ranch," I clarified. "Known him my whole life."

"Not your whole life," Bishop mumbled.

"I mean, as good as," I laughed. "What? I was like, four when Dad brought you on? Anyway, we're practically family."

The lie was bitter and horrible like cough medicine being forced down my throat, but I swallowed it either way.

"Black Springs, right? Heard some of the boys talking 'bout it when y'all walked in. That's a damn fine outfit. Y'all hiring?"

"Nope," Bishop said, popping the P. "Even if we were, don't think you'd cut it."

"What's that supposed to mean?" Case asked, puffing out his chest.

Bishop stared at him, the corner of his lips tipping up. "You ever rounded cattle?"

"Well, no—"

"What about branded? Ever helped with that?"

"Not exactly, but—"

"Have you ever driven a tractor? Or pulled anything in that fancy truck I'm sure you've got sittin' out there?"

Case was silent, teeth grinding so hard I swore I could hear them scraping against one another.

Bishop chuckled. "Then why the fuck do you think I'd hire you to work on my ranch?"

"It's not your ranch, though, is it?" Case snapped back. "You may be the second in charge, but you don't have a say in shit at the end of the day."

I'll say this about the kid… He'd found his balls but found them at the wrong time.

"Okay," I said, dragging out the word. "Case, it's been great —*really* wonderful—but I think it's time you head back to your friends."

"Yeah, okay," he scoffed, grabbing his beer. He muttered something under his breath, but I didn't hear it. Or maybe I did, but I wanted to pretend otherwise.

"Lennox!"

I turned to see Cleo scurrying over with her drinks, but her eyes were wide. Panicked.

"What's up? What's wrong?" I asked, placing my hands on her shoulders.

"Ellis," she panted. "He's here. He's at the door." Her eyes slid to where Josie and Lincoln were cozying up on the dancefloor.

"I'm on it," I said, stepping around her. "Stay here."

Josie needed to kick that asshole to the curb, but now wasn't the time to do it. I didn't know why Ellis was here, and I didn't care. All I wanted to do was make sure my sister was okay.

She and Lincoln stood in the center of the dance floor, looking at one another like moon-eyed fools, lost in their own world. I almost hated to intrude.

Almost.

I marched forward, skidding to a stop as I rested my hand on his shoulder. "Hey, cowboy, mind if I have this dance?"

I quickly gave them a rundown, telling Josie she sure as hell didn't want Ellis to walk in and see what I had. She took off toward the table, leaving Lincoln and I alone out on the floor.

The house band who'd been playing was saying their good-byes, packing up their instruments to clear the way for the next act. The bar switched to one of their tried-and-true playlists of old country tunes.

They'd played it so many times, I'd memorized the order. The owner never switched the songs to shuffle, even though most of his regulars had tried to show him how. I didn't mind, though. It was comforting to know that no matter how hard people tried to change things, he'd basically told them all to go to hell.

It feels like something I would've done, honestly.

Lincoln's movements were stiff, his muscles coiled and ready to strike beneath my hands. He didn't take his eyes off Josie for one second, not until she was safely sitting down at the table with Cleo and Bishop.

I glanced up at him, envious of the way he watched her with such fervor. No one had ever looked at me like that. Not that I had ever let anything grow past the point of lust-filled glances and heated moments in the back of my truck.

I told myself I never had the time for more, that I was too busy with life on the ranch and the circuit to share what precious moments I had with someone else. Even though we were in the heart of cowboy country, it was hard to find someone who understood.

I think they found it attractive at first—how I could hold my own in the arena and kick most of their asses while doing it. But there was some deeply rooted belief that all of that had to go away when a woman settled down. Suddenly, it was unbecoming.

I was never going to be the type to be barefoot and pregnant, turning in my reins for a spatula while my partner was out tending to the things that needed to be done. I wanted to be beside them, fixing fences and rounding up cattle. I wanted to be seen and treated as an equal, sharing the load of life's hardships instead of becoming an accessory on their arm.

My mom always said I had too much of my dad in me. At first, I thought it was a negative comment, something I always challenged her on. As I got older, though, I realized it was the best compliment I could've been given.

I squeezed Lincoln's hand, bringing his attention back to me. "Don't break her fucking heart."

He looked confused, brows pulling together in question. Yeah, it may have seemed out of left field to him, but it wasn't to me. "Pardon?"

I'd watched Josie, my sweet, overly anxious, falls-in-love-too-easily sister, get hurt more times than I could count. I was always there to pick her up when she was down. We'd go out to the Lone Star, tearing up the town until the cycle started again, and she caught the eye of some new heartbreaker.

Only now did I realize we'd never done that after her trip to Tennessee. I hadn't understood what was different about that time than any of the others, how she seemed more distraught after a five-day fling than she had finding out her boyfriend of over six months had been cheating on her.

But I understood now, and I reckoned love didn't give a shit about conventional timing.

"You heard me, cowboy. I mean it. If you break her heart, I'll kill you. There's a lot of places to hide a body on the ranch, and I won't think twice about shoving your dick back up—"

"I'm not gonna break her heart," he mumbled, sliding his

eyes back toward the table. "But I'm afraid she's gonna break mine."

I followed his gaze, stomach dropping as I noticed Ellis standing where Lincoln had been moments ago. He leaned forward, relying on the table to steady him as he swayed on his feet.

As Josie leaned away, every muscle in Lincoln's body grew taut. We'd stopped in the middle of the dance floor, earning our share of rude looks from couples passing by. "Don't go making a scene," I warned. "You don't want to get tossed out on your ass."

"I don't give a shit about that," he said, rolling his neck as Ellis sneered down at my sister.

He said something, and Josie slammed her hand down on the table. I didn't need to hear her words to know she was tearing into his ass. It would've been funny had Bishop not sat up straighter and looked over his shoulder at Lincoln and I.

Ope. This wasn't going to end well. Someone was going to end up with split knuckles or a broken nose. My money was on Ellis for the latter.

And then, just like I'd predicted, all hell broke loose as Ellis reached for Josie, pulling her off the stool and getting in her face. She reached for the hand firmly curled around her bicep, trying to loosen his white-knuckled grip.

Lincoln was gone, storming toward the table in a murderous rage. His boots thundered against the concrete floor. I followed, hot on his heels because if he didn't get to him first, I'd be the one security was dragging out, kicking and screaming.

I'd always hated Ellis, but that was because I thought he was an arrogant piece of shit who thought he was better than everyone around him. I'd never clocked him as the violent type, but sometimes, you didn't see a snake in the grass until you got bit.

Laying a hand on any woman was a mistake, but laying a hand on Josie?

Huge. Fucking monumental.

Cleo shouted for security as Lincoln pulled Ellis off Josie, internally cheering as he landed a hard blow to the fucker's nose. I stopped beside Cleo, watching with glee as blood began trickling down his upper lip. "What'd you do that for?" I asked her, grabbing what was left of my beer off the table and downing the rest.

We both cocked our heads as Lincoln pushed Ellis against a table. "Because I don't want to have to call Dad and explain why he's going to need to drive down to the county jail and bail everyone's ass out."

"Davey doesn't call the cops for shit like this," I said, just as the man in question came bounding up. He'd worked at this bar for as long as I could remember, and I'd gotten to know him pretty well.

"Hey, hey!" he called, trying to break up the fight, but Bishop put his arm out to block him. "Bishop, what the fuck?"

"Aw, come on... Let the man get a few good hits in," Bishop said, jerking his chin toward the spectacle. "He put his hands on Josie." There was a smirk on his face as he watched Ellis try in vain to break out of Lincoln's hold. I didn't know why, or if there was even a reason, but he hated the fucker almost as much as I did.

And maybe it was the alcohol, maybe it was my adrenaline, but there was something about that simple move that was stupidly hot.

I was clearly not in my right mind because there was no way I was letting myself daydream about Bishop Bryant.

"Can't risk the bar being sued, dumbass," Davey muttered, barreling through Bishop's blockade. Lincoln stepped back with his hands up, welcoming Josie as she wrapped her arms around him. Two other men grabbed Ellis, trying to drag him out, but he broke free and made a dash toward my sister.

Lincoln tried to break their fall to no avail. They both landed in a tangle of limbs. Ellis lunged forward, calling my sister a bitch and shouting promises of lawsuits from the top of his lungs.

Fuck that.

I stepped between them, reaching Ellis before Davey even had a chance. Without another thought, I placed my hands on his shoulders and smashed the toe of my brand-new boots into his balls. "Piece of shit," I spat as two large arms wrapped around my middle. The scent of sage and honey and very bad decisions filled my senses as I was pulled tightly against a warm chest.

"Easy there, killer," Bishop chuckled. His deep, throaty tone sent shivers down my spine. "I think you've done enough damage."

I watched Davey pick Ellis off the floor and drag him to the front doors. The crowd parted, some laughing and clapping the moment his wailing was gone. Josie pulled Lincoln to the corner, fussing over him like he'd been in a knock-down, drag-out brawl when it barely was classified as a bar fight.

"Lemme go," I said, struggling in Bishop's hold.

"Have it your way," he said, untangling himself from my middle and letting me drop.

The sound I made was somewhere between a yelp and a squeal—I couldn't be sure. I wasn't in the habit of making it.

I spun around, ready to dig into him for letting me fall when I saw a smile on his lips. An actual smile—not that fake, public shit. No, this had wrinkles forming near his temple, and his eyes had a weird playfulness. He covered his mouth with his hand, shoulders shaking with restrained… *laughter?*

"Was that a laugh?" I asked, peering up at him. He rolled his lips together, dropping his hand and tucking inside the pocket of his jeans. "Like, an honest-to-God *laugh*? Oh my god. Who are you?"

Bishop closed his eyes. "Why do you have to be weird about shit?"

"Because I don't know if I've ever heard that weird sound from you. Should I be worried? Do we need a doctor?"

"It was just a laugh, Lennox. Nothing to make a fuss over."

I crossed my arms over my chest. "You're not programmed to laugh, so this obviously means one of two things."

He leaned his elbow on the table. "Alright, let's hear them."

"One," I said, holding up my pointer finger, "you've been abducted by aliens, and this is some kind of body double situation."

He blinked. "*What*?"

"Or two, you've been possessed. I'd wager it was some kind of demon. Does thinking about hell make you homesick? Have you experienced any projectile vomiting recently?"

Bishop shook his head. "Where the fuck do you come up with this shit?"

I shrugged. "Unlike some people—and I'm not naming names, of course—I read books with *words*, not just pictures. I know it's a crazy concept. Maybe if you tried it some time, you could learn a thing or two."

"Are you saying I can't read?" he asked. He seemed offended, which was weird because that was exactly what I was saying. I'd never seen Bishop read anything besides whiskey bottles and feed labels.

"I already told you I wasn't naming names, Bish," I said, raising my hand to mimic zipping my lips tight.

Out of the corner of my eye, I noticed Cleo walking up. She placed her hand in the crook of my elbow. "Let's go check on Josie," she said, chewing on her cheek. "I want to make sure she's okay."

"Yeah, I guess we'll need to settle our tabs. Davey doesn't

call the cops but has a no-bullshit policy. Lincoln'll be kicked out for the night," I said.

Bishop stuck his hands in his pocket. "Well, are y'all wanting to stay? There are plenty of familiar faces here tonight. We could probably catch a ride if you wanted to."

I shot Cleo a grin, ecstatic because I wasn't ready to go home. There was a restless energy coursing beneath my skin. I wanted to set it free, to see where it would take me.

"Don't you think we should probably cut our losses and go home?" She pulled away from me, fidgeting with her fingers like she had earlier.

I reached out and grasped her hand, and gave it a quick squeeze. Her eyes met mine, verging on panic or hope. I couldn't tell which. "Do you want to go home, Cleo?"

"I don't know, Len." Her voice was little more than a whisper. I barely caught her words over the din of the crowd.

I pulled her in tight, aware of Bishop's curious gaze bouncing between us. "You say the word, and we're gone, okay?"

"Sure," she said, nodding slowly. "But maybe we could get a few shots?"

I clapped my hands together. "Fuck yes, we can! That's my girl. What's your poison? Whiskey is my personal favorite, but there's also tequila—"

"Tequila," she blurted out. "Lots of tequila."

Bishop groaned. "This is gonna be a long fucking night."

I turned toward him, standing taller as his eyes slowly raked along my body. He dragged a thumb across the bottom of his lip, shaking his head.

Yup. The alcohol was getting to me, but that didn't mean I couldn't have fun with it.

"Oh, you have no idea."

GRAB THROUGH THE DUST HERE!

also by amber palmer

acknowledgments

Wow. I just wrote and published a damn cowboy book... Bet none of y'all saw that coming, did you?

Neither did I! I grew up in that world, and when someone asked me if I'd ever read or write in this genre, I always answered with a big, loud, resounding NO.

But never say never, right?

To my readers, thank you for sticking with me for this change of pace. Thank you for telling me I would be your first cowboy romance and showing genuine excitement every time I posted online. Y'all kept me going when I considered scrapping everything and burning this manuscript.

To my husband, thank you for not balking when I came to bed at 2:00 AM and said, "I think I'm gonna write a cowboy book..." Thank you for waving food and water in my face while I wrote and edited, as I was too lost in this story to move.

To Lauren and Holly, this book wouldn't have happened without y'all. Hands down, no questions asked. Thank you for pushing me outside my comfort zone and encouraging me to follow this crazy (for me) story idea. Thank you for the endless freak-outs and late-night texts, for making me believe in myself when I didn't. Thank you for encouraging me to find what makes *me* happy.

To Heather, you're the LOML—my sweet little capybara. I'm sorry I made you read and edit cowboy smut, but you had so much fun, and you can't tell me you didn't. Thank you for your fancy words. Thank you for turning this story into one I am eternally proud of.

To Liz, thank you for always making time for me and never making me feel like a burden. Thank you for your endless support. (You're welcome for all the giddy flutters; I will write that on my headstone.)

To Rose, thank you for laughing at my corny jokes and being one of the first to show excitement over this story.

And thank you to every single person who picked up this book. This has been a wild ride in the best way possible, and I am so grateful you welcomed me with open arms.

meet amber

Amber Palmer is an American fantasy romance author. She was born in Arizona, but raised in Texas. She is the proud parent of three (evil) cats and one puppy dog, and when she isn't nose deep in a spicy fantasy novel, she's listening to her bookish Spotify playlists and making notes for her next project! A passionate advocate for mental health, Amber features characters processing various traumas in her work. She is an unapologetic lover of anything spicy, while also making time to game with her husband.